Hostile Territory
A Blackbridge Security Novel
Marie James

Hostile Territory 2

Copyright

Hostile Territory: A Blackbridge Security Novel
Copyright © 2020 Marie James
Editing by Marie James Betas & Ms.K's Edits

EBooks are not transferrable. All rights are reserved. No part of this book may be used or reproduced in any manner without written permission, except in the case of brief quotations embodied in critical articles and reviews. The unauthorized reproduction or distribution of this copyrighted work is illegal. No part of this book may be scanned, uploaded, or distributed via the Internet or any other means, electronic or print, without the publisher's permission.

This book is a work of fiction. The names, characters, places, and incidents are products of the writer's imagination or have been used fictitiously and are not to be construed as real. Any resemblance to persons, living or dead, actual events, locale, or organizations is entirely coincidental.

Cover Credit: Najla with Qamber Designs and Media

Hostile Territory **4**

Acknowledgments

Readers! Thank you for jumping on this ride! It means the world to me that you're joining me on this new journey with the men of Blackbridge Security!

Shoutout to Christine Estevez and Wildfire Marketing for having my back on these releases! Couldn't do it without them!

Thanks Natasha Carrere and Read.Review.Repeat for the help with this release!

Shoutout to my BETA's (Laura, Brittney, Brenda, MaRanda, Michelle, Jamie, and Shannon for keeping a close eye on this and making sure I start off this world on the best foot possible!

Mary with Ms.K Edits, you lady are absolutely amazing! Keep that shit up!

Bloggers! Thank you a million times over! I couldn't do this without you!

~Marie James

Synopsis:

Can you call someone an enemy if you haven't seen them for the better part of a decade?

Deacon Black is perfectly content with the status quo—work, sleep, repeat.
Who cares if he's rigid, structured, and set in his ways?
It's a job requirement that keeps his men safe and his company's doors open.
One phone call is all it takes to upend his life and land him right back into a past he has tried to forget.
Revisiting old ghosts is the last thing he needs.
Especially when the forced trip down memory lane includes the only woman he never wanted to see again.

Annalise Grimaldi hit the jackpot with her life—from her trust fund to her best friend, she has it all.
But her world comes crashing to a halt when her best friend vanishes—leaving behind an apartment in tatters and more questions than answers.
There's only one person she can think of that can help in a situation like this.
She hates to make the call, but there isn't a thing she wouldn't do to make sure her friend is found.
Even setting aside her hatred for Deacon Black.

Prologue

Deacon

So this is what broken promises look like. A room filled with people I don't know and won't ever see again. Nameless faces who have no clue about the turmoil swirling in my gut. People surrounding me for a variety of reasons, none the wiser that my world is imploding, or would be caving down around me if Dani was ever on time.

I know she's late just to spite me, but even with her chronic pettiness, I can't help but feel saddened by my tasks today.

I promised to love Daniella Altieri for the rest of my life.

I made those vows before God and our families.

She was it for me.

I hate that she still is.

I hate that I've been gone, serving a country that rewards my loyalty with paltry pay and gripping nightmares, instead of at home loving her and holding her in my arms.

Can't she understand that I'm doing exactly what we talked about?

We wiled away the nights for years, setting up our goals and dreaming about what our future would look like.

She was never happy about my need to join the Army, but she accepted it. Or at least I thought she did.

Can't she see how lonely I've been without her? How it kills me to leave her at home alone when I'm gone for work?

If only she'd been lonely, too.

My bed was empty.

Hers hasn't been.

I could've forgiven her, eventually.

She wasn't interested. She was quick to cut ties, and that cut me like a knife, wounding me more than the other scars covering my body from war.

The low chatter of the packed courtroom only serves to irritate me, but the sight of Dani finally walking in with a ridiculous entourage has my jaw clenching enough to ache.

I understand Annalise being here. Those two are connected at the hip and have been since I met my wife freshman year of high school. There's no need, however, for her parents and a couple other friends to bear witness to my annihilation.

Six years of marriage and Dani can't even look in my direction as she sits down on the other side of the room surrounded by her support group.

As we wait our turn before the flustered judge, I take a good, long look at my wife. Her hair is longer, but her once always smiling face is twisted up in a mask of indifference that's become all too familiar recently. Her eyes are no longer bright and shining, gazing around looking for some sort of trouble to get into. There's a hardness to her features right now that makes me hopeful. Is she regretting being here? Is she having second thoughts about throwing our love in a fire and watching it turn to ash?

My attorney clears his throat beside me, no doubt a warning to stop glaring across the room, but I ignore him like normal. He's a placeholder, a requirement for today's proceedings, and that's it.

Dani nods mechanically when her father leans in to speak to her, shaking her head in response.

I just need one glance, one sweep of her eyes in my direction and I know I can pull her back in. One quick second to change her mind. Our love hasn't been a fairy tale, but it's been close. Meeting in high school, all it took was that one look before we knew we were going to be important to each other. I just need that contact one last time to make her realize she's making the biggest mistake of her life.

Her eyes aren't the ones that meet mine.

Annalise Grimaldi, Dani's best friend since diapers and shit-stirrer extraordinaire, turns her head and sneers in my direction. The woman would be a knockout if she wasn't evil incarnate. She's always hated me and going by the animosity flowing from her amber-colored eyes, nothing has changed.

Without thought, I tilt my head up in a nod, a challenge, the very same way I did years ago when we were teens. Only back then, I had the girl. Back then, Dani would smack her friend on the arm and tell her to chill out. I won the battles between Anna and me years ago.

Today, that doesn't happen.

Today, I lose everything.

Ten years together, the last six married to the woman of my dreams ends with a fifteen-minute session in front of the judge. A couple of signatures, not one word spoken between the two of us, and I walk out of the courthouse a changed man.

Walking to my truck stiffens my spine and my resolve, but it's the sight of Dani wrapping her arms around a man's neck in the parking garage that will change me forever. Her dad, beaming down at his little girl as she embraces the man is something I never experienced.

Both of her parents hated me from the jump, and if I ever took a step back and examined the relationship I had with Dani, I'd realize that it started out as rebellion on her side and it's ending with her going home. Her sacrifice, her choosing me was temporary, and somehow, deep in my gut, I always knew it would be. I was never enough for her, and no matter how hard I worked to be the man she thought she deserved, I was always going to come up short.

Somehow, my eyes drift away from my now ex-wife to her best friend. Time has been good to her, and the two-and-a-half years since I last saw her sneering face have changed her from the teen queen she thought she was to the woman she has always pretended to be. Gorgeous, thick in all the right places, the face of an angel with a heart as black as midnight. She's finally gotten what she wanted, but when her eyes meet mine, there's a shimmer of sadness in her eyes, a hint that maybe she feels sorry for me, and that's worse than her animosity.

I don't need pity, and certainly not from a woman who has spent the entirety of her adult life trying to rip a hole in my relationship with Dani. Knowing that she's finally succeeded, I look away just completely done with the entire day.

The heartbreak I felt in the courtroom waiting for Dani to show hardens. The grief washing over me as we signed the paperwork all the while she refused to look me in the eye dissipates, and by the time I climb into my truck and pull away, I'm a changed man.

I'm impenetrable, untouchable, my heart caged in concrete, wrapped in chains, and tossed into the depths of the ocean never to feel the warmth of the sun again.

Chapter 1
Deacon

"Casing the joint?"

A smile is on my face before I can even turn around.

"Nothing around here worth stealing." Facing Jake Lincoln fully, it only takes a few heartbeats before his arms are wrapped around me.

I clap him on the back twice, but he seems more reluctant than usual to let me go.

"Never stopped you before." He grins wide, the corners of his eyes and laugh lines on his face deepening. The man is always smiling, always happy, always the first one to step up to help someone out. It was like that the day I met him at fifteen and it still rings true today.

"One time." I hold up a finger for emphasis. "I stole something once."

He doesn't need the reminder since he brings up our very first meeting each and every damn time I see him.

"You stole a gun, Deacon." His brow furrows, face growing serious, much the same way it did seventeen years ago. Only today he's not in the familiar uniform I've seen him wear more times than I can count. There's no holster belt on his lean hips, no badge pinned to his proud chest. Today he's dressed to the max in a navy suit and a tie.

I grin back at him when it's clear he's struggling with taking the serious route. "It was an airsoft gun. You make it sound like I broke into a car and jacked a drug dealer's arsenal."

"That would've happened a few days later if I hadn't stepped in."

We both pause for a moment, letting reality sink in. He's probably correct in his assumptions. At fifteen, I was wild and rebellious, ready to prove to myself and everyone around me that I was a badass, that I was street smart and could survive in any situation.

It didn't matter that I grew up with two loving parents in a nice middle-class neighborhood. It didn't matter that I laid my head down at night on clean sheets with a full belly when most of my friends didn't have those luxuries. None of that mattered. I'd started down a dark road, and if Jake hadn't been called when I was caught red-handed with a stolen toy gun at a local retailer, my life could've been dramatically different.

"You're right," I finally agree, smiling wistfully with the memories of just how hard I thought I was back then. It doesn't even come close to the way I am now, but life experiences make things different. They set you on a path no one could've predicted.

I'm now officially a badass, at least those around me say that I am. Only I'm on the right side of the law, mostly anyway.

"How's your mom and dad?"

People swarm around us, interrupting to shake Jake's hand and tell him congratulations on his retirement as we talk, but it's always like this around Jake. He's the sort that draws people in. Without even knowing why, people gravitate to him, much the same way I did all those years ago when he offered me something different, something I never thought I'd long for. He offered safety in his mentorship, safety to be around friends who didn't judge and more importantly didn't tempt me into doing all the wrong things. Positive peer pressure changed my life and kept me from making mistakes that would eventually be too hard or impossible to correct.

And he did this with numerous young men and women. Many of those people from my teen years are the ones walking up and greeting him like family, most all of them successful in their own right.

"You didn't answer me," Jake prods as another person walks away. Like always, he never leaves a question unanswered, and he expects the very same from those he interacts with. *Accountability is key*, according to him.

"Mom is thinking of retiring. She claims kids are brats more so now than ever before, and there isn't one conversation we have that she doesn't lament about how much better things would be if she had gone into accounting rather than teaching. Dad is still working down at the shop, and says he'll continue until the day he dies, especially if Mom retires."

We both smile, knowing Dad is full of it. He loves Mom like I've never seen before. I grew up watching that, wanting that for my—

I clear my throat, refusing to let any of those thoughts infiltrate my head. Eight fucking years since I walked out of that courtroom, and I still get agitated, more over the wasted time than anything else.

"She still teaching in Ellendale?" I nod. "If she thinks those kids struggle, she hasn't seen the kids I work with."

Jake shakes his head, and I know exactly what he's talking about.

Growing up with a mom teaching at one of the best private schools in St. Louis meant free tuition to said school. It also meant I was the poor kid amongst the rich brats, which in turn lead to the constant need to prove myself, only I went in the opposite direction. Instead of working hard to do better, to be better, to show those idiots that I belonged there with them, I gave them exactly what they expected. I was a hardass, skipping school, disrespecting teachers, being an all-around jerk. That is until Jake. The changes were gradual, but eventually Mom's job was no longer threatened by my behavior and I grew up to be a man that was almost respectful.

The Army only lasted eight years. There was no point in staying in after my divorce. I only joined to provide stability for the family we were supp—

Another throat clearing. Another smile at Jake.

"What are you planning to do with yourself now, old man?"

He scoffs, both of us knowing that he's still a badass on the basketball court and could chase down a criminal in full uniform if he were challenged to.

"Retirement just means I can spend more time down at the rec center."

"And that means I'll probably never see him again."

Jake softens, opening his arms immediately as his wife Connie steps up beside him. He presses smiling lips to her cheek, and I watch as her hand settles over his stomach, the move so practiced it's rote.

"He's going to have to find a compromise, right?" I grin at Connie. "Maybe you two could volunteer there together."

My phone buzzes in my pocket as Jake raises an eyebrow at his wife, as if they've already had this conversation and I'm a voice of reason.

My phone flashes an unfamiliar number, but I press decline even though it's a local number. I can only be fooled by robocalls so many times. Before I can shove it in my pocket, the phone rings again. For the second time, I hit ignore for it only to ring again.

"Give me a moment, please," I tell them as I walk away, accept the call, and hold it to my ear.

"What?" I snap, angrier at myself for bringing the damn phone in with me than anything else.

"Deacon?" The voice is an unfamiliar screech, clearly an upset woman. "Is this Deacon Black?"

Oh hell. A phone call from a hysterical woman is never a good thing.

"Speaking," I snap.

"It's Anna."

"Okay." I don't give much away, still trying to figure out what's going on.

"Annalise Grimaldi."

I nearly drop the damn phone. Never in a million years did I think this woman would call me.

"I can't believe you still have the same number." Her words don't fit the hysteria she displayed a few seconds ago, but that doesn't stop the wave of cold chills rushing down my spine.

There's only one reason that Anna would call me. I haven't seen her or heard anything about her in the eight years since my divorce, and we only have one connection.

"It's Dani," she sobs.

I clear my throat, swallowing multiple times to ward off the lump forming there. "What happened?"

I squeeze my eyes closed, waiting for her to deliver the terrible news. People die every day, some suddenly, some slipping away gradually. Some after years of no contact, but somehow that doesn't stop the twinge of pain, the thoughts of regret. Years of separation and no contact doesn't stop the grief of losing someone you once loved.

"What happened?" I repeat when all I can hear on the other line is whimpering and pain.

"The police are all over the place. There was so much blood. They won't talk to me. They carried her out on a stretcher. I think she was shot."

Her words come out in short puffs of breath between sobs.

"Shot?" I say because that doesn't make any sense. "Where?"

"In her condo."

Rich girls don't get shot in their condos. Rich girls end up with coke problems and either die from an overdose or car crash from driving under the influence. Levels of violence involving guns doesn't make sense.

"I-I didn't know who else to call. Can you come here? Maybe they'll talk to you." Anna's voice is almost begging, but it's almost like she's at the other end of a mile-long tunnel.

"That won't work," I tell her. "Go to my office."

"Office?" She sounds surprised but assures me she's got the address when I spit it out.

I hang up before she can say anything else. Police at an active crime scene won't talk to me, but it so happens that I know a couple of guys who can get me the info I need within minutes.

I wave to Jake, and he nods in my direction, well aware of my line of work. He won't be offended that I had to duck out early.

A couple of drinks and telling a dear friend congratulations on his retirement has somehow managed to turn into a night I have the feeling is going to change my life forever.

Chapter 2
Anna

I can't help but think calling Deacon was a mistake, but the second that stretcher passed in front of my peephole it was almost instinctual.

I didn't call my dad or one of my many cousins. I didn't even call someone in Dani's family to seek help. He was my first and only thought. He's the man who always knew what to do when things got crazy in the past, and here I am shoving him right back into our present, a man I haven't seen or talked to in nearly a decade.

I thought he'd hang up on me, and I'm certain that's exactly why he sent me to voicemail twice before answering. Even after years and years he's willing to help, and that says something about the man. I don't have time to think about what any of this means. Why he's so willing to help with just a short strangled conversation. I push the memory of his sad face after his divorce from my head.

My hands tremble, making it nearly impossible to pack a bag and gather my things to leave. Not paying attention to what I'm shoving into my overnight bag, I just grab things at random so I can get out of here.

Anxiety over not knowing a thing is slowly morphing into fear for myself even though I have no reason to be afraid. As time ticks by, I grow scared that whatever happened with Dani could happen to me. It settles in my stomach like a brick and speeds my hands as I pack.

Voices flow into my apartment, letting me know that the hallway is still filled with uniformed officers loitering around long after the EMTs left with her bloody body.

There's a good chance my best friend is dead or dying on her way to the hospital, but the cops wouldn't tell me anything. All I got was a couple of inquisitive looks, ones that told me they'd have questions for me later when they discover that I'm not just a nosy neighbor. The thought of answering questions right now when they refused to answer mine is more than a little unnerving. I feel guilt even though I had nothing to do with what happened next door.

I'm not just some intrusive person next door. Dani is my best friend, and she has been since we were babies. We haven't seen or spoken much to each other in recent months, but we've been as close as sisters for as long as I can remember.

Go to my office.

Those words from Deacon's lips don't even make sense. Last I knew, he was a military guy, still in the Army when he and Dani divorced. No matter how much I try to picture him working in an office to quell my frantic thoughts, I just can't. I was privy to his goals since Dani and I were inseparable, and he made it clear from about sixteen that he was planning a career in the military. There's no way at thirty-two that his military time is over.

I'm inches away from reaching out to open my front door when the banging begins. I jolt, the sound of hard knuckles rapping against the wood frightening me more than I thought it could.

Instead of opening the door and demanding answers, I run through the apartment and head out the back. I know it makes no sense. I know I'm not in trouble, but I also don't have answers. I can't open that door and have those men tell me that my best friend was murdered. I can't face that alone.

The back stairway is thankfully empty. Cops have better things to do than walk up several dozen flights of stairs when the elevator to the top works just fine.

In my haste, I stumble and nearly fall more than once. Heels, speed, and stairs don't mix, and I'm panting like I ran a marathon and my shoes are ruined by the time I make it to the lobby of my building. Genaro looks at me like I've lost my mind, but I don't have the ability to care about my looks right now. The sympathy in his eyes as he looks in my direction while holding the front door to the building open, however, does make me pause. Does he know more than I do about what happened to Dani? He might since he would have had to direct the police to her condo when they arrived.

"Ms. Grimaldi?" Genaro holds out his time-worn hand, but I know if I take it, I'll just break down. He doesn't look insulted when I look away to gain some control.

The sight of his hand makes me realize I've left everything in my condo except for my phone. At least with that, I can pay for a cab. Thankfully, there's always one idling nearby, and Genaro flags it down, holding the door open for me until I slide inside. I'm trembling from top to bottom, but the tired cabbie doesn't seem to care, and for that I'm grateful. There's nothing worse than having to talk to a stranger out of common courtesy.

I realize I sound like a complete asshole in my head, but I just give the driver the address to Deacon's office and press my back to the seat, keeping my eyes on my building until it fades from sight. I don't realize until I shift in my seat just how bad my feet are. Blisters line the back of my heels from my shoes rubbing them running down the stairs.

My hiss of pain draws the cabbie's eye to the rearview mirror, but he still remains quiet. Kicking off my shoes, I gather them from the floor knowing I'm going to have to find a trashcan to dump them in. I hold them in my lap like a lifeline, toying with the delicate straps to try to keep my fingers from shaking, but it doesn't help.

I have no idea what Deacon can do to help, but not being alone right now would at least calm me a little.

The sight of the high rise as the cab driver slows in front of the tall building shocks me. This isn't some rinky dink office. This isn't a small travel trailer housing the office of a lawn care service or a struggling mechanic's office—both things I considered I'd be facing once I let myself think about it. This is upscale and expensive. Two things I would never attach to a man like Deacon Black.

The cabbie sighs for wasting his time, and I quickly pay, having made the entire trip without speaking other than to provide the address. I climb out of the cab, still unsure if I'm in the right place, but the doorman assures me I'm correct, and lazily points in the direction of the elevator.

Chapter 3
Deacon

The drive back to the office was spent with my fingers tapping on the steering wheel in frustration, irritated that only idiots seem to be occupying the roads at this time of night. Then, I realize that whatever shitshow I'm about to face is more the cause than anything because the irritation doesn't drain away as it normally does when I take the private elevator up to the Blackbridge Security office.

Of course a couple of the guys are here just hanging out. Some never seem to go home, even after a long day of work.

Jude Morris, my medic and biological science engineer, is frowning down at a length of rope as he tries to perform some ridiculous knot.

Ignacio Torres, the team's translator, is reading a book, the title in a language so unfamiliar I can't decipher.

Brooks Morgan, the best covert ops guy I know, is staring into his phone, no doubt taking selfies like always.

"Boss man!" Jude snaps. He's the first one to see me walk in the room. *"Queso!"*

"It's *qué pasa*, you idiot," Ignacio mutters without even looking up from his book.

When I don't tell him he's stupid, like I normally would, it draws the eyes of all three guys in the room. Jude drops the rope, Ignacio lowers the book, and miracle of all miracles, Brooks slides his phone back into his pocket.

It's then that I realize I need to check my face. These guys have been with me for a while, and I don't know that I've ever had such a quick response from them all at the same time outside of working a serious job.

"There's a woman coming. Let me know when she gets here." They all nod, and I'm once again floored they don't give me shit about hooking up with chicks at the office. I don't and they know it. They better not be bringing chicks back here either. "Is Wren in?"

They all answer in the affirmative, but I'm already heading across the room to his office. Wren Nelson is my tech guy, and if he wasn't the best in his field, I'd be less inclined to put up with the irritation that comes along with his working here.

Swinging his office door open without knocking, the first thing that hits me is how damn cold he likes to keep his office. I understand that some A/C is required with all the equipment, but you could probably hang meat in this damn place. Most days it's no big deal, but this evening, it's just one more damn thing that annoys the shit out of me.

The second thing I'm prepared for...

"This motherfucker."

I snap my head to the right, glaring at the bird that always has something to say. He turns his head, angling it to the side so I can only see one yellow eye surrounded by stark white feathers.

"What did I tell you about that fucking bird?"

"That's he's amazing," Wren says without even turning away from his stupid video games to look in my direction.

"Pretty bird," the African grey parrot says, and even now I can hear the fucking sarcasm in his voice as he walks back and forth on his perch, head bobbing up and down like there's a song playing only he can hear.

"Wren," I snap, and that's all it takes for my surveillance guy to drop his controller and turn in my direction.

"Fuck," he grunts when he sees me. "What's wrong?"

"I need you to work up a complete dossier on Daniella Altieri. Start by finding out what went down at her condo tonight."

His fingers are already working over the keyboard before I complete my demand. He's efficient like that when he has to be.

I tap my foot on the ground as if it will help Wren pull the information faster, but I go rigid when I notice that Puff Daddy—stupid name for a stupid bird, if you ask me—is stomping out the exact same beat with his beak. He turns his head to the side once again when I glare at him.

A low, insanely humanlike chuckle escapes from his throat. He doesn't possess an ounce of self-preservation, considering how many times I've threatened his life.

"There's not much about tonight." All of my attention turns to Wren. "Gunshot wound. Considered critical. Last update was him heading to the hospital."

"Him? As in male, or are you assuming?"

"Male victim," Wren says, pointing at the words on a screen I'm certain he doesn't legally have the right to be reading.

Relief like I've never known washes over me.

"What the hell have you gotten yourself into, Dani?" I mutter to myself as Wren goes back to work.

"Holy shit," Wren whispers. "Dude. Is this you?"

My eyes narrow on the computer screen, following the track of his finger to the picture there.

"Fuck off," I hiss. "I need a full workup."

"Look how much hair you had," he continues, not giving up. "Look at those curls. I prefer it over the buzz cut, man."

Even though I'm still irritated, I'm not as pissed as I would be if I hadn't just found out that it wasn't my ex-wife that was shot in her apartment. Of course, there are a million questions running through my head, but I give that relief a little time to breathe.

"When was this taken?" he asks, not pulling his eyes from the screen to the right which is running through screen after screen of information faster than my eyes can even focus on. He's fucking with me, but he's also managing to do what I need at the same time.

"Senior prom," I mutter.

"You look like a baby."

"I was."

Things were so different back then. There's a hopefulness in that kid's eyes as he looks down at the girl in his arms, but that hope burned away so long ago it seems like a handful of lifetimes have passed since that photo was taken.

"Wow," Wren mumbles. "Your wife, man?"

A wedding picture pops up, and I have to turn away. For the longest time, I thought that day was the best day of my life, until Dani bitched afterward about the simplicity of it all. She didn't get the dress she wanted. She had to settle with a ceremony in my parents' backyard instead of a huge party at a five-star hotel, or the destination wedding in Fiji she always hoped for. She only had two bridesmaids because I spent all of my time with her and didn't have any other guys to stand at my side while I promised the rest of my life to her.

She didn't see what I saw. She didn't see how her beauty shined through in her simple white dress, or how my mother's yellow rose bushes provided the perfect pop of color when compared to the bouquet of lilies in her hands.

I sigh in irritation as Wren sweeps through another set of images from the wedding. How did this shit even end up online?

"Your wife is smoking—"

"Ex-wife," I snap.

"—but this chick is every man's wet dream."

A smiling image of Annalise Grimaldi covers the screen, and for the life of me, I have no idea why her picture makes my breath catch. Maybe because I never remember her smiling. Maybe because the sun is reflecting off her golden pupils in a way that makes her seem ethereal. Maybe because in this image she doesn't look like the evil villain set out to ruin everyone's lives.

"She's on her way here," I murmur.

Wren turns his chair to face me, his unruly hair falling haphazardly over one eye. "Really? She's pretty."

"Hey, pretty girl! Wanna fuck?"

Wren's mouth spreads into a grin, but all I can do is roll my eyes at the stupid fucking bird.

"Bringing girls back to the office?" Wren's eyebrows waggle comically. "Naughty boss."

"Find me the information I need or you're going to be out of a fucking job," I snap.

He chuckles, knowing I'm full of shit. My entire operation would go down in flames if it wasn't for his computer skills. Technology is the future, and he damn well knows it.

"And teach that stupid bird something besides vulgar words."

Wren and the parrot are cackling like the fools they are when I let the door slam behind me.

"Not here yet?"

Ignacio shakes his head. Jude is nowhere to be seen.

"What does she look like?" Brooks asks with way more interest than I'm comfortable with.

A body like a god and a soul darker than Satan's. If memory serves me correctly.

"Like a woman."

Brooks turns, a smile on his face I know has pulled more chicks than the average man. I've intrigued him, but I don't have time for his bullshit right now.

"She's upset and dealing with some shit. Just come get me when she arrives."

Brooks, realizing I'm serious, nods his head and turns back to face the front office. I arrow to my office, needing a moment to wrap my head around the fact that Dani isn't the one hurt, but apparently, she's in some deep shit. Shootings and acts of violence don't happen often in her area of town. All I can do is wait. Wren is an ace at what he does and I know he won't bring me a dossier until he's one hundred percent sure he's obtained every ounce of information that he can scour from every single database he can access.

With the limited information Wren has on the victim, I type out a text to my second in command, Flynn Coleman, giving him Dani's address with a request to find out what he can. Flynn is former FBI and has managed to maintain many contacts at the bureau that benefit BBS.

Quickly, I change out of the damn dress shirt and jacket I had on for the retirement party, thankful I keep spare clothes in my office. We all do, actually. There's no telling what any given day will bring around here and we always have to be prepared.

Now all I can do is wait for the information to roll in, and that annoys me even more because waiting is the fucking worst. I'm a man of action, and this part sucks.

Chapter 4

Anna

My bare feet slap the polished concrete floor as I step onto the elevator, but I don't have the wherewithal to worry about germs right now. Besides, the floors are gleaming, as would be expected in this part of town. My destroyed heels hang from my still trembling fingertips as I press the button for the ninth floor.

I'm nearly in tears, stuck in my own head by the time the doors open to reveal a solid marble wall, only interrupted by a single door. Carved in the wall are the words BLACKBRIDGE SECURITY AND CONSULTING.

Shock immediately stops my pounding heart, quivering lip, and tears as I stare at Deacon's name carved into the wall.

But before I can do a double take or rub what I'm no doubt hallucinating from my tired eyes, a smiling man with gorgeous blue eyes pushes the door open for me.

"Annalise Grimaldi?" he asks as he sweeps his hand through his corn-silk blond hair.

"Y-Yes," I manage. "I'm here to see—"

"Deacon," he interrupts. "Come this way."

His voice is low and calm, somehow serving to lighten my load a little.

My eyes wander everywhere—to the sleek but functional reception area and the wide, no-frills hallway leading past offices. All the doors were closed for privacy; I imagine.

"I'm Brooks," the handsome man tosses over his shoulder as he directs me to a huge room with sofas, a massive television on the wall, and a coffee station fit for a king in the far corner.

"Anna," I tell him idiotically, because he knew who I was when he first opened the door. I blame it on the events of the night because any other given time, I'd have more control over my words and responses.

He gives me a kind smile, somehow reading my uncertainty as we make it to the center of the room.

"Would you like a cup of coffee?" Brooks asks when he sees my eyes dart in that direction.

I honestly don't, but the tranquil tone of his voice almost makes me say yes.

"No, thank you," I answer instead. I couldn't hold a cup of coffee without spilling it all over my hands right now if I wanted to.

"That's Ignacio." Brooks points to another handsome man on the phone. He's speaking in a language that's not even close to Spanish even though he's clearly of Hispanic descent.

Ignacio raises his hand in greeting, never missing a beat of the conversation he's having.

"Jude." Brooks points to the other man in the room who merely nods at me before looking back down at a length of rope in his hands.

Is Deacon breeding hot guys down here? Is that his new specialty since clearly, he's no longer in the military? Military guys don't have their names emblazoned on marble walls.

"And you've already met me." This charming bastard grabs my trembling hand and presses his warm lips to the skin there, and like an idiot who hasn't met dozens of celebrities and most of the kings and princes around the world, my cheeks flush at the contact.

"Brooks!" a man snaps behind me, but the charismatic guy doesn't jerk away. He simply lifts his head and winks. The mini-spell he cast on me doesn't break until he releases my hand and walks away.

In a daze and questioning everything in my life, I turn in the direction of the gravely angry voice only to be floored again.

I could tell you a million things I remember about Deacon Black. He's an asshole for starters, but more than that, he's always had this kind of jokester aura about him. Although it drove me crazy in high school, he was always doing something silly to make Dani laugh.

I hardly recognize the man standing in front of me. I'm not a good judge on size, but he's much larger than he was at the courthouse that day. His arms are thicker, his chest broader and testing the limits of the gray t-shirt he's wearing.

The only things that haven't changed are the sneer on his face and the fire shooting from his eyes.

"Deacon." I stand tall, knowing that I'm asking this man for help but also not willing to cower from him either.

His eyes are focused over my shoulder, and when a soft chuckle reaches my ears, I know that he's glaring at Brooks who doesn't seem at all intimidated by the angry man glaring at him.

"Deacon," I repeat, never the one to appreciate being ignored. My sister is much older so I practically grew up an only child, and of course I have all the selfish issues that come along with that position in the family.

"Anna," he grunts, still not looking at me.

I'd say he's snarly, if that's even a word, but if I'm being honest with myself, it's not altogether unappealing. The man has really grown into himself since I last saw him.

When his head turns and our eyes finally meet, I feel like I've been slapped in the face. Seeing his bright blue eyes as he watches someone else and having their attention solely on me are two different animals. Chills race over my skin, something that has never happened to me where he's concerned. Most of our interactions in the past have been actively avoiding each other even though our relationships to Dani put us in constant contact. It was a challenge we both excelled at, yet here I am coming to him with purpose and having the gumption to ask for help.

Suddenly, I feel like I'm in the wrong place. His divorce from Dani was ages ago, and I'm a fool for thinking he'd even care that she's hurt.

"It's not Daniella," he says, his eyes boring into me as if he can read my mind.

"Wh-What?"

"The injured person in her condo. It was a man, not a woman."

"How do you know?" Why did I just take a step closer to him? Is it relief? An invisible pull?

He doesn't answer. He simply pulls his eyes from mine to look around the room once again like he's scanning the space for threats. A tattoo of three crosses stretches down his neck from nearly the bottom of his jaw and disappearing into his shirt.

I wonder what Mrs. Black thinks of that? His mother was a no-nonsense English teacher at our high school, but she was well loved and respected because students knew exactly what they were getting. I don't think she'd be very impressed with him marking his body this way.

I clear my throat. "Are you sure?"

"One hundred percent. I have shit to do, Anna."

"Typical fucking Deacon," I mutter, but make sure to keep my voice loud enough for him to hear.

He huffs an indignant, humorless laugh but he still doesn't look at me.

"Thanks," I hiss, but when I turn to leave, I'm reminded of the sores I have on my bare feet.

"What the hell happened to you?"

I don't even have to turn back to know his eyes are on me. I can feel them drilling into my back like heated lasers.

Before I can tell him to fuck off, he grunts.

"Jude can you take care of this."

This.

Like I'm a nuisance, and he can't wait to be rid of me. Yep, definitely a mistake coming here.

If it were humanly possible, steam would be rolling out of my ears with how pissed he's making me. Apparently, it's only his looks that have changed. Now he's not just forty more pounds of muscle, but clearly, he's twice the asshole I remember as well.

"Really?" I ask as I turn back to face him.

I wonder how much jail time I'd get if I clawed his damn eyes out.

"Tell me about Dani's involvement with other men," Deacon demands before the guy on the sofa across the room can make it in our direction. He pauses, almost comically once Deacon begins talking again.

I glare at him. "Her relationships with men are not any of your damn business."

How shitty of a friend does it make me if I tell him I haven't spoken to her at length for quite a while, and I don't have a clue who she's been dating? Some damn best friend I am, right?

"Jealousy didn't look good on you fifteen years ago, and it still isn't winning you any awards no matter how strong your damn jaw is now."

Internally, I kick myself for letting that slip out.

Deacon's lip twitches, but the fire never stops burning in his eyes. His face returns to anger when someone on the other side of the room tries to cover a laugh with a cough. If I had to put money on it, I'd say Brooks was the culprit. He seems like the type to enjoy winding this man up.

My back stiffens, and I hope it makes him believe my refusal to give him any information.

"I'm not a jealous ex, Anna," he seethes. "You called me for help, remember? Dani wasn't the one injured in the condo. I've had one of my guys try to reach out to her and the cops answered her phone from inside her apartment. They don't know where she is. Do you?"

He had one of his guys try to call her.

For some reason that seems to make a lot of difference right now. Maybe I was mistaken on the jealousy.

I look down at my own phone in my hands. I hadn't tried to call my best friend because I was so certain that she was the one being taken to the hospital. Knowing the police have her phone will keep me from ever calling her number again.

"Where is she?" I ask like he didn't just tell me he didn't know.

"Anna," he growls.

Knowing that I'm irritating him just as much as he's irritating me makes me stupidly giddy. Just like old times.

"Who was the guy in her condo? Is she dating thugs now?" He shakes his head on a huff. "I wouldn't put it past her. Slumming has always been her kind of thing."

I could argue with him, remind him that he's the only man without money Dani ever showed an interest in, but right now doesn't seem like the time. It was always a point of contention between the two.

"I don't know who it was. I thought it was her, remember?"

This conversation is going absolutely nowhere.

"If it wasn't Dani, then I'm just going to go home."

I don't exactly relish the idea of walking out of here on bare, injured feet, but the fear I felt in my apartment earlier has been replaced with anger at being around Deacon once again, and that's enough irritation to keep me going for a lifetime. The relief that it isn't Dani also makes my lungs seize and my eyes burn with unshed tears. I'd like to have my breakdown in private because I don't put it past this jerk to gain comic relief from my pain.

"You're not going anywhere," he snaps before I can even get fully turned away from him.

"Excuse me." I spin around and nearly lose my balance. Deacon lifts an arm to catch me, but I'm lucky enough to manage it on my own without his putting his hand on me. I wouldn't be able to stand even that miniscule amount of help from him.

"You're hurt—"

"Blisters from shoes aren't exactly a fatal wound."

"—and until we know what the hell—"

"I'll be fine."

"—is going on, it may not be safe going back to your building."

We talk over each other, but I still hear what he says.

"Not safe?" I question, and just with his simple words, I grow frightened again.

I may lose my mind before all of this mess is over with. My emotions are firing a million miles an hour, and I don't have a damn clue where it's going to land next.

"There was so much blood, Deacon." I lower my head and look down at my phone and shoes in my hands. "The EMTs' gloves were covered in it. Cops were everywhere. If it wasn't her, where is she?"

His throat works on a swallow as tears begin to roll down my cheeks. "I don't know, but you're stuck here until we figure it out. Let Jude get those wounds cleaned up. You won't be walking any runways if they get infected."

My jaw hangs open, but he doesn't even notice because in a blink, he's disappearing into an office on the other side of the room. How much does he remember? How much did he pay attention to me way back when? He knew I wanted to be a model? A pipe dream that never came to fruition, but still. He remembered? I can't even allow myself to be angry that his words were another barb, another insult about the differences in our lives.

"Follow me," Jude says as he walks past.

Looking around the room, I find Ignacio off the phone and staring in my direction. When I notice the charming Brooks doing the same, I duck my head and follow the guy back down the hallway. The second he shoves open a door, the lights flash on, revealing a room stuffed with enough medical supplies to make most free-standing clinics jealous.

He points to an exam table on the far wall, and like the obedient child I never was, I hop up on the table without argument.

After washing his hands, he gathers supplies and spreads them out on a small rolling table.

"How long have you known Deacon?"

He doesn't say a word as he pulls on latex gloves, unwraps some gauze, and pops the top on a new bottle of saline.

I hiss when the cool fluid flows over my sores, and I expect him to grip me hard when his free hand presses to the back of my calf to hold me steady, but surprisingly his touch is gentle, much the same way I'd expect a doctor in a hospital to be.

"I didn't even know he was out of the military," I continue.

I'm left without a response once again.

"You're not curious about me?"

This causes his eyes to lift up to mine, but he still doesn't open his mouth.

I give him a sweet smile, one that has worked for me numerous times in the past, but he doesn't seem fazed by the miniscule charm I'm trying to lure him in with. I want details on Deacon. I want to know what he's been up to for some reason. Is he even up to the challenge of locating Dani? Is she even missing? Did someone take her and hurt her? Was her blood in the condo as well?

I keep the questions coming before my mind can run through every episode of *CSI* I've watched and start coming to horrific conclusions about my best friend.

"Not curious at all?" I prod because talking seems to help with the insane thoughts racing through my mind.

Jude only gives me another small smile.

"Is it often that women show up here off the street in crisis?"

His lip twitches. "You'd be surprised just how often that very thing happens."

And things just got a lot more interesting.

What exactly have you become, Deacon Black?

Chapter 5
Deacon

"You're a dick."

I take a long slow breath, keeping my eyes off the stupid fucking bird as I enter Wren's office again.

"I'm going to put that bird in a fucking stew," I threaten.

"At least he didn't call you motherfucker," Wren says as I pull up a chair beside his. "Give him some time to change. It's a slow process."

"Speaking of slow," I mumble, angling my head toward the computer. "What do you have for me?"

"Quite a lot actually."

I spend the next hour going through the copious amounts of information Wren has discovered online, and my eyes are nearly crossing when I stand to leave. After finding out that Dani wasn't the one hurt, I was hoping this would end up being an open-and-shut case, but the shit Wren just explained to me makes things much more complicated.

"Compile the rest of it for me. Shoot it to my phone and print a hard copy."

"You got it."

I turn and glare at the bird, challenging the bastard to say something. Unconcerned and using his beak and foot to open a sunflower seed, he simply does that head tilt shit before shooting me a *later* as I open the door.

"He's going to eat you one of these days," Wren says.

"Eat it hard," Puff says before I close the office door. "You know what Daddy likes."

"Stupid fucking bird," I mutter as I walk across the room.

"She's in your office," Jude says before I can even open my mouth to ask a question.

Normally, I'd be ecstatic at his ability to get me information before I have to waste energy asking for it, but there's something about the glint in his eyes that makes me cautious. Also, I didn't want that damn woman in my office. We have a waiting area in the back for instances just like this. He'd never let another client into my semi-personal space. I guess I should just be grateful he didn't send her upstairs to my apartment on the tenth floor.

Client.

I realize as I think the word, that's exactly what Annalise Grimaldi is. She isn't an old friend. Enemy would be closer to the definition, but this is still personal, right?

She didn't call me to hire Blackbridge. She called because when there was an issue with my ex-wife, I'm the first person she thought of.

I clench my teeth, looking over at my medic, wondering who's going to provide his treatment when I jab him in the damn nose for the way he's looking at me right now.

His grin only grows wider. I expect this kind of shit from Brooks, but it seems he just can't leave it alone. "She had a lot of questions about you."

That news doesn't really upset me, simply because I know he didn't tell her a damn thing. No matter how personal a case is, he's a professional through and through. The other guy loitering around the room however…

My eyes hitch toward Brooks. The smiling bastard simply raises an eyebrow at me.

"You need to tone down your fucking charm while dealing with clients."

"Can't," he says with a wide smile. "It's literally uncontrollable."

"I know better," I mutter. "Ease up a little on the charisma and keep your fucking eyes off of her."

"She's off-limits." It's not a question, and I know he's not finished. "I knew that much when you pissed a circle around her when you first saw her."

"Never seen you growl at a client before," Ignacio says, walking into the room with a beer in his hand.

"Don't you assholes have anything better to do than hang out here? Anything on the Hughes case?"

Ignacio takes a seat next to Jude on the sofa. "Nothing yet, boss, but I'm working several different angles."

I tilt my head, popping my neck, but it doesn't bring the same sweet relief it normally does.

"You know what would ease some of that tension?" I don't even look at Brooks. I know exactly where his head is—in the gutter like usual. But nothing will ever happen between Anna and me. Like *ever*. We can hardly stand to be in the same room with each other.

I release a long sigh and turn away from them.

"Exactly," Brooks says as I head to my office.

They couldn't possibly be further off the mark right now. The only reason Anna is here is because her friend is in trouble. Probably more trouble than she even realizes after the information I just got from Wren.

They're only looking at skin-deep shit though, and when a woman walks in here crying and asking for help, looking like a four-course meal, they're bound to read things wrong.

The woman in the parking garage eight years ago has nothing on the Annalise Grimaldi that showed up here tonight. Even then, she'd changed from the day of our wedding, but now she's somehow managed to get thicker, sexier with her long brown, almost black hair. Her eyes are brighter, more honey-like, even red-rimmed with tears and fear muting them.

"Jesus," I hiss, rubbing my hands over my face before opening my office door.

I need to figure all of this shit out with Dani so I can send her angry little friend on her way.

"Like fast," I whisper when I walk in and find her asleep on the sofa in the corner.

No longer resembling a snarling bear, Anna is curled up in a protective ball, her small hands under her chin. I'd say she looks like a child, but the woman is way too stacked for anyone with working eyes to make that mistake. Bandages from Jude's care are the only things tainting her perfect skin, and somehow even those don't detract from her appeal. They make her real, less perfect, more approachable which is something I never pictured her as before.

I shake my head, forcing any thoughts of how she looks from it. I'm just tired, and maybe my dry spell has been a little too long. That's the only reason for letting her somehow invade my thoughts in any form other than working toward getting her the hell out of my life, again.

I clear my throat, but she doesn't even stir, so I find another gentle way to wake her. I slam my office door, and she jerks like she's been shot.

"You're such an asshole," she hisses as she lifts the top half of her body off the sofa and stretches.

Fuck my life. Has her belly button always been pierced?

I sneer in her direction. What self-respecting woman in her thirties has body jewelry?

My throat suddenly dry, I try to convince myself as I walk across the room, leaning on the front of my desk with my arms crossed over my chest that asking her for a better look at the glinting stone would be a mistake.

"What?" she snaps when she looks in my direction to find me watching her.

I want to ask how her makeup is still perfect. She's been sleeping. She came into the BBS offices with tears running down her cheeks. Yet, here she is, lipstick still in place and not even the hint of a smear under her eyes.

"Did you reapply your makeup?" Damn it. I'm a fucking idiot.

"Huh?" She touches her face with soft hands still throwing daggers my way. "I left my apartment with nothing but my phone. I don't even have my keys to get back inside. Why in the ever-loving hell would you think I reapplied makeup?"

Because you're gorgeous.

Like a smart man, I keep my mouth clamped closed. She's managed to tilt everything upside down, and I know if I open my lips to speak, something crazy may have the chance to slip out.

"What?" She's glaring at me, eyes narrow and ready to cut me with her scathing words. "Don't look at me like that."

I drop my eyes to the table in front of the sofa, unsure of what my face is actually doing.

"You came to me for help," I tell her evenly.

"You're not concerned about Dani?"

"Of course I am. That's why I'm helping."

"Do you still love her?"

Unable to decipher her tone, I raise my eyes back to hers. She stares back at me with a blank expression, like the question she asked means more to her than she's wanting to let on.

"This isn't about love," I assure her. "It's an obligation."

"What kind of man—" She snaps her mouth closed before looking down at her hands and taking a deep breath.

I will her with my eyes to finish that sentence, but she doesn't.

"You know what, none of that even matters."

"What's going on in her life?"

She bristles with my question, but she doesn't taunt me with the same bullshit she did earlier.

"We haven't talked much lately." I see a flash of pain fill her eyes, and it's easy to see that there's some regret there.

Those two were thick as damn thieves, and although I shouldn't be because that chapter in my life has been closed for a while now, I'm curious about what could've happened to cause distance between them. Did Dani go after Anna's boyfriend? Did my ex hurt her friend the same way she hurt me?

"How long?" I ask instead of opening gates that I may never be able to close again. I wouldn't be surprised if Dani did something unforgiveable. She's always been an expert manipulator and unrepentantly selfish.

"What?"

"When was the last time you spoke with her?"

"We haven't really hung out in months, but I spoke with her a couple of weeks ago."

"Did she talk to you about her money problems?"

Anna laughs like what I just disclosed is absurd. "She doesn't have money problems."

"Her credit cards are maxed." Her shock-filled eyes snap up from her hands. "Her rent is late, and she's on the verge of eviction. She has nothing left. No money in the bank, nothing."

It's apparent by the look on her face that she had no idea about any of this. Just how much distance is there between them?

I don't mention Dani's dad's problems or the fact that all of his accounts have been frozen due to a pending federal corruption investigation. If she didn't know Dani was no longer rich, she wouldn't have heard about any of that either.

A knock on the door interrupts, but before I can tell them to wait, Wren shoves open the door and hands me a folder.

"This is what I found so far. I'm still running some other checks."

I nod at him, and he turns to leave. He merely gives Anna a passing glance before walking out the door. Unlike Brooks who could charm the panties off a nun, Wren is all talk behind his computer screen, growing shy when around beautiful women in person.

Anna doesn't speak as I flip through the dossier Wren just handed over. Silence fills the room before my eyes land on a piece of information that makes my jaw clench.

"Tell me about the Russian Dani's been dating."

Chapter 6
Anna

"Russian?"

Deacon tilts his head, giving me that *don't bullshit me* look.

"Listen." I hold my hands up. "I saw a guy she was recently dating a few times in passing, but he never spoke in front of me. She didn't even introduce him. I don't know if he was Russian or not."

"Yet you don't seem surprised."

I huff. "Why would I be? Last year she was dating a guy she swore was a Saudi prince. She isn't exactly selective so long as the guy has money."

Deacon looks back down to the folder of information, cracking his neck to either side before looking back at me. The sound makes my skin crawl just like it always has.

"Is that who was in the apartment?" He nods. "Is he dead?"

"Not yet." There's no emotion whatsoever in his voice, like it won't bother him at all that the man could die.

"She was spooked," I recall, saying the words out loud as the memory floods my brain.

"When?"

"When I talked to her on the phone last week. She answered the phone but only stayed on the line long enough to tell me that she couldn't talk. The phone call was so brief, I only just now remembered it. I didn't think much of it. Dani has always been sort of a drama queen. She could've been spooked because Neiman's was having a sale she didn't have time to make. You never know with her."

Deacon snorts in agreement. "When did you speak to her before that conversation?"

"Ten days before that, maybe? So, like three weeks ago. She wouldn't give me much information, just that she was going on vacation to a beach. I think the next time I spoke with her was right after she got back from that trip."

Even though he's still looking down at the paperwork in his hands, I know he's listening to me, so I continue.

"I stopped by her apartment a couple of days ago after she didn't show up for a gala, but she didn't answer the door."

His eyes find mine, and he doesn't look impressed at all. "Still living your life from one party to the next, I see."

"Do you just wake up in the morning and decide to be an asshole?"

He blinks in my direction.

"Or maybe spin a wheel to determine your level of dickheadedness for the day?"

"According to the information Wren found, you don't seem to be in any danger."

Of course he'd just ignore my questions. It's not like I fully expected him to give me an answer anyway.

He doesn't say a word before walking out of the office. Stubbornly, I stay on the sofa. He didn't tell me to follow him, and even if he had, I wouldn't trail along behind him like some damn lost dog waiting for bits and pieces of information.

I don't really want to go back to my place, but I can't get a hotel room for the night without returning there for my purse.

"Here."

I look up to see a pair of basketball shoes in his hands.

"I imagine they're going to still be too big, but these are the smallest pair we have here."

Instinctively, I scrunch my nose at the sight of the shoes. I'm not at the country club about to play tennis, so these just won't work at all.

"I'm wearing a Prada dress."

"And we're all out of fucking matching Jimmy Choos," he growls before dropping the sneakers near my bandaged feet. "Go barefoot for all I care but hurry the fuck up. I have other shit to do."

"Where are we going?" I snap as I regretfully tug the shoes on my feet, tying them as tightly as I can manage to help prevent them from creating more blisters.

"I'm taking you home." He's irritated to the max but pissing him off has always been fun for me. It's been years, and it's only taken a fraction of time to get right back to where we were all those years ago.

"Taking me home? How do you know I didn't drive?"

"You don't have any fucking keys."

"Whoa there, detective. Calm down."

He grumbles under his breath, but I'm on his heels when he leaves the room for the second time. The quicker I get my purse from my condo, the faster I can see the back of him. I never should've called his ass in the first place, and I'm kicking myself for doing just that when we're caged alone together in a different elevator from the one I took to get up here.

When the doors finally open, we're not in the lobby of the building I entered through but in a parking garage lined with vehicles more fitting for war than downtown St. Louis.

"Is that an armored truck?"

"I'm parked over here," he says, once again ignoring my question.

"What the hell are you into, Deacon? I was thinking you left the military, but it doesn't seem like it's that far in your past."

With the flick of his wrist, a huge black truck roars to life. I resist the urge to cover my ears as the grumble echoes off the concrete surrounding us.

"You know what they say about guys in big trucks—"

The words die on my lips when he turns and glares at me. "Do you want to walk home?"

"I'd take a fucking cab, jerk. Just like I did to get here." After all the stairs I took out of my own building, I never want to walk more than a few feet for the rest of my life.

He sweeps his hand in the direction of the guarded exit ramp. "Move your sweet little ass then."

Sweet little ass?

Before I can ask him if he's paying me a compliment, he climbs in his truck, honking the horn when I don't immediately follow. I jump like I've been hit with an electric pulse.

"Fucking jerk," I mumble as I open the door and nearly break my neck trying to get inside.

He doesn't laugh at me for having that reaction to the horn or my shoddy attempt to climb in his jacked-up truck like a normal person would. He's too intense, too reserved for that kind of stuff, I guess.

What happened to the boy with the quick smile?

I click my seatbelt in place and stare out the window. Of course he was never smiling my way back in high school, so why should things be any different now?

"I see you still have a filthy mouth."

"Wouldn't you like to find out just how filthy it can get?" I say before I even think about who I'm talking to. My cheeks heat, and I know I'll beat myself up later for it. If he wasn't so infuriating, I'd have better control over my stupid mouth.

Thankfully, he doesn't tease me about the slipup. Putting the truck in drive, he rolls toward the gate that automatically opens when he draws closer. His truck is dark, functional, and surprisingly clean. There isn't a speck of dust on the dash or an empty fast food bag to be seen. There's nothing in here that even hints at his personality or what he's been up to since we last saw each other.

I have more than a million questions about him, his life since the divorce, and his job.

But I can't ask any of those. We were never friends in the past, and we sure as hell aren't friends now. We drive in silence, and the questions just keep piling up.

Has he had any contact with Dani?

Does he keep track of her?

Does he care what she's been doing the last couple of years?

Does he want to rescue her from her money troubles? He doesn't seem to be hurting for cash these days.

I want to confess how scared I am, how my hands are literally shaking with the lack of information about what's going on with my best friend. He said there are no threats to me that his friend found, but how can he be sure?

When I squeeze my eyes closed, all I can see are the distorted images of the EMTs rushing past my peephole with that man on the stretcher. I don't even know if the man they took out of there was the same guy she was dating.

Feeling his eyes on me at the red light, I look up and glance in his direction, but Deacon is staring out the front windshield. It makes me wonder if I'm losing my damn mind, but then the stark brightness of his eyes makes everything else fade away.

Were his eyes always so blue and mesmerizing? Was his jaw, now covered in thick, dark stubble, always so strong and defined? Surely not. The man I remember was a jerk, an asshole to the ultimate extreme, making me cringe every time I saw him. From our interaction earlier, he's still a huge jerk, but so long as this guy keeps his snide comments to himself and the snarky comebacks at bay, I can admit just how damn handsome he is.

The masculine jaw in question clenches when his eyes dart in my direction. He's not impressed with catching me watching him, but he keeps his mouth closed as the light turns green.

I'm an absolute fool for even noticing how good-looking he is. My best friend is missing, could possibly be hurt, and here I am wondering what his stupid hands would feel like on my skin.

Heaven help me. I've lost my damn mind.

Chapter 7
Deacon

Anna's condo is only six miles from the office, eleven minutes in traffic to make it there, yet it seems like a decade has passed before we pull up outside the overpriced building.

For a man whose job is to literally keep an eye on people, to track people down, I'm hit with the knowledge that I didn't know where my ex-wife was living until Wren pulled the information online. When I said I wasn't looking back eight years ago after getting divorced, I meant it. It wasn't an immediate break, of course. I was too weak for that, but last I knew she was living back with her parents, planning her wedding to some mogul that her elitist parents approved of. Hell, she was wearing his damn ring that day in court if I recall correctly.

"She didn't marry Charles Warren?"

Anna looks from her building back to me.

These are the first words I've spoken since we left the parking garage, and I feel like an idiot for even asking. I just want to shove this woman out of my truck and drive off. I have every intention of forgetting I even saw her today, and the sooner she leaves my vehicle, the quicker that can happen.

I don't know why I even asked, morbid curiosity maybe?

"The man wasn't very happy when he found out Dani was keeping a guy on the side."

I'm surprised she even answered my question without questioning my level of concern, but more surprising is the look she gives me when I nod my head in understanding.

"She didn't—did she cheat on you, too?"

"I'll walk you up," I say instead of answering.

Anna is Dani's best friend. I find it impossible that she doesn't know the details of our breakup.

"I'll be fine," she mutters in irritation, but before she can climb out of my truck, I'm already out and around to her side.

"My mother would kick my ass if I didn't see you to your door."

She grumbles, completely unimpressed with the minimal level of courtesy I'm trying to provide. I won't tell her that I hope the cops are gone so I can take a look around Dani's apartment in an attempt to figure out more about what's going on. Letting her know that would only lead to another barrage of questions, and explaining my job and what I do every day isn't any of her concern. I don't want details about her life, and she sure as hell isn't getting any about mine. Finding her watching my face on the drive over with a weird look of curious infatuation was enough.

After a quick hello to the doorman, Anna scurries across the expansive lobby like she's trying to hide from everyone. No doubt she's embarrassed about her uncoordinated shoes. The woman never would leave home without being completely dolled up, and she must be dying a little on the inside knowing that people are seeing her in a designer dress and plain black Nikes.

A smile tugs up both corners of my mouth as the elevator opens. I don't say a word even though I want to taunt her and make her feel even more out of place. That would be petty, and I'm a grown ass man.

"Think he's going to share a picture of you in those shoes to TMZ?"

Ha! Obviously not grown enough.

"Genaro is a professional. He'd never do that to me."

"Anyone will do anything for the right price," I mumble. "Trust me."

The elevator opens up on the twenty-sixth floor to silence. The police that Anna mentioned were bustling around earlier are no longer loitering in the halls.

"It's eerily quiet up here," Anna observes as we step out.

"The police are gone," I tell her. "There were no cop cars out front."

"I'm sure the staff made them park out back. Genaro wouldn't allow even the cops to cause a spectacle out front. He's—" Her words catch in her throat, and it doesn't take but a split second for me to realize why.

I pull my gun from my hip, unsure of what I'm going to find on the other side of Anna's ajar door.

"You have a gun!" she screeches. "Why do you have a gun?"

"Shut up," I snap, instinctually moving my body so she's behind me. "Did you leave your door open?"

"Of course not, idiot," she snaps, and even though I know she's scared, she still manages to insult me. Same old Annalise.

Maybe I should let her go in first.

The thought makes me smile, but the sight of the police tape on the door down the hall reminds me just how dangerous the situation is.

"It's been kicked in," I tell her as I inch closer, noticing the fractured wood at the door frame.

"The police kicked in my door?"

I stop her from moving around me to see the damage.

"Probably not the police. Stay out here."

For once in her damn life, the woman listens to me, and by the time I push her front door open fully, I can hear small sobs coming from the hallway.

Bringing her back here was a mistake, and that's made obviously clear when I look around the trashed room. It definitely wasn't the police, unless they were looking for a needle because her belongings are the haystack. The entire room is trashed. The television has been kicked in and ripped from the wall. The expensive sofas have been slashed. There isn't a single piece of furniture that hasn't been toppled. Every drawer in the kitchen has been pulled out, several on the floor upside down. There are utensils strewn everywhere. This place is a damn mess.

Even the fridge has been opened and divested of its contents all over the marble floor. Her bedroom has met the same fate, the mattress slashed and her clothes scattered all over the damn floor.

"Fuck," I grumble as I make my way back to the living room. "And to think my night was almost over."

"Oh my God."

My eyes snap up to find Anna standing in the doorway with her hands cupped over her mouth and tears streaming down her cheeks. Her eyes are glued to a painting on the floor. It's destroyed, but it couldn't have been more expensive than all the other things combined, but it seems to be her sole focus.

"Was it a Monet or something?"

"Zeni painted that for me."

On second look, I can tell it's one of those cheap paint by numbers canvases, but after hearing her, it hits me in the gut like an anvil. Zeni was her cousin, only two years younger than us who killed herself our senior year in high school. They found no note, no explanation or reason why the pretty girl took her own life, and the pain it caused Anna back then was astronomical. It was the only time the girl broke her tougher than nails façade in public. It was the only time I wrapped my arms around her, and she let me as she cried into my shirt. It didn't last long before Dani pulled her away.

I don't reach for her now. I don't think she'd appreciate me touching her, but the longer she stands there staring down at the ruined painting the easier it is to see that she's still haunted by her cousin's death even after all this time.

"I'm sure it can be fixed," I say, almost placing my hand on her back, only to pull it away at the last second.

We both know it will be impossible to repair, but she nods anyway.

"We need to get out of here. The police didn't do this."

As if in a trance, Anna follows me out of the apartment. I have my phone out, texting Flynn to come check out both apartments before the elevator opens up in front of us.

"Where are you taking me?" she asks when we climb back inside my truck.

"To a hotel."

"Can I stay with you?"

Abso-fucking-lutely not. "No."

"I can't stay alone." Her tears haven't stopped since she stepped inside of her apartment, but it'll take much more than some crying to get me to let this chick invade my private space. No one, and I mean *no one* is allowed in my apartment or back on the ranch.

"You'll be fine," I assure her. "I'll book you under a different name. I don't know who trashed your place, but until we get more info, you can't use any of your credit cards in case they're tracking you."

"They're all back at the apartment anyway," she manages through her crying.

I make a mental note to have Wren track Anna's shit too. I wouldn't put it past someone petty enough to do that to her belongings to use her credit cards.

"This has to be related to what happened in Dani's apartment."

"Impossible." I almost smile at the fire in her voice. Her anger I understand and can deal with. Crying women have always made my skin crawl.

"And why is that?"

"I don't have any enemies." I cock an eyebrow at her because we both know she and I aren't friends, but she just scoffs. "Everyone loves me."

I nearly laugh at those words but decide I'm just glad that the tears seem to have stopped for now.

"You can't be serious." Her eyes are wide as she peers at the hotel sign.

"They have a complimentary breakfast."

"I don't eat carbs and grease any time of the day."

"Your snobbery is showing."

"I'm not staying here," she growls, and right then I know if I go in and book a room it'll only be a waste of my damn time.

"I'm not paying for you to stay in some five-fucking-star hotel. I can take you to your parents."

"I don't want them knowing anything about this. I want to go to sleep. I'm exhausted, and my dad will grill me for hours."

"Not my problem." I put the truck in drive and take off toward her parents' neighborhood.

"Take me to the Four Seasons."

"I'm not—"

"Fucking bill me for it," she hisses.

"No one would expect you to be at that other hotel," I explain.

"Because they know I'll already be dead if I'm forced to stay there."

I grip the steering wheel until my fucking hands ache. There isn't one single thing about this hoity-toity woman that I missed.

Chapter 8
Anna

After demanding a suite with a view, I practically throw myself on the sofa in the lobby and wait for him to finish booking the room. With the way my luck's going tonight, he'll be back in minutes letting me know that his credit card was declined. The lady working the front desk keeps a pleasant smile on her face even as he clenches his jaw so tight, I'm fearful he'll crack his teeth.

Thankfully, I keep my eye on him because he doesn't even look my way before turning from the counter and heading to the elevator. I barely have time to slide my arm through the gap before the damn elevator door closes.

"Very mature," I hiss when I step inside with him. "Did you get a suite?"

I honestly don't expect him to have gotten more than just a basic room, but they're all nice here so it's really no big deal. I just need about three days' worth of sleep.

"The Presidential Suite." There's laughter in his tone, as if he's somehow sticking it to me by getting one of the very best rooms they have to offer. He hands me the printed receipt with a wicked grin on his face like I'll be upset at the price. "The room is booked for the week. Non-refundable. I'll make sure it all goes on your tab."

I don't even bat an eyelash. I'm not so much a diva that I need over twenty-five-hundred square feet in a hotel suite, but I'm not going to turn it down either. His smile has fallen with my lack of response by the time the elevator opens up on the nineteenth floor, but even as irritated as he is, he still unlocks the door, holding it open for me to enter first. Despite his prickly attitude, his mother did raise him right.

I'm surprised he doesn't kick me in the ass and walk out of the room the second I cross the threshold, but by the way he's standing just inside makes it very clear he has no intentions of staying. Normally, I'd feel safe looking out onto the Gateway Arch, but it doesn't bring the same level of security tonight. Not after what happened in Dani's condo. Not after what happened to my own condo.

"I'll update you if we get any new information." Deacon hands me the plastic key to the room before returning to the door. "I suggest staying here until you hear from me."

My hands are trembling too hard to hold the key before the door clicks closed behind him. Being alone has never been an issue for me. If anything, I prefer silence over being in crowds or around others. I know it doesn't appear that way to most because I have a very active social life, but those obligations are more because of my parents than anything else.

The tears I thought had dried up in the truck on the way here come back full force, and I rush around the suite turning on every light to try to gain more comfort. It doesn't come. The fear doesn't abate when I snap on the light in the media room. It doesn't fade when I do the same in the study or the bedroom.

The king-sized bed doesn't look appealing. It looks lonely, like it will swallow me whole if I even get near it. The knocking on the suite door sounds all too familiar to the knocking on my condo door before I bolted out of there to go to Deacon's office, and after coming home to find my entire condo destroyed, all I can picture is that someone followed me here. What would've happened to me if I hadn't left as quickly as I did? Were the guys knocking on my condo door before I left, the ones wanting to hurt me?

The blood on the EMT's hands flash in my mind, and it only takes seconds for my brain to register the fear. The suite bedroom closet isn't exactly tight quarters, but I throw myself in there anyway. At least there's a door that closes even if there isn't a single thing in here to use for protection against an intruder.

The knocking stops, but less than ten seconds later, the door to the suite whooshes open. I'm on the verge of a heart attack, whimpering and terrified when a shadow crosses in front of the door. It fades away only to return a few seconds later.

I screech when it's tugged open, burying my head in my bent knees and trying to prepare myself for the worst. I don't know shit about survival or how to defend myself. I only attended one of the self-defense classes my dad wanted me to take in college because I ended up with bruises on my legs after that one session. There was no way I was going to walk around campus looking like I had been beaten. I'm regretting that decision now.

"What in the hell are you doing?"

I snap my face in Deacon's direction, expecting from his tone that he's going to call me an idiot, but he must see the fear in my eyes because he closes his mouth and stands outside the closet door.

No doubt he's still pissed, his default for as long as I've known him, but there's a flash of sympathy in his eyes as well. I nearly bristle with the look he's giving me but bite my tongue instead. I don't want him to leave again, and I know opening my mouth to tell him he's an asshole for scaring me would increase that chance.

"Get in the bed and get some rest." He walks away, and I find him standing in the middle of the living room looking out onto the Gateway Arch when I gather enough courage to leave the closet.

"It's pretty, isn't it?"

I've always taken the architecture in St. Louis for granted. It's always just been there. Yeah, I've ridden on the tram to the top and looked out the tiny windows way up in the sky, but that was more for the video and for social media, the ability to mark it off some contrived list of experiences. I didn't take a moment to enjoy the actual beauty of it. Somehow though, the sight of the Arch, which right now includes Deacon's reflection in the window glass, is an absolute thing of beauty.

"You bitched the entire time we were up there," he mutters, crossing his arms over his chest and spreading his legs. He doesn't bother to turn around and face me directly.

How could I forget that Dani, he, and I did that together? Hell, we did everything together despite our contempt of the other. Dani was our North Star. We were both pulled to her, spending nearly every waking moment we could with her. Thinking back, I can't even remember when the shift started to happen, when she was more interested in doing things for herself than spending time with me and him.

"Get some sleep, Anna. I'm waiting for some information. I'll stay here until it comes in."

Since it doesn't seem like he wants to take a trip down memory lane, I turn and walk away without another word, kicking the ridiculous sneakers off my feet before climbing in the bed. After a few minutes, I realize just how uncomfortable my dress is, so I toss back the covers and tug it off over my head, tossing it to the floor. I don't turn off the lights in the room, but I can't imagine sleeping at a time like this.

A guy was shot, my apartment was ransacked, and Dani can't be found.

Was she abducted? Are they going to want a ransom?

With the financial trouble she's in, that means her dad is suffering too. He probably wouldn't be able to pay, but even though my own parents aren't Dani's biggest fans, I know they wouldn't let her be hurt over money.

What if Deacon doesn't find her in time? What if something happened to her long before tonight?

A shiver rolls down my arms remembering how she didn't answer her door the other day. How she missed the annual Star Light Gala last week. She loves that event and hasn't missed one since its inception ten years ago.

"Deacon!"

It only takes seconds before he's standing inside the room. I swallow, the lump of fear lodged so deep in my throat I don't know if I'll ever be able to speak again. Tears burn the backs of my eyes, but I do everything I can to keep them from falling. I know he's tired of me, tired of seeing me cry, tired of having to even be near me, but somehow, he's still a comfort to me.

"I-I don't want to be alone," I croak.

His eyes dart from the sheet clutched to my chest to the empty spot beside me on the bed, and then he looks physically sick at the thought of crawling under the same blankets with me.

Instead of crossing the room to join me, he walks to the chair in the small seating area and sits down, pulling out his phone and ignoring me. Overlooking the small wave of disappointment washing over me, I watch him. What did I think? That he was going to join me, wrap his arms around me and tell me everything was going to be okay?

"Thank you for helping me," I say, my eyes still glued to his stupid handsome face.

He merely grunts like a caveman rather than bothering with actual words.

"I know you hate me."

His jaw clenches, but he still doesn't look up from his phone.

It seems like an eternity before he speaks.

"I don't hate you."

Liar.

I don't believe him, but then his shoulders relax, and he looks calmer than I think I'll ever feel again.

Nope. He's telling the truth. He doesn't hate me. He's indifferent to me, and that hits me harder. We no longer had a forced connection until I called him and dragged him right back into Dani's whirlwind of drama.

I doze off watching him, but immediately begin to dream of being in the condo when whoever it was came inside. They were a blur, a face covered in a ski mask, but terrifying, nonetheless.

I wake with a gasp, hot tears already rolling down my cheeks.

I'm near the point of having what feels like a panic attack, something that I've never before suffered from when Deacon's huge frame fills my vision.

Surprisingly gentle hands cup both sides of my face, and he forces my chin up until I'm looking in his bright, blue eyes. His thumbs skate over my cheeks, wiping my tears away.

"Shh. You're fine. You're safe. You know that, right?"

I nod my head as much as I can manage with his grip on my face.

"I'm not going to let anyone hurt you. Understand?"

I nod again, my focus drifting to his mouth as he says the words. Lips too pink and perfect to belong on any man's face are less than a foot away from mine, and I'm entranced by them.

"Go back to sleep," he whispers, showcasing his perfect teeth.

All I can do is nod in answer, hating that he releases me and goes back to the chair across the room.

Chapter 9
Deacon

I'm in the chair kicking myself for touching her face, beating myself up for noticing the way the soft, billowy sheet floated to her waist, revealing her jaw-dropping breasts covered in dark lace when a silent text rolls across my phone. How is her damn face that soft? How does she smell like a small slice of heaven? How did I let myself be drawn right back into this bullshit?

I'm tired as I stand, knowing where I'm heading next. It's five in the morning, and the sun hasn't even begun to think about casting its light on our part of the world yet, but sleep isn't going to happen anytime soon.

Grabbing the extra keycard from the table near the door, I slide it into my pocket before walking out of the ridiculously expensive suite. She wanted more room, and being the asshole that I am, I got the most expensive room they had available. She didn't even give a shit that the room cost more than two grand a night. Fucking rich people. I mean, I'm not broke, but what a damn waste of money. The economy hotel I was going to book would've been fine, but for the princess it was like even suggesting she walk inside was a slap to her face.

I head to the office, and when I get inside, I'm not at all surprised to see the usual suspects sitting around the breakroom area. In addition to Jude, Brooks, and Ignacio, Quinten Lake, my extraction expert, and Gaige Ward, my acquisitions guy, are there as well.

"Don't you fuckers have shit to do?" I complain as I walk across the room.

"It's not even six," Brooks says with a yawn from near the coffee pot. "Want a cup?"

"In a minute."

"You're not acting like someone who left here with a hot piece of ass last night," Brooks grumbles, but I ignore him.

Quinten snorts.

"I can find you something better if she didn't work out," Gaige offers, but I just flip them all off over my right shoulder.

Chuckles follow me into Wren's office.

"Put your dick away! We're being invaded!"

I grumble under my breath. The first fucking time the stupid bird said that when I walked in, I legit thought Wren was in here with his meat out, but then I realized he has cameras all over and there really isn't a way to surprise him by walking into his office. Not that I wouldn't put it past him to take his dick out in here when he's bored. The man spends way too much time in front of computer screens.

"Puff Daddy," Wren warns. "We talked about this."

"Talk to the hand," the bird snaps back.

"Doesn't even fucking have hands," I mutter before flopping down in the chair beside Wren. "Lay it on me."

Wren hands me another folder, a different color from the one he gave me last night.

"His name is Nikolay Petrovich."

"The guy she was dating or the guy in her condo?"

"They're one and the same. Haven't been together long, a couple of months maybe. I don't have a ton of details, but if there was ever the wrong guy for your wife—"

"Ex-wife."

"*Ex*-wife to get involved with, this is the one. He's got ties to bad shit all over the world." He turns to look at me. "How did it go last night?"

His grin is enough for me to grip the papers in my hands until they crinkle.

"How much work do you think you'd be able to get done with two swollen eyes and a broken hand?"

"No!" he gasps, dramatically holding his hands back protectively. "Not my moneymakers!"

"This is fucking serious shit," I seethe.

"It's always serious shit, D. You're going to have a stroke before you turn forty if you don't lighten up."

"What else?" I ask, ignoring the last jab because honestly, I'll be lucky to make it to thirty-five at the rate I'm going.

"Chatter is that the Russians are looking for Dani."

"How up to date is that info? Are you sure they don't have her already?"

"As of," he looks back at one of his computer screens and taps away, "three this morning, they still haven't found her."

"How do you know?"

He shrugs, a small smile curling up his lips. "I tapped into Daniella's phone and all the phones she's had contact with and it just spread from there.

"The Russians aren't using burners? I find that hard to believe."

"Crazily enough, most of them are on a family plan."

"Fucking idiots."

"I agree, but not everyone can have our latest tech. Anyway, they aren't only looking for your ex-wife, they're also looking for a fuckton of diamonds."

"What?"

"Diamonds, blood diamonds to be more specific. From the information I have, Nikolay went to confront her about them being missing and shit went down in her apartment. There's no record of them being recovered by the police or on Nikolay when he got to the hospital."

"Was it only his blood in the condo?"

"Too early to tell. Forensics aren't back yet."

"I can get Flynn to light a couple fires to make it happen quicker."

"Last night I would've argued that her father's recent run of bad luck was the reason all of this shit is going down, but Daniella has been all over the place with Petrovich."

"I want a list of every place they've visited since they met."

I stand from the chair.

"Already on it."

"I need you to find her, Wren."

When he looks up at me, he doesn't crack a joke like he normally would.

"I will," he vows, and when I walk out of his office, I know the man won't sleep until he's scoured the world to locate her.

Even the damn bird must sense the seriousness of the situation because he doesn't say a word as I walk out.

"Here." Brooks shoves a travel mug of coffee into my hand the second I step inside the break area.

"Thanks, man." I take a sip and wince at the tar-like beverage, but I don't bitch. I'm going to need every damn milligram of caffeine I can get today.

"Where are you headed?" Flynn asks, his British accent making his voice sound deeper this early in the morning.

"Altieri, Inc. When did you get here?"

"I've been here since I finished up at the condos last night. I was in the back when you arrived."

His hair is still wet from a recent shower, and I'm envious of him.

"What did you find?" I wave at the other guys as I walk out of the office and head to the elevator.

"Not much more than the police did. Wren found some security footage of the Russian boyfriend showing up, but somehow Daniella made it out of the building without being spotted. He couldn't find her leaving on the cameras."

In the parking garage, Flynn climbs into the passenger seat of my truck without even asking if he can tag along. I don't argue because I know he won't get out even if I threaten him. I may possibly be losing control of my own men, but that's an issue to deal with at another time.

"Less than an hour after the police left the scene, he tracked two big guys to the floor, but could only track them as far as the elevator. There aren't any cameras in the hallway on that floor."

"With what they're paying to live there, they should each have armed guards."

"No doubt," Flynn agrees, resting his arm in the windowsill. "I don't know if you went to Daniella's—"

"Dani," I interrupt. She hated her full name, and for some reason I feel like I need to respect that right now since I have no fucking clue what's happened to her.

"Dani's apartment was trashed worse than Annalise's."

For some reason it doesn't bother me as much when my closest friend uses Anna's full name. It's like I'm also protective of her and his using the shortened version gets him too close. I'll work my mind through that bullshit later.

"Looking for the diamonds," I muse.

"Probably."

This is what I love about my team. They're so efficient and up to date on everything, I don't have to waste my time retelling information.

"How was the Four Seasons?"

And then there are times when they're too damn efficient.

"Overpriced and pretentious."

He chuckles.

"Brooks says she's a real looker."

I huff a laugh. "Brooks thinks everyone is good-looking."

"True. The man has an uncanny ability to find the positive in everyone." I keep my eyes trained on the road. Flynn does too, but I don't even for a second think he's giving up on the topic of conversation. "Are you agreeing or not?"

"About Brooks? I just did."

"About Annalise Grimaldi," he corrects, his tone making it clear I'm not fooling him.

"She's my ex's best friend."

"Still not an answer."

"What does it matter?"

"A lot now that you're refusing to answer the question. You're the one making it a bigger issue, not me."

He smacks my hand when I reach to turn on the radio. "I'll fucking shoot you."

"Don't get all fucking growly with me. I watched the damn video. Wanna tell me what's going on?"

"The video? Are you fucking kidding me?"

I gun the engine harder than necessary when the light we're stopped at turns from red to green. His laugh makes me even closer to fulfilling the promise. The only thing stopping me right now is the cleaning bill.

"Yes, the video. The guys were in an uproar when I stopped in last night, and when Wren offered, I watched."

"Of us in the breakroom?"

His silence makes me want to grind my teeth together before breaking his nose with my fist, the cleaning bill be damned.

"You watched video of me in my office?"

"Hey, all of those cameras were your idea, not mine."

"And if I were fucking her?" I seethe, my cock somehow making himself known in my jeans. He doesn't seem to hate the damn idea. "How long would you have watched then?"

"All the way up to the money shot."

He's smiling at me, and I can't help but grin.

"That would never happen."

"Because she's your ex's best friend?"

Because Annalise Grimaldi would never get on her knees for a man, much less let him paint her perfect face with cum.

"We don't exactly get along," I explain. "We never have."

"Thin line between love and hate."

"You're ignorant," I mutter as we pull up past the valet guy standing in front of the building that houses Altieri, Inc.

"To be continued," Flynn says as he opens his door.

"Sir, the keys?" the young guy prompts when I walk right past him. "Sir, you'll be towed."

"Touch my truck and see what happens." The boy swallows hard, but the quick nod of understanding tells me that pickup will sit there unmolested until I return.

"You are in a super shitty mood," Flynn mutters as we walk inside the building and arrow straight to the bank of elevators. "Oh, this shit is swanky."

"Her father is in a load of trouble. This time next month, he'll probably be begging for change on the street or locked up in jail awaiting trial rather than living the high life."

"The rich are always greedy."

I grunt my agreement as the elevator closes and takes us to the very top of the building. Facing my ex-father-in-law isn't even close to the top of my list of fun things to experience all over again. The last time I came inside this building, I asked for Dani's hand in marriage. I know if I closed my eyes and focused, I could still hear the sound of him laughing me out of his office.

"Sir!" The lady at the front reception desk isn't pleased when I walk past her. "You can't go back there!"

"It's okay, love," Flynn says, staying behind to keep her busy. "He's just gonna chat with an old friend."

His accent gets thicker when he's trying to calm someone down. She isn't impressed.

"I'll call security!"

Ignoring her, I walk straight back to Jeno Altieri's office. He seems more frustrated than surprised when I shove open his office door. He also looks thirty years older than he did the last time I saw him, and I imagine that has more to do with the heat he's facing than actual aging.

"I thought I'd never have to see you again," he mutters when he looks up at me.

"Believe me, the feeling is mutual." I don't step but a few feet into his overly large office, and I never take my eyes off of him.

"Why exactly are you barging in here like the damn police?"

"I hear that may have happened a time or two recently." I can't help the small smile that tugs up the corners of my mouth with knowing the man is in trouble. He's always been too flashy to avoid detection for long.

"Get to the fucking point, Black. I'm sure security is already on the way up to forcibly remove you from my property."

"And how much longer will you own the property?" I take a few steps closer and find joy in the way he slinks back.

I'm not the scrawny guy I was nearly two decades ago when I came here for the first and only time.

"Deacon," he growls, but there's more fear in his voice than anything else. "I didn't think the feds were hiring lowly security businesses as muscle these days."

I'm not surprised he's kept tabs on me over the years. I knew deep down he always saw me as a threat to his empire, or at least to the one and only heir he managed to have, but hearing it from his own mouth makes me damn near fucking giddy.

"Tell me about the Russians."

Clear confusion draws his brows in and before he can even open his mouth, I already know coming here will be fruitless.

"I don't have any business with the Russians."

I turn to leave, no longer interested in wasting my time with the idiot.

"Wait!" he screeches. "What's going on?"

"Does the name Nikolay Petrovich ring any bells?"

"No. Who is he?"

Dani has always been one to keep secrets, especially when she thought her trust fund was going to be compromised.

"Dani is missing. I'm pretty certain a Russian Syndicate has her."

He falls back into his office chair as if he's been shot in the chest.

"You'll find her," he demands. "I'll do anything."

"That might actually mean something if I thought you had the ability to pay for my services."

I turn to leave once again.

"Deacon, please!"

I don't turn back around. I don't tell him that no matter how big of a piece a shit he is or how broken his daughter left me that I'm already on the case. Let the bastard stew in his own shit for a little while.

"Let's go," I grunt as I walk past Flynn.

Chapter 10
Anna

Deacon glares at the delivery guy leaving the suite when he finally decides to show back up. He's been gone half the damn day, and I don't even want to think about the fear that tried to settle back in when I woke up and he was already gone.

"What the fuck is going on here?" His eyes scan the numerous packages spread around the living room of the suite. "Did you buy out the damn mall? I fucking told you to stay here."

"Nieman's delivers," I tell him with an eye roll and ignore his irrational anger. "Are you hungry? I had the kitchen stocked as well."

His eyes continue to dart all over the room, and I inwardly smile when I see them pause on the lingerie piled up on the coffee table. From my experience, every man is a sucker for satin and lace.

"I put it on your tab," I tell him just to amp things up a bit, a little retaliation for leaving me alone here all day.

"I'm not paying for all of this shit." His voice is much calmer than I'd like.

"It's not shit," I snap. "That's the entire Agent Provocateur spring line."

"It looks like a waste of a thousand dollars."

I snort a laugh. "If only it were that inexpensive. It's the softest satin you'll ever touch. Go ahead. Pick a piece up and feel."

His eyes dart from me back to the lingerie, and even though I know he'd never do it, I love that he has to think about it for a second before he spins around and heads to the kitchen.

"You're paying me back," he yells from the kitchen amongst the snapping and opening of several cabinets. "You have enough food in here to last a month. I doubt you'll be here that long."

Just the threat of being stuck here for that long makes my body seize up. I fly off the couch and rush to stand in the doorway. Deacon is bent at the middle, looking in the refrigerator, and God, the things those jeans do to his ass.

I snap out of that thought when he stands back up, a half of a turkey club making its way to his mouth.

"Still wanna complain about the food?" I tease when he takes a bite big enough to engulf half the sandwich.

He glares at me as he chews, swallowing before speaking again. He points his half-eaten sandwich past me to indicate the living room area. "There's no reason you need all of that shit out there. There has to be a dozen bags filled with shit."

I clench my teeth, trying to calm down before speaking again. Yelling will get us nowhere. Besides, he still hasn't seen the bags in the bedroom, and I'd like to diffuse this situation before he does.

"Deacon," I begin, channeling my most cajoling tone, "I didn't have anything other than the clothes I was wearing yesterday and those awful sneakers."

"Normal people would grab sweats or something."

"I'm not normal, and Walmart doesn't deliver." I shudder at the thought. I don't think I've worn a pair of cotton panties a day in my life, and I'm sure as hell not going to start now when I'm in a crisis.

He grunts his agreement, stuffing the rest of the sandwich in his mouth, but I don't know which part of what I said he was agreeing with.

"Don't give me attitude about liking nice things. Those Diesel jeans hugging that tight ass of yours didn't come from Target, buddy."

His lips lift, and it would be sexy as hell on him if it weren't for the glob of mustard sticking to his top lip. Okay maybe even now, he's sexy.

I clear my throat, but I refuse to turn away even when I feel my cheeks begin to heat.

"Looking at my ass, Anna?"

"Don't be ridiculous. It wasn't by choice. You were bent over when I walked in here." Seems plausible, but the grin that grows on his face says he doesn't believe a word of it.

His eyes sweep me from top to bottom, and I hate that I changed into soft lounge pants and a tank top after my shower an hour ago. I'd be better prepared to fight this battle if I were in heels and a dress.

There's just something wrong about arguing over his nice ass when I'm looking homeless. The lounge clothes may be Olivia Von Halle, but even the finest cashmere isn't doing my plump ass any favors. I'm not exactly dressing to accentuate my shape right now.

I close my eyes and take a long-suffering breath. "What were we talking about?"

"You were complimenting my ass." Is that humor in his tone? I look down the hall toward the bedroom, if only to avoid the trip down memory lane when his laugh and jokes were an everyday occurrence. I hated him for it then, but they sure would be a nice change from the surly man he's become.

"Before that."

"I was letting you know that you're responsible for paying me back for all of that junk you *had delivered* from Neiman's." I roll my eyes and blow out the puff of air I was holding. "Add that to what you owe me for working on finding your friend, and it's looking to be a hefty damn fee."

"You're charging me to find Dani?" I snap my head back, but honestly, I'm not all that surprised. "No love lost there, huh?"

His eyes dart away, and almost like a tangible thing, the fun we were having and whatever wall that was beginning to crumble is fortified once again.

"There are eleven men working on this shit, and we don't work for free."

My lips form a flat line. I would've paid him even if he didn't insist because the last thing Dani or I need is owing this man. Knowing that doesn't keep me from wanting to argue with him about it.

It's the look on his face, the challenging raise of his eyebrow that tells me that doing so would be a mistake. He takes pride in his work and even joking about him doing it for free is an insult I'm not willing to play with.

"So, what happens next?"

He turns back around and begins digging in the fridge again.

"We can order pizza," I offer.

I won't eat it, but he seems like a guy that would enjoy something like that.

"There's a ton of food here," he argues without pulling his face from the fridge.

"Make yourself at home," I grumble.

He chuckles but there's no humor in his snippy laugh. "Women. You fucking told me about the food, don't get pissed when I take you up on the offer. I'm not one of your little richy-rich guy friends who doesn't eat."

He moves things around on the shelves before deciding on a fruit, meat, and cheese tray.

"As for what comes next," he begins, pausing to take the time to lift the plastic lid and open the various dips, "you'll stay here until things calm down or we have a better idea of what's going on."

"I have obligations, Deacon. I can't just hole up in a damn hotel room for the foreseeable future."

"It's a suite. You make it sound like it's not larger than the average American home. Besides, you can miss a few parties."

"It's not just a few parties!" I cross my arms over my chest, but when his eyes laser focus on my breasts, I drop my hands to my sides. "I have places my parents require me to be."

"Anna." Deacon props his arms on the counter and drops his head between his shoulders. "This is more serious than a few social obligations."

"And how am I supposed to know that? You won't tell me shit."

When he lifts his head, his lip is twitching but not with humor. "Your best friend stole a couple million dollars' worth of uncut blood diamonds off a notoriously violent Russian mobster. He's not dead, and all of his little buddies are looking for Dani and those stones."

"Oh God." My hand covers my mouth.

"Yeah," he snaps. "So forgive me if I'm more concerned about trying to get her spoiled ass home safe than your parties. This is life-and-death shit right now."

I clear my throat to ward off the tears that are threatening. I've cried a lifetime of tears in front of this man, and I refuse to keep doing so.

"Okay," I tell him before turning and walking out of the kitchen.

As quietly as my shaking hands can manage, I close the bedroom door and lean against it. The room is in complete disarray from all the things I had delivered, and I was in the middle of pulling tags from the clothes when Deacon showed up. I haven't even made it to the makeup, hair and bath products yet. I don't have the energy for any of it now, so I head back to the closet, shoving aside the things the concierge hung in there and sit down.

I don't even know what to try to focus on right now. There are too many things in my head warring for attention.

Dani has gotten herself into a world of shit, and just like old times, she's managed to drag me right back into the middle of it. As I close my eyes and rest my head against the wall, I try to think of things that make putting up with the drama worth it.

I come up empty.

Chapter 11
Deacon

An hour of reprieve, that's all I got when Anna disappeared into the bedroom. Just enough time to finish eating and settle on the couch. I barely closed my exhausted eyes before she came into the room sighing like I'm the reason her world is crumbling down around her.

"What now?" I snap, finally over it when she sighs for what seems like the millionth time.

She shrugs, never pulling her eyes from the baseball game playing on the muted television. She's not paying any damn attention to the game. I'm pretty damn certain her only goal in life right now is to irritate the hell out of me.

I'd leave, but there are a couple of reasons I'm still sitting here. One, she was terrified last night, and she seems calmer when I'm around. God only knows why. Two, I'm fucking beat, and even the twenty-minute drive back to my apartment above BBS headquarters seems like an impossible task right now.

I should've left when she first sat down before my muscles relaxed and I let the past couple of days sink into my bones. Now I know I'm planted here for the rest of the day and possibly all night unless Wren calls with some form of usable information.

She doesn't answer my question, but I cut my eyes in her direction when she sighs once again.

"Do that one more time and I'm going to hogtie and gag you," I threaten.

Without pulling her eyes from the commercial break on the television she pops an eyebrow up. Is that interest? I can't imagine a woman like Anna even considering the idea of being bound, but that doesn't explain the way her face lit up when I said it.

"Just go to bed." I nudge her legs splayed out on the table with the tip of my booted foot.

"It's too early," she grumbles.

"You didn't sleep well last night."

"How would you know?"

Because I watched you toss and turn, and I didn't bother to comfort you because the more you wiggled, the more the sheet drifted away from your body revealing so much tanned skin, I had to bite my knuckle to keep from groaning and waking you.

And it's official. I'm the biggest creep on the planet. I didn't feel so bad watching it last night, but replaying it in my head makes me feel like I should be on some predator list splashed on the front page of the local paper.

"You look tired," I say instead.

She snaps her head in my direction, narrowing her eyes but not saying anything.

I know what I just said, and I've been married, so I know what it sounds like to a woman. *You look tired*, to them, translates into *you look like shit*. Somehow, females, with a very clear understanding of the English language translate those few words differently than any other words a man could use.

She doesn't take it as concern from me but as an insult.

"Tired, huh?"

"Just a little," I placate because Lord knows I don't have the energy for another verbal sparring session with her.

"Okay." She pops up from the couch and walks away.

"Crap," I mutter, turning my head just in time to see the bedroom door snap shut.

After twenty minutes of not hearing anything from her, I finally settle back into my sloth position on the couch. The game is over by now, but I just can't muster the energy to reach for the remote and change the channel or turn it off completely so I can sleep.

My lead-heavy eyes flutter when the bedroom door opens, only Anna isn't popping out for a bottle of water or something to eat. She's dressed to the nines in a sleek blue dress that moves like waves of the ocean when she walks.

"What the fuck?" I hiss, sitting up fully on the sofa and glaring at her. "Playing dress up or something?"

I default to agitation because that emotion is ten times better than wondering which set of sexy lingerie she's wearing under that amazing dress. I had to hightail it out of the living room earlier this afternoon at the sight of it in order to prevent her from getting an eyeful of what seeing it did to me.

"I'm going down to the bar for a drink."

"Like hell you are." I almost add *not dressed like that*, but that would only encourage her to ask more questions. I still haven't gotten the sound of her saying *wouldn't you like to know what this filthy mouth can do* out of my head. On the surface my answer is never in a million years, but truthfully, I wanted to unzip right there and—

I shake my head, looking from the tips of her painted toenails to the layers of shiny hair floating around her shoulders in sleek waves.

Do not think about wrapping that around your fist.

Don't do it, Deacon. Be strong. Be—

"What?" Her knowing grin reminds me of the way I imagine a female octopus would look at her mate before strangling him to death while they're mating. It's all coy and alluring when really, it's just a trap.

"You need to stay in the room."

"I need a drink."

I point to the phone on the table. "Call room service."

"I need the ambiance," she says with a wave of her hand before she breezes away.

"You need your ass whipped for being so damn stubborn," I mutter.

I doubt she heard me because the door to the suite closes with a mocking hiss before I get the words fully out of my mouth.

I've taken enough precautions to get her here that I highly doubt she's in danger, but it isn't the threat of Russian mobsters hurting her that has me standing from the sofa and cursing under my breath. It's the knowledge that once she sits down at the bar that she's going to be swarmed by assholes that have a much greater chance of deciphering the lingerie question I thought of earlier than I would, namely by having a chance to pull that silky blue fabric from her body.

My pulse is pounding in my ears by the time I step off the elevator and head to the bar. Soft music plays overhead, and surprisingly the bar is fairly calm. A few guys dressed in expensive suits lean in close telling bullshit stories over a bottle of Glenlivet. An older couple people watch, each holding a glass of red wine. The bartender wipes down the counter with a bored expression on his face.

Anna sits in a corner booth away from them all, peering down into an amber liquid-filled rocks glass. She looks lonely and desolate, and I should turn to leave. Other than the businessmen jaw-jacking about times gone by, there isn't anyone here I can picture Anna leaving the bar with, but I don't go back to the room.

I spend a moment unnoticed just taking her in. From the top of her head to the tips of her toes, the woman is gorgeous. The sun-kissed, no doubt chemically enhanced tones of her multihued dark hair glitters under the soft light over her head. Her pouty lips are meant to be kissed, and if we didn't have a history, if she was just a girl in a bar, I'd be on her in a split second. Even though she looks high-class and too expensive to get tangled up with, I'd take my shot. Not only would I try to pick her up, I'd count my lucky stars if she looked up and smiled at me before she told my ass to get lost, which she no doubt would. Because Diesel jeans or not, there are just some traits to people who grew up with money that those who didn't can ever fake, and Anna doesn't seem like the type of girl to go slumming with a man like me.

After gaining the attention of the businessmen, and the way they dart their eyes from me to Anna, I know it's only a matter of time before one of them builds the courage to walk up to her.

I belly up to the bar and order a glass of whiskey before carrying it to her table and taking a seat. I don't know if she looked up while I was at the bar, or if she doesn't give a damn who sat down with her, but she doesn't lift her eyes in question or to greet me. I'm fine with it. I'm not one for conversation anyway.

After sitting quietly for ten minutes, Anna pulls her clutch from some magical pocket in her dress. I guess the glass of whiskey she's drowned didn't provide the answers she was hoping for. She thanks the bartender when he comes over and refills her glass, but other than that she doesn't take her eyes from her phone.

"Please tell me you aren't updating your social media with your location."

Her lips twitch, but she doesn't answer. I think she was scared enough last night that I won't have to worry about shit like that, but then again, this is Annalise Grimaldi sitting beside me. All I have to go on is my knowledge of who she was in the past. I don't know a damn thing about her other than what I had Wren pull for me. He gave me shit about it when I requested it after getting back from Altieri, Inc. earlier.

As suspected, Anna doesn't have a single thing in her current life or in her surprisingly squeaky-clean past that would make me suspect that she's got something going on that would lead to her apartment getting ripped to shreds. Her world is being turned upside down because of her friend.

Her phone chimes with an alert, and like an overprotective bodyguard, I bristle when she doesn't immediately tell me who she's getting a message from.

I stew in my irritation, downing what's left of my drink and signaling for the bartender to bring me another.

"I have a gala to attend in three days."

"No."

"What do you mean, no?" Her eyes lift, meeting mine for the first time since I sat down at the table.

"It's not a good idea. There's too much shit going on right now."

"I'm not just going to stop living my life because Dani is in trouble."

"I'm not asking you to stop living your life," I snap because this sounds much like the argument I had with Dani a million years ago when she was going out every night instead of spending time with me when I was on leave. Fuck, why didn't I see the signs back then? They were like flashing red lights, but all I could see was my beautiful wife. "You just need to hit the pause button for a while."

"I'm obligated to go, but if you're so concerned for my safety in the middle of a huge crowd, feel free to tag along."

Not a chance in hell.

"That won't happen," I spit. "Those events aren't my thing, but I'll send one of the guys."

I can't believe I'm conceding right now but going by the look of pure determination in her eyes, short of locking her in a room, she's going to that damn party whether I like it or not.

"Good." She smiles wide, and it's a look I've seen a hundred times when her and Dani were getting ready for some trouble. "I suggest sending Brooks because he's smoking hot and beyond charming."

Chapter 12

Anna

It's been an hour since our conversation about the gala, and Deacon might as well be made of stone. Other than lifting his glass to his lips, he's made no other movements, including his mouth. Not one single word has left his lips. I don't know if he took my suggestion under advisement, or if he's pissed.

Let him be mad, just like I was when he shot down my idea of him attending the gala with me. I wasn't asking him out on a date or anything, but that still didn't ease the biting sting of rejection. He didn't even take a moment to consider it… just *no*. Hello wounded ego. It's been a while.

But no worries because I'm curing my shattered self-esteem with every sip of whiskey I take.

The more I drink, the worse I get at hiding the fact that I can't stop looking at him. When did he go from the goofy guy making Dani laugh to this serious-as-hell commando guy? Of course he was more serious at court that day, but the situation didn't really call for jokes and ridiculous dancing.

Right now? The way he watches the door like he expects ninjas to fly in with samurai swords swinging is something I never thought I'd see. I guess we've both changed though, more him than me.

He's always been good-looking. I can admit that in my head, but he's somehow managed to take those boyish charms I used to roll my eyes at and turn them into a muscled guy with more sex appeal than a stage full of oiled-up strippers. Like seriously, is it hot in here or is the sight of him lifting his glass to his lips making me overheat?

Maybe he thinks this tough-to-crack hard exterior will keep me away, but honestly it just makes me want to drill down under the toughness and find all of his mushy spots. The more I drink, the better of an idea it seems.

"What exactly does your company do?"

"Security and consulting."

I clench my jaw. "I knew that from reading the wall outside your office."

"Then why did you ask?" He rolls his head on his shoulders to face me, and damn if the pink in his cheeks from the alcohol doesn't make him just a little more human and appealing.

I grin at him, resisting the urge to bite my lip when he smiles back. Yep, he's just as tipsy as I am.

"Deacon," I grumble. "Tell me."

"We do all sorts of stuff."

"That explains everything. Please, say no more. I'm suffering from information overload right now."

His chuckle washes over me, and I take a moment to just let it settle around us.

"We're hired out for personal security." I nearly reach out and squeeze his bicep but have enough control over myself right now to drop my hand before I touch him. "Sometimes, we have to find people. Sometimes, we have to find information."

"Like a PI? You follow cheating spouses and stuff?"

"Sometimes," he answers with a shrug, but from what I can gather, there's more to it than what he's letting on.

"I bet the women just flock to your team."

He lifts his glass back to his mouth, and I'm entranced until he lowers it back to the table. Has he been running his fingers over the rim this whole time? If so, why do I only now feel that same caress like he's swirling that thick tip on the inside of my thigh?

"Are you denying it?" I shove his shoulder, and he either lets me move him a few inches or he's wasted.

"No." His grin widens. "Brooks is quite popular. Quinten doesn't ever have trouble finding fun."

"What about you?" I empty my glass, filling it once again with the bottle the bartender left at our table to hide my embarrassment.

"Me?" He runs his hands over the scruff on his chin, but I can tell from the look in his eyes that he's actually considering the question and not rubbing himself there in that douchebag way college frat guys do right before they wink at you and say something ridiculous like, "Bet."

"I don't do relationships." His tongue snakes out, sweeping over his lips before he looks back to the front entrance to the bar. "Not really my thing."

"I bet you just haven't found a woman you're sexually compatible with." My eyes widen. Did I really just say that to this man?

He doesn't answer, and the alcohol swimming in my system tells me that now isn't the best time to let it go.

"I mean, it's hard to find a woman who likes to be hog-tied and gagged." He shifts in his seat, but I know he heard me. He's the one who put the thought in my head earlier when he threatened me with it.

"I bet you're a man who takes charge, really makes a woman beg for her own pleasure."

He clears his throat, but I can't look up from my glass to gauge his reaction. I shouldn't be saying any of this shit to my best friend's ex-husband, but I can't seem to stop myself either. Ignoring the arousal throbbing down south with each filthy word, I continue.

"Lots of hair-pulling and choking." I hum my approval. "Taking what you want from their bodies."

"Wow." He slaps his glass down on the table and stands suddenly. "I think you've had enough to drink. Let's head back up."

A thousand different scenarios race through my head in the flash of a second. What will happen up in the suite? Will we make a mistake? Will I even have the courage to try? Am I building him up in my alcohol-ridden brain to be hotter than he actually is? Would Dani forgive me if we crossed a line?

As I stand and follow him out of the bar, I come to the full understanding that nothing will happen once we're locked safely away in the suite. Even drunk, Deacon is too reserved, too closed off to ever let anything happen between the two of us. From his silence at the table, I know he isn't interested.

Why should he be? We've been more enemies than friends for the last seventeen years, and our recent reconnection was born from necessity rather than any desire from either one of us. Once this is over, we'll both go back to our separate corners of the world and will probably never see or hear from each other again.

I blame both the alcohol and the movement of the elevator for leaning closer to him as we begin to ascend.

He, on the other hand, is like a statue standing in the corner waiting for his chance to get away from me. Once the elevator stops on our floor, I don't waste a second getting away from him, but he's instantly at my back to insert the room card into the electronic reader.

"Crap," I mutter when my heel catches on the threshold when he shoves the suite door open. He could just let me tumble forward. It's not like I'm going to remember much of tonight in the morning anyway. He probably thinks a goose egg on my forehead will make his job easier by keeping me locked away in the room since I'm too vain to go out in public with such an injury. What he doesn't know is I'm an expert with makeup and could probably lose an ear and still feel confident enough to walk out of here with a ponytail swinging.

"Easy," he says, gripping me with an arm around my waist instead of letting me rocket forward and get hurt.

"Such a gentleman."

He scoffs at this because it's something I'd probably never direct at him if I were sober, even if he saved me from smacking the floor with my face.

"Let's get you to bed."

"Umm," I slur. "Yes, please."

Jesus! Does my brain to mouth connection just completely sever while drinking around this man?

Instead of telling me to kick bricks, he just groans deep in his chest, probably ready to be clear of me since I'm so annoying to him.

The walk to the bedroom seems extra long and filled with distractions and enough obstacles to have my legs not wanting to work properly. I fully expect him to shove me in the direction of the bed and vanish, but he crouches low, one hand on my calf, the other working the straps on my heels loose.

I curl over him, trying to convince myself that I'm only doing it to maintain my balance, but he smells amazing, and the warmth his body is emitting is too much to resist.

"Lift," he says with a quick tap to my right foot once he tosses my left heel away.

When he stands again, we're nearly nose to nose. I read this as interest because the man is much taller than I am and if he were standing to his full height, I'd be pressing my face against his chest.

"Looks like you have magical fingers." In my head the words come out buttery soft and filled with enough innuendo a guy even ten years younger than him could hear the suggestion in it.

He must not be very quick on the uptake because he backs away and frowns at me.

Ignoring yet another rejection, I lean in closer with my fingers tangled in his shirt.

"I've been wondering all night what your mouth tastes like," I whisper, lifting my chin and letting my eyes flutter closed.

His hand caresses the side of my face, but he never closes the distance. When I look up at him, he's looking away, his strong jaw clenched tight.

"Get some sleep, Anna."

And then he's gone, the bedroom door snapping closed behind him. I flop down in the bed, certain I'm going to have a mile-long list of regrets when I wake up in the morning.

Chapter 13
Deacon

I'm not used to waking up and feeling less than my best. I normally eat clean and take care of myself. It's a requirement for the work I do. I have to be on my game all the time, ready to take on the world at the drop of a hat, but I blame both the whiskey and Anna for opening my eyes to the sun blazing into the suite and wanting to do nothing more than roll over and go back to sleep.

I don't, simply because I can't. There's a laundry list of things that need to be done, and the first is getting out of this fucking suite before the temptation sleeping in the other room wakes up.

I've been wondering all night what your mouth tastes like.

Fuck my life.

How I managed to back away without giving in or agreeing that I'd been suffering with the same question for much longer than we'd been drinking last night is beyond me.

I'm going insane. That has to be the reason. There's no other explanation for the way my body reacts around her. I must be in desperate need of a long vacation, a way to recharge and regain control of my damn life.

I groan, my head reminding me of how big of an idiot I was last night. Drinking so much whiskey, the constant lift of my glass to my lips was the only thing keeping me from saying something that would later lead to regrets, or worse yet, using my mouth for other things. The end result? I was hammered when I fell asleep. Too drunk to pop some painkillers or drink a couple bottles of water to stave off the hangover, my head is now pounding like a snare drum.

Climbing off the sofa that's too swanky and small to fit my frame, I hit the bathroom first, then grab a couple bottles of water out of the fridge. I should be running out of here like my ass is on fire, but instead of turning right, out of the kitchen, I make a left and slowly open the door to the bedroom.

As I look into the dim room, I tell myself that I'm doing the courteous thing by making sure she didn't choke on her own vomit last night, but when I hear her soft snores before my eyes adjust to the lack of light, I don't turn away.

I become that creep again. The one standing too far into the room to be gentlemanly, looking down at her sleeping. In my experience, most women curl up under the covers and bury their faces, making sure no draft in the room can touch an inch of exposed skin.

Anna doesn't sleep like that. Anna, apparently, also doesn't sleep in many clothes either, but I don't slither out when I see her dress from last night tangled on the floor alongside her bra. God, did she really have the red lace on under that blue dress. Who knew she was so patriotic? I smile when a flash of fantasy invades my head of her smiling over her shoulder only wrapped in an American flag.

"Jesus," I mumble when the sight of her lying on the bed shoves that half-cocked image from my brain.

Nothing, and I mean *nothing,* could be better than reality. Although she's mostly covered, the long line of her back is open to the air, one thigh pulled up and showing inches and inches of bare skin. Her arm is curled under her chin, tucked in close to her body, preventing any real indecency, but sweet Uncle Sam is she enticing.

I snap back when she grumbles and begins to move. As much as I want to see her turn over—

I'm shocked at how hard it is to walk away and not crawl into bed with her right now. Fuck, just the feel of her warm skin against mine would probably be enough to make me blow in my damn jeans like a teenager.

I bite my lip, at first with regret of backing away and then as punishment because I clearly have a serious problem and I get the fuck out of there. I don't know that I'd be able to resist her if she woke up and looked at me all sleep-tousled. I'd be a damn goner, and the last thing I'll ever need is getting tangled up with this woman.

When I make it across town, I get off on the tenth floor instead of the ninth, needing a shower and something in my stomach to soak up all the liquor I drank last night more than anything else. My apartment seems almost foreign even though it's only been a couple of days since I've been here.

I take my time in a cold shower and scarf down food that has no taste before heading down to the office. For the first time in days, none of my guys are hanging out in the break area. I almost miss those idiots as I make my way to Wren's office.

"Come give Daddy a kiss," Puff Daddy says as soon as I shove the door open.

For some reason I grin when he starts making smooching noises instead of wanting to wrap my hands around his little gray neck.

"Aww, don't be an asshole about it," he squawks when I ignore him.

Wren is smiling when I take the chair beside him.

"You look tired," he says when I run my hands over my face. I agree that I am with a low murmur.

See? That's how normal people handle being told that. I didn't give him a dirty look and run away, unlike some people I know.

"We have a little more information, but I don't know how helpful it will be."

Instead of handing me another file, Wren pulls up information on the huge screen directly in front of us.

"Dani," he must've gotten the memo from Flynn not to use her full name, "went to West Africa with Petrovich last month."

When images flash on the screen, I realize this must be the beach Dani told Anna she was going to vacation at.

Other than obtaining intel, I don't have any other emotions to seeing my ex-wife, in a white bikini, wrapped around a tall man. He's frowning down at her, but it isn't real anger I see in his eyes. He's protective over her, and I can only imagine the hell he gave her for wearing her barely there bikini to the beach where other men could see what he's so clearly possessive over.

"See that look on his face?" I ask.

"The one that says he's seen her naked?"

"The one that says this is more complicated than just a man missing a bag of rocks."

"I wouldn't call millions of dollars in diamonds a bag of rocks, but okay. Yeah. I guess."

"Bling bling, motherfucker."

We both huff a laugh at the stupid bird but keep our attention on the screen.

"I know you don't get out much past your online hookups, but that," I point to Nikolay's face, "is a man in love."

"Twitter pussy!" Puff Daddy squawks before laughing at himself.

I glare over my shoulder before looking back at the image on the screen. Dani's familiar devious smile makes my skin crawl, partly because she looked that way around me often but mostly because it only means trouble for her. Life is a fucking game to that woman, and so far, she's been lucky. I'm pretty sure that if her luck were to run out, it's going to be with the man in the picture with her.

"That could be good, right? If he loves her, he won't hurt her."

"You don't understand. Men don't like to be hurt. Men like Petrovich are more likely to kill her for her betrayal than forgive her for her indiscretions."

Silence fills the room as that news settles around us.

"He spends more time in West Africa than any other place as far as I can tell, which means—"

"It's probably where he'd take Dani if he got his hands on her," I finish for him.

"That's a little outside of our realm."

"What chatter have you heard from the Russians?" I don't ask for details about how he gets his info. I'm certain someone in the government wouldn't be happy with where he likes to dig. I'm working on plausible deniability.

"They've been silent. Not one peep. As of yesterday evening, it's like they all just disappeared."

"Or they're on to us," I mutter with another scrape of my hands down my face.

"I'm more careful than getting caught by a handful of Russian mobsters, boss," he grumbles. "You know that."

"Still. I'm going to call Cerberus for help. They're much better with international interactions, and we helped them a while back in Venezuela."

I stand to leave, needing to make this call in private in case Tug gives me shit and I have to pretend to beg. I don't need my men seeing me fall so far from grace.

"One more thing," Wren says before I can step out of the office, "Petrovich checked himself out of the hospital yesterday. It was against medical advice, but the bullet missed all major arteries. He'll be sore for a while, but he'll make a full recovery."

"That fucking complicates things."

"Maybe not," Wren says as he turns in his seat to face me.

"How so?"

"Maybe since no one died, they won't be so inclined to take a life." He shrugs, and I wish I had his optimism.

"I've seen guys kill over a can of soda and the last cigarette in a pack. Believe me, a couple million dollars in missing diamonds is more than enough reason to put a bullet in someone's head."

I shoot off a text to Tug, one of the guys that works for Kincaid, the president of the Cerberus MC in New Mexico. They do a lot of recon and recovery, mostly tracking women down that have been abducted and removed from the United States and forced into sex trafficking, and they have the resources I'll need if we're going to West Africa to get Dani.

As I wait for the return text, unsure if the Cerberus team is even on American soil, I can't help but feel like we might already be too late. I lock myself in my office, disable the cameras so Wren can't watch me, and have myself a little breakdown. I've gone years without Dani even popping up in my head, but I'd never wish her dead. I'd never want harm to come to her. I can admit that I wanted her to feel half of the emotional pain she caused me, but I'd never wish for something like this to happen no matter how much of it is because of her own actions.

Chapter 14
Anna

"Maybe it was something I said," I mutter as I look down at the still folded pile of blankets Deacon used the other day.

I know it was something I said, and unfortunately, I remember every stupid word that came out of my drunk mouth. If there were ever a time to turn back the clocks for a do-over...

He hasn't been here. He was gone when I woke up, stayed gone the entire day, was still MIA when I went to bed last night, and telling from the untouched linens, he never came back last night either.

We've declined maid service since being here. Deacon's idea of course because we can never be too careful about who we let in the room.

Me: Where are you?

That's the text I sent fifteen minutes ago that has still gone unanswered.

So, I made a comment about his mouth and tried to kiss him. Who cares? Is he like a man-child or something? He said no, I sort of accepted it. Now it's time to move on. He knows I was drunk. I'd planned to tell him I was joking when I woke up yesterday, only to find him gone. Things don't have to be weird. Things weren't weird until he made them that way by taking off and hiding away.

Deacon the Dick: Working.

I narrow my eyes at my phone, squeezing it in anger until I accidently take a screen shot of the text.

"Stupid mother—" I make quick work of deleting the image and then erasing it from my recently deleted folder, all the while wondering if his boy genius of a hacker caught it in time before I got rid of it. Knowing that messy-headed kid, he's been tracking my phone and location since the second I got off that first phone call with Deacon days and days ago.

Like an idiot, bored out of my mind, I run from one end of the suite to the other and back again, wondering if he can track the motion with his super-secret, high-tech spy computers. I mean, I'm only assuming he has that shit, but any guy worth his weight in the computer world would. I've watched *Criminal Minds*; I know how efficient Penelope Cruz is.

I try yoga, but it isn't the same at getting rid of tension alone in a room rather than in front of that sexy instructor down at the country club.

Television does nothing for me, and since I already spent a ton of time alone prior to this recent mess, I've already binge-watched just about everything on Netflix, and I don't care how much people were talking about it a while back, I refuse to watch a show about a dude with a mullet playing with tigers and working his way through straight men.

But of course, I love tigers, which in my bored state allows memories to come rushing back from a teenage trip to the zoo.

"He's an idiot," I mumbled, chewing bubble gum and glaring at the guy on the other side of the room.

"I don't know why you two can't get along." Dani didn't even turn her head when she spoke.

Of course she didn't. Her eyes were glued to Deacon, who was on the other side of the herpetarium, swaying back and forth in front of the glass separating him from the king cobra on display.

"Don't hold your breath or you'll die, because that's never going to happen."

She sighed and finally took her eyes off her man long enough to look in my direction.

"Please?"

I was honestly shocked. Dani didn't say please to anyone. She had been handed everything in her life, much the same way I had, but she was never grateful for it. Expectant was a better word to describe my best friend.

"You're like a sister to me." She pointed to Deacon who had moved on to the next enclosure, and from the way he was tilting his head, he hadn't found whatever creature was supposed to be inside yet. "He's the love of my life. I'm going to spend the rest of my life with him, and since I don't plan on giving you up, I need you two to make an effort."

I resisted the urge to get mad about sounding like the second choice she had to even *consider keeping.*

"Have you even told your parents about him yet?"

She shook her head, her eyes drifting back to Deacon.

"You've been dating for almost a year, Dani. Don't you think it's time?"

"You know how my dad is." I did. He was a complete asshole. I didn't think Dani and I would've been so close or spent so much time together if she didn't hate being at home. "I have to ease him into it."

"Babe!" Deacon turned around, his eyes shining in the low lights above his dark-haired head. "Come look at the tongue on this thing."

Without looking back, Dani glided from her seat beside me to join Deacon on the other side of the room. As I watched them, I understood that I may never have what those two have found in each other. Even though I'd never be caught dead letting a guy nuzzle my neck like a fool or squealing like a pig because of it, which is reminiscent of the sound Dani was making, I couldn't help but envy their closeness. Deacon was protective of her, and other than my own father, I had never had someone who looked out for me. When they left the room without a glance in my direction, it was the moment I understood that the description didn't even fit my best friend. How was it possible to feel so alone when you were surrounded by people?

It's too much. Being here is too much. Having Deacon around is too much.

If he's the love of her life, that means the second they're within eyesight of each other again, nothing else is going to matter. Dani hasn't been the best of best friends to me recently but we have a history, just like she and Deacon have a history, only their bonds have always been tighter than ours. I'm not competition, not that I really want to be, but being stuck here with no one to talk to and no one to interact with is going to drive me insane.

I had on full makeup and nice clothes before I even walked out of the bedroom this morning in anticipation of finding Deacon lounging on the couch, so all I have to do is grab my phone before heading to the door.

I squeal when I tug open the door to find a guy standing just outside.

"It's okay, Anna. I work for Deacon."

He must see the fear in my eyes.

"You're British, not Russian," I say like an imbecile.

"Hence me saying I work for Deacon."

"I'm going out."

He doesn't touch me, but he shifts his body to block my way. "I'm afraid I can't let that happen."

"Am I a hostage now?"

A grin slides across his handsome face, and once again, I'm wondering about what the physical requirements are for working for Blackbridge Security and Consulting. There have to be laws against requiring these guys to be so good looking.

"I'm Flynn Coleman." He holds out his hand, but I'm still a little too pissed at being told I can't leave to shake it right now.

"I can't stay here. I'm going crazy all alone." I snap my jaw shut because I shouldn't have admitted to such a weakness so quickly. I imagine this guy thinks I'm an uppity bitch like Deacon does even though his boss has never actually said those words to me. Well, he said it a couple times in high school, and apparently, I'm still butt hurt over it.

"I'm right out here. You're not alone."

Sighing with my growing frustration, I cross my arms over my chest and glare at him.

"I'm not scared. I'm bored." Then I have a genius idea.

"What are you doing?" he gasps as I grip his forearm and yank him inside the suite.

"Why are you here?" I ask when the door closes behind us in the entryway. He doesn't answer me, and I think he's still in shock that I had the audacity to pull him inside. "To make sure I don't leave, right?"

He gives me a reluctant nod.

"Problem solved then. I'm bored, and you have to be bored just standing out there all damn day. So, I'll provide you with a place to sit, and you'll provide me with company."

"Is that so?" God, I just love a British accent.

"Sit," I tell him before heading to the kitchen. "Do you want sweet or salty? I can do both if you prefer."

"Umm."

I peek my head around the corner and look at him. "Chips and popcorn or frozen yogurt and grapes."

"Popcorn."

"Sit."

Thankfully he does, and my mood lightens immediately with the anticipation of just having someone around.

Stiff as a board, he sits on the far end of the sofa as I drop a huge bowl of popcorn in his lap and find some stupid movie on the television.

"I love Wayans brothers' movies," I tell him.

"They're an acquired taste," he murmurs but half an hour in he's struggling to hide his chuckles.

"Told you, you'd like it." I stretch out, laying my head in his lap like we've known each other for years because well, I want to and it's more comfortable.

He stiffens again, but eventually he relaxes enough to rest one arm over my stomach as the other drags fingers through my hair. I'm torn between asking him if he has a girlfriend and taking a nap when the suite door swings open.

Standing there with that strong jaw twitching is Deacon, clearly pissed like he has any right to be.

"I'll meet you at the truck, Flynn," he grinds out, his eyes staying locked with mine.

As if he doesn't have a care in the world, Flynn lifts my head from his lap and stands, bending in the middle to brush his lips across my forehead.

"It's been a pleasure." He winks before pulling away and leaving the suite.

Deacon doesn't pull his eyes from mine. We glare at each other. Well, he glares. It takes everything I have not to grin at his ridiculous reaction.

"Your party is sorted."

Those are the only words out of his mouth before he turns and leaves.

"Where are you going?" I hiss.

"I have work to do."

And just like that I'm alone again.

Chapter 15
Deacon

I wait patiently for all of the Cerberus guys to gather around the table. This is Kincaid's show, and I'm just grateful he's promised me the help I'm going to need in West Africa. Leaving the States to work always gets my blood pumping. We don't get to do it often, and I know my guys are going to be hypervigilant in the field. The president of the Cerberus MC expects the same level of professionalism from his own guys.

After Kincaid introduces the newest member of the team, surprisingly a tall woman, he steps aside and I have the floor. On the flight over here, I spent hours trying to figure out what I'm going to say to these guys to get across the importance of this case to them. At first, I was going to leave out all the personal details, but if the roles were reversed, I know I'd want that info, so that's what they're going to get from me today.

I nod at Kincaid as I step forward and clear my throat.

"It's not easy standing up here and admitting that I've failed, but here I am. This mission is more than a little personal for me, and I thought it was in my best interest to come to you guys for help rather than fucking everything up by letting my emotions control the outcome," I explain.

"Who are we looking for?" Grinch asks. I've met him before, but we haven't had much interaction.

Shadow, the guy in control of the computer system, uses this moment to put Dani's picture up on the screen behind me. I gave them several from her social media, and I'm grateful he chose one where she isn't hanging on the arm of some rich asshole. I don't want anything to detract their attention from the mission.

"My ex-wife."

Everyone in the room stiffens, and even though I know they were all paying attention before, they're even more attentive now.

"Daniella Altieri and I have been divorced for over eight years, but after being contacted by her best friend last week about an altercation that happened in Dani's condo, I got involved."

The screen flashes again with an image of Nicolay.

"Nikolay Petrovich was shot during that altercation and left for dead. He survived and has recently checked himself out of the hospital."

"They're looking for your girl," one of the Cerberus guys deduces.

"I've not had any interactions with my ex since we signed our divorce papers." I don't know why that distinction matters, but for some reason I feel the need to tell them. "If her friend, Annalise Grimaldi, hadn't called me, scared, I probably wouldn't even know she was missing. There has been no action on any of her accounts since the shooting."

A grim expression washes over several of the guys' faces before they can stop it. They're thinking the same thing I can't get out of my head either, but I can't not try to find her. If she's gone, her family is going to need closure. I'm going to need closure. Fuck, Anna will need closure.

"My guy has found info that the Russians are looking for her."

"Because of the shooting?" one of the guys asks.

"Because she disappeared with something they want."

A throat clears, but no one outright asks what it is.

"Chatter obtained through Russian text messages and phone calls leads us to believe they think Dani took off with some diamonds." I swallow again. "A lot of diamonds."

"The bag of blood diamonds they're looking for has a street value of three-point-two-million dollars," Shadow adds.

A whistle rings out as several of the guys shift in their seats.

"Our access to their phone calls and texts dried up two days ago, but as of the last transmission, they hadn't found her yet," I continue. "Petrovich frequents West Africa. His family has a compound there. Your expertise with international raids is why I'm here today."

"We'd like to do this with non-lethal force," Kincaid says, and this is the point the men around the table all grow agitated.

Tug shakes his head when I make eye contact with him.

"Non-lethal?" one guy scoffs. "The Russians don't know that. We go in with guns blazing loaded with plastic bullets and bean bags and they're going to come at us with the full force of the Bratva."

"Sounds like fucking suicide," another guy mutters.

Despite their outburst, everyone grows silent when Kincaid holds his hand up.

"Other than distant ties, we haven't been able to tie Petrovich to the Bratva," Shadow informs them. "Hence the reason they're operating out of West Africa rather than Russia."

"We're not trying to start a war. That's why we're not going to fill the place with bullets," Dominic, Kincaid's older brother, says as he steps forward. "We've gathered some intel from a couple guys we know in that area and according to them, there aren't many people on the property. Other than three guys and some house staff, the place is practically deserted."

"One of my guys was able to get a travel restriction placed on Petrovich so he can't leave the US right now, so if his guys have her, they're working with a skeleton crew," I add.

"This mission is voluntary due to the risk," Kincaid tells the guys, and every eye in the room turns to me.

I can see them sizing me up, trying to determine if it's worth the trouble.

"By a show of hands," Kincaid says.

"Seems like a good day to die," Tug says and raises his hand first.

"Fuck yeah," Grinch says with an insane smile on his face.

"You can still kill 'em with a plastic bullet if you hit them right," another guy adds as he lifts his arm.

Before long, every man, and the new female member have a hand in the air.

Kincaid slaps me on the back after dismissing them. He's smiling while I'm still standing there with shock all over my face.

I know my guys would do this for me, but I had my reservations about the Cerberus team being so willing to put their lives on the line for Dani.

"I'd say they're all fucking crazy," the president says, "but we have a very thorough vetting process including psychological testing."

"Have a couple of beers with the guys. We're heading out at four in the morning," Shadow says as he walks around the computer equipment to join Kincaid and I at the front of the room.

***

"Is it like this every night?" I ask as I lift my beer to my lips.

"Not really," Tug answers. "We work a lot."

"Seems distracting," I mutter, watching women walk around with happy smiles on their faces and dirty thoughts in their eyes.

"I'm not distracted," Shadow assures me, and when I look, I see his eyes locked across the room on Misty. I was introduced to his wife an hour or so ago, and even though there's thirty feet separating them, they are somehow right here with each other.

"Yeah?" I prod. "You and Misty? Even after all this time?"

Tug told me they have two grown children, but this man is looking at Misty like she's a snack that's about to get eaten. I can't help but smile. Some fuckers have all the luck.

"All this time." He taps the side of my beer bottle with his own. "Maybe you and Dani can make up once we get her back home."

I snort a laugh. "Yeah. That ship sailed a long time ago."

Tug nudges my shoulder and indicates a guy walking across the room toward Rivet, the female member.

"Is he Cerberus?" The predatory look in his eyes doesn't reflect the disposition I've seen from the guys.

"That's my stupid-ass son," Shadow says, disapproval in his voice.

"Kid doesn't have a fucking chance," Tug whispers as the others in the room grow quiet and watch him approach her.

Shadow snorts a laugh. "I hope she embarrasses the shit out of him."

"He seems pretty sure of himself," I observe.

"That kid gets more ass than any guy I know," Tug interjects.

"My kid, remember," Shadow grumbles.

The blond guy, bearing an insanely striking resemblance to the man sitting beside me, spits out a beyond stupid pickup line. No one around him laughs, and after a cursory glance, Rivet goes back to the conversation she was having with Grinch.

"Idiot doesn't know when to quit." I can feel Shadow's irritation growing by the second. "If he touches her, I'm going to kill him."

Just as the words leave his mouth, Shadow's son reaches his hand out and trails a finger down Rivet's arm.

Faster than lightning, she spins, and in a combination of moves I've not seen outside of a kung fu movie, she has him on his back on the floor. Like a bug she had to scrape off her windshield, Rivet takes a step to the side. The guy on the floor says one last thing to her, but she ignores him and picks up her conversation with Grinch as though they weren't interrupted.

"I knew we made a good choice with her," Shadow says proudly before taking a long sip of his beer.

It takes several long minutes before the kid picks himself up off the floor. He doesn't even look in Rivet's direction when he slinks back off to sit with a group of people.

"See you in a couple of hours," Shadow says before crossing the room with determination. It's only minutes before he and Misty disappear.

"Pretty sweet place you guys have here," I tell Tug. "Where are your people at?"

"Max and Jasmine?"

I nod, not at all weirded out that my friend is in a polyamorous relationship with a guy and girl.

"They're around here somewhere."

"I'm surprised everyone agreed to help me."

"Shouldn't be," Tug says draining the last of his beer. "It's what we do."

Chapter 16

Anna

I feel like a fool for winking at myself in the mirror, but I'm killing it in this dress. The floor-length black silk is like a sensual caress on my skin, and not only do I look sexy in it, I feel phenomenal. It's doing great things for my injured ego.

My mom picked it out and as much as I hate to admit it, she always has the perfect eye and picks the things I never would've looked at. Nine times out of ten, they work out, so I can't really complain that even at thirty-two my mother is still buying me clothes.

The ringing of the doorbell outside of the suite keeps me from thinking about the conversation I had days ago about Deacon's Diesel jeans. I'd wondered more than once if his mom grabbed those for him on sale, but I know enough about fashion to tell they were from the latest line.

I shake my head and plaster a smile on my face. With a deep breath in and a long slow breath out, I reach for the doorknob. This will be the first time we're seeing each other since he got pissed about Flynn being in here with me, and I just don't have the energy to fight with him again tonight. He was gone last night, and I didn't sleep well.

"Hey there..." The words die on my lips when I see that it's not Deacon standing on the other side of the door.

If I had taken a moment to consider the facts, I would've known that Deacon would've either used the key he managed to pilfer or he would've texted me from the damn truck and told me to get my ass down there so we could get this night over with.

"Hi, I'm Wren," the shaggy-haired guy says with a quick smile. I don't miss the mild tremble to his lips. "I'll be escorting you tonight."

"Is that so?" I barely catch myself before I cross my arms. Doing so would wrinkle the dress, and the last thing I need tonight is disapproving looks from the other people at the gala.

The only part of tonight I was looking forward to was seeing Deacon, and coming to that realization in the shower while I was shaving every damn inch of my body has been enough to deal with.

"I figured he'd send Brooks."

Wren's smile wilts.

"Or Flynn."

And the smile falls completely off his face. Now I'm an asshole for hurting this guy's feelings.

"They're not—" He swallows, and it makes me wonder what Deacon told this guy about me. He legit seems like he's seconds away from turning around and running. "—he sent me."

Even with his messy hair, and the numerous years separating us in age, I can see the appeal of this guy too. Add another hot guy to team Blackbridge for heaven's sake. His tuxedo is pressed to perfection, and there's a glimmer in his eyes that tells me there's a wild child waiting to escape. Tonight may end up being a blast even without Deacon Black.

"Well, Wren," I say as I grab my clutch and step fully into the hallway, "let's go have a great time."

He releases the breath he was holding when I scoop my arm through his and turn us in the direction of the elevator.

"Are you old enough to drink? I'm planning to drink my weight in whiskey tonight and we need to preplan our night if you're getting drunk, too."

"I'm twenty-six," he mutters as we wait for the elevator, "but I'm not drinking tonight. It's not allowed while we're working."

It only takes a few words to be reminded that to Deacon, I'm nothing more than a job.

Question is, what happens when we find Dani? I don't know if I'll be able to handle going back to a world that doesn't include that surly bastard.

***

Despite the awkward foot Wren and I got off to, he managed to loosen up some during the limousine ride. He'd never been in one, and I watched with glee as he enjoyed it for the first time like an awe-struck kid. I also managed to convince him that pre-gaming, including a couple of shots, were a necessity to get through a night like tonight. His work excuse flew out the window the second I held up the bottle of liquor.

This is the first Starfish Gala, and since my parents are huge advocates of helping ocean life, it was one of the events I didn't have a say in attending.

I don't think Wren is going to be who she's expecting when my mother insisted I bring *a nice man as a date* when I spoke with her earlier. I still haven't spoken to them about what happened with Dani or how my apartment was trashed. If we're able to find her safely, I may never open my mouth to have that conversation with them. It wouldn't be the first time I kept secrets from my parents for Dani.

"What just happened?" Wren asks with a silly smile. "Your face just transformed from happiness to depression."

I quirk my lips back up into a half-smile. "I don't really like attending these kinds of things."

"Really?" He honestly sounds surprised. "It seems so glamorous."

He sweeps his arms to indicate the luxury car we're traveling in.

"It grows tiresome after a while," I mutter.

I expect him to get that same look on his face that Deacon gets, the one that says *oh you poor spoiled brat*, but he just looks wistfully outside the dark-tinted window to watch the building move by slowly.

"I guess glamour isn't always glamorous," he whispers.

"Tell me about yourself." I nudge his shoe with the tip of my heel. "Do you have a girlfriend?"

"No."

"Single and looking?"

He turns his head back in my direction. "I game."

"Like hunting?" I tilt my head in confusion.

"Not hunting. Games. Online stuff mostly." He frowns. "I'm awkward when it comes to women that aren't aware of the score."

"The score?" Is he drunk after just a couple of shots?

"I, umm…" He lifts his hand and squeezes the back of his neck. "I meet girls on hookup apps. I find it difficult to walk up to women in person without having set up arrangements previously."

"Hmmm."

"You can say it. It's weird. I'm fucking weird."

A laugh erupts from my throat before I can stop it.

"Ha, ha," he deadpans before looking out the window again.

"No," I scoot closer and grip his arm until he's turning back around, "I'm not making fun of you. I just thought you were joking."

"I'm not."

"What about the girl you lost your virginity to? You approached her, right?"

His cheeks beat the land speed record for turning red as an apple. "Oh, Wren, no. Really?"

He shrugs, breaking eye contact, and I think he may be close to tears. "She knew, so it's not like it's a big deal."

"There are girls online looking for that sort of thing?"

He refuses to look at me again when I tug on his tux sleeve.

"She was a professional."

Another bubble of laughter threatens, but I manage to hold it back. This poor guy.

"Are you saying you hired a hooker to lose your virginity to?"

Finally, he looks in my direction, his brows drawn together tightly.

"Don't be so crass, Annalise Grimaldi. They're called escorts. It's not like I drove around town in my mom's Camry with twenty bucks in my pocket looking for chicks on the street corner. It seemed normal at the time, and I'll have you know she thoroughly enjoyed herself that night."

"I bet she did," I agree wholeheartedly. "It's jus—"

"What? I swear I'll never talk to you again if you tell Deacon what I just confessed."

"I'd never tell Deacon." And I mean it, because despite just having met this guy, I feel like we could eventually become real friends. "It's just that I've met Brooks and Flynn and Ignacio. They all seem very *sure* of themselves. I didn't expect your story to turn out like it did."

"Those guys have mad skills picking up women. Quinten is great too." He's grinning again, and I'm certain we've managed to avoid a meltdown. "Those guys spend time traveling, and I'm always sitting in my office on the computer. It takes a lot of time to do what I do. I don't always have the time to socialize."

"Well," I tell him with a smile of my own, "we're going to socialize you tonight, my new friend."

The car rolls to a stop at the front of the building where the Starfish Gala is being held.

"Are you ready to rub elbows with the rich people of St. Louis?"

Expecting a smile, I can't help but laugh when he seems to turn greener than he was when I found him standing outside of my hotel suite half an hour ago.

"Come on, handsome. If you're going to start learning how to pick up women, there's no time like the present."

I reach over him and shove open the door. He steps out, reaching for my hand without even being instructed to help me out.

"You're off to an excellent start already," I mutter through a smile as cameras flash all around us. "You may just have it all down before the night is over with."

"Don't count on it," he mutters, eyes squinting with each rapid click of the flashbulbs.

Chapter 17
Deacon

Being this close to the beach with the ability to smell the ocean, knowing we aren't even going to get a chance to dip our toes in the salty water is its own form of punishment. Standing outside the Petrovich's family compound, not knowing if Dani is inside or if she's alive or dead is hell—a torture I wouldn't wish on my worst enemy.

I'm no longer in love with her. What I told the guys yesterday was the absolute truth. That ship sailed long ago, but Dani and I will always be connected. We'll always have a history.

"You ready?" Tug grunts, his hand on my shoulder.

His question is more than two words, more than just checking in to make sure I'm physically capable of heading inside.

He's asking me if I'm in the right headspace. If I'm mentally capable of handling business without getting myself or the other guys killed. It's reference to the long conversation we had on the plane ride to Africa and the brutal facts of what we may be facing once we get inside.

"Yeah, man," I answer on instinct, but the calm I would normally feel in a situation like this is absent.

I know I'm capable of doing my job. I know I won't freak out and lose my shit if we walk into a tragedy, but it's the after that I'm worried about. If Dani is here in any shape or form, she'll be recovered. Of that, I'm one hundred percent certain. The aftermath is going to be the challenge.

"You're sure?"

I grind my teeth but keep my eyes forward. I don't need anyone doubting me, but I also understand where he's coming from. It's not only my guys in danger if I fuck up. His team, his friends will be compromised if I can't keep it together.

"I'm good," I tell him, and after a long look into my eyes to be sure, he nods and gets into position.

"There are three men inside. One is the groundskeeper, but I have no doubt he's as thoroughly trained as the guards. There are two female house staff as well," Shadow says into the headset. "We need to go in hard and fast. We have the element of surprise, so this should be over in minutes."

Shadow, along with Kincaid are still back in New Mexico. It's very rare that the entire team leaves the Cerberus compound. They have family and loved ones on the property and don't like to leave them unprotected.

We move forward like wind whispering through the trees when Hound gives the command to his team. The house isn't as big as one would expect with the amount of illegal business the Petrovich family does, so that keeps one team on standby in the tree line at our backs so we don't bottleneck our way inside. Tug urged me to stay with the second team but gave up that recommendation with one scathing look from me.

Hound did step in and refuse to let me lead the team. I'm at the mercy of Cerberus and beyond grateful for their help, so I really couldn't argue that point. This is how they work. He leads the team and gives the commands.

"Thirty feet," Hound whispers, his voice heard by everyone through our headsets.

"Movement to the east." Tug's voice is calm, and in a flash one of the guys ahead of me splits off. After a grunt, silence once again fills the air.

"One down, four to go," Hound assesses.

Most people would think these situations look a lot like they do on the SWAT shows on television but banging loudly and announcing our entrance isn't the tactical way to handle things. Stealth is key, and both my team and the Cerberus guys are experts in the field.

I'm seventh in line behind the Cerberus team, and by the time my feet cross the threshold into the house, all but one of the people inside have been seized.

The last woman, an old lady of about seventy who was still asleep on the second floor is bound with her head covered in a hood within a minute of the entire team making entry. She sighs loudly, mumbling something I don't understand in Russian as she's urged to sit on the couch. Each of them seems so unaffected that I have to wonder how often people burst into the house and tie them up.

Ignacio explains to them in Russian that we aren't there to hurt them, urging them to tell us where Dani is.

"She said she isn't here," Ignacio explains.

It's almost too easy, and my blood pressure spikes, my pulse pounding in my ears as we clear every other room.

"I'm not getting any other heat sensors," Tug says as I follow him from room to room.

"That doesn't mean—" Shadow clears his throat, the rough sound traveling through his mic, and I know if this weren't a personal crusade, he would've finished that sentence. We all know the possibility of what we may find and dead bodies don't give off heat. "Keep looking."

I stand a little taller with each area that is cleared without finding my ex-wife. The grief I was already preparing myself to feel slowly dissipates to a manageable level by the time the entire compound is walked through and she isn't found.

"There are no soil disruptions on the property," someone says.

So, she hasn't been buried here.

"The basement?" Shadow asks.

"Cleared."

"Both floors?"

"Cleared."

"The outbuildings?"

"Cleared."

I tilt my head, hearing a growl come through the mic.

A slew of angry Russian spills from the living area where three guys are holding the house's residents.

I don't understand but one word and that's Petrovich's name.

"What's he saying?" I ask Ignacio as I make my way through the house in that direction.

"She's not here," my guy answers.

"Torres," I snap.

I can't be placated right now.

"He says Dani isn't here, but Petrovich is looking for her." The long pause before he continues makes my skin crawl. "Nikolay is looking for her, and she's as good as dead if they don't recover what she took."

"And now?" I ask when the guy starts talking again.

"Whores who don't know their place end up only one way. He urges us with every curse word in Russian to come back in a few weeks and we can dig her body up from the backyard."

Tug grabs the shoulder of my flak jacket before I can make a move against the guy.

"All clear?" Shadow interrupts, and I can tell by the tone of his voice that he's seconds away from insisting we get the hell out of there.

"Every inch searched," Hound responds.

"Roll out."

The command is law. The Cerberus guys turn to leave, but Quinten finds my eyes from across the room.

All it would take is a simple nod of my head and my team would stay behind and spend the next week getting every ounce of information from these people as possible, no matter what it takes.

"Black," Tug snaps with another jerk of my vest. "Roll out."

I nearly jerk away from him, but then the old lady on the couch yawns, and with that one action I know they'd die before they gave anything up, and that's if they know anything at all.

I hitch my head to the side, my guys understanding my meaning. We all exit the building, one Cerberus guy left behind a little longer so he can cut the old woman's restraints. There's no doubt that Petrovich will be pissed when he hears about what went down here tonight, but we used soft cuffs, not one single weapon was discharged, and no one was injured. It should count for something, but it doesn't keep the pit in my stomach from growing. There will be some form of retribution, and I get the feeling that it's going to hit on a personal level.

"Sorry, man," Tug says as we near the airstrip to leave.

The drive takes a little more than an hour, but we're still on guard. Phone calls move faster than the SUVs we're traveling in, and a counterattack is expected before the plane will have the ability to take off.

"We always knew finding her there was a long shot. There were no travel plans for her or anyone connected to Petrovich."

I nod my understanding because it's true, but not finding Dani in West Africa means I'm pretty much back at square one. Being anywhere in the United States is just as bad as the possibility of her being on foreign soil.

There's a collective sigh of relief as we pull up to the tarmac without altercation, but the guys don't settle until we're a mile in the air over the Atlantic Ocean, and even then, most squirm in their seats. It's the adrenaline that built up that wasn't used with the mostly calm mission that keeps them from fully relaxing. I can't imagine what the next couple of days are going to look like back in New Mexico when they get home and search out ways to release all the extra energy.

I once again scour the dossier Wren compiled for me, hoping that there's something I overlooked, something I missed the first hundred times I went through it. Nothing jumps out. I'm right back where I started.

Chapter 18
Anna

If I get that same damn *Working* text from Deacon again, I may scream.

It's been days since I've seen him. Days since the gala. Wren and I had a blast laughing, drinking, dancing, and ignoring all the looks we got from people who couldn't believe we had the gall to show up at an event and have a good time. It's what's been missing in my life for a while now. Fun and games at those types of events were frowned upon when I was younger, but there were concessions because of my age. The older I got, the stricter the rules. By the time I made it out of high school, the expectation was to mingle and smile, two glasses of champagne max, and dancing was only suitable occasionally in ballroom style. Wren wasn't suitable two nights ago, and his insistence that the running man was acceptable with every song played was frowned upon by many in attendance.

I avoided eye contact with my parents, but the few times I did happen to look in their direction, I found Mom smiling and Dad shaking his head with a sparkle in his eye.

Needless to say, we had a blast, but then he dropped me back at the hotel before disappearing again. I haven't had human contact in two days other than a quick phone call from Mom asking who my date was and if I'm going to bring him to their house for dinner. I put a big X on that suggestion and told them that he was just a friend doing me a favor by attending. When she wouldn't let it go, I lied and told her that he was married and his husband wouldn't appreciate me taking him away again anytime soon. She then suggested I bring them both. In the end, I agreed but didn't give her a timeframe. It's my hope that she'll forget all about it.

It's been weeks since someone has reached out to me other than family members, and it was in the early morning hours a day ago when I realized I've been the one to always reach out to the people in my life. If I don't call them, they can't be bothered to contact me. Being my stubborn self, I decided that I'm done with people like that. I don't need people in my life that don't value me.

That mental declaration led to deeper thinking about the kind of person I am, and I spent hours in my head reflecting on my life. Let's just say it's a scary damn place to be trapped.

I'm at my wit's end. Seclusion doesn't work for me because I don't like myself or who I've become in the last ten years. Staring at all the stuff I bought when I first came to the hotel makes it even harder to deal with. I didn't need the entire lingerie line. I wanted it. I didn't need eight different bodywashes and four types of shampoo. I'm not going anywhere and have nothing planned for the next couple of weeks, so I didn't need a dozen new pairs of shoes and a closet full of clothes. I hate myself right now. It's no wonder Deacon doesn't even want to see or talk to me.

My best friend is missing, and I'm a petty idiot who's worried about clothes and the scent of my hair. I know all of the stuff is a distraction because thinking of Dani makes me think of all the horrible things she could be suffering from. Thinking of her makes me think of him and the way I acted like a complete idiot in the bar and in the bedroom days ago.

Walking around the hotel suite, I shake my hands by my sides but nervous energy wins out. After a quick peek through the peephole and realizing there isn't someone standing guard out there, I make the decision to leave. I'll just head to the park and maybe go for a walk. A coffee sounds like an amazing idea right now. Even if I don't talk to anyone, just being around other people will be better than going crazy all alone up here.

I change out of my lounge clothes. Just because I may be having an existential crisis about the direction my life has taken, I'm nowhere near the point I can go out in public looking like a train wreck.

My phone rings in my purse as I reach the elevator. It's a local number, but instead of sending it to voicemail, I accept the call, desperate for even a robocall right now.

"Where do you think you're going?"

My hand freezes above the call button to the elevator.

"Umm..."

"Anna." The warning is clear in Wren's voice, but it still doesn't hold the same power as it would if it were Deacon on the other line. "You're not supposed to leave."

"I can't stay here!" I screech.

"Overdramatic much?"

"You don't even understand." I sag against the wall in defeat.

I'm not trying to cause problems for Wren. I don't want Deacon jumping on his ass because I can't do what I'm told but staying here isn't an option.

"I'm going crazy. Before long I won't even have to worry about Russian mobsters because I'll be in a secure institution on twelve different psychotropic drugs to manage my insanity."

He sighs, but it ends with a chuckle.

"How did you know I left the room?"

"I don't divulge my secrets."

"Oh my God! Do you have cameras in the suite? Did you watch me doing yoga earlier?"

My cheeks heat because I attempted yoga sans clothes a couple of hours ago, both wanting Deacon to show up and praying that he didn't. Like I said, my mind is a scary place right now.

"Were you..." he clears his throat. "Why, would that bother you?"

"I didn't have my hair fixed," I say stupidly, and when he laughs again, I know there aren't cameras in the suite. At least not in the media room.

"I'm tapped into the hotel's system. I know when the door opens. The suite to your door opened and the elevator wasn't triggered prior. There's no order to your room for room service and no one has checked in for a delivery to your room."

I close my eyes, taking a deep breath before speaking. He's only doing what I'm sure Deacon told him to, but I'm not used to having someone so invasive in my life.

"If you're keeping such close tabs on my every move, why would it be unsafe for me to go down the street to get a coffee?"

"We have coffee here."

"I'm not there," I mutter.

"You could be."

My mood shifts immediately. "Really?"

"If you go back inside and give me twenty minutes, I can have a car there to pick you up."

My pulse begins to pound with the prospect of getting out of here even if it's to head to the BBS offices for a little while.

"Deal," I squeal and turn back to the hotel suite.

***

"I don't think I've ever seen a woman so happy to see me before."

I scoff at Wren when he meets me at the elevator outside of the BBS office.

"I find that hard to believe," I tell him with a smile.

"How so?" He tilts his head a little, intent on hearing what I have to say.

"Fishing for compliments?" I slap him on the shoulder because running up to him and hugging him for helping me escape the hotel suite would be weird, right?

He winks at me before holding the door open for me to enter.

"This is Pam."

"Anna," I tell the middle-aged woman at the front desk, holding out my hand.

"She's our mother hen. The only one around here who can keep all of us guys in line."

Pam rolls her eyes as she takes my hand.

"I'm the office manager and client liaison."

"Lovely to meet you."

Pam wasn't here the other night when I arrived, but it's nice to know that it's not just the guys running this place.

"We're going to hang out," Wren says as if he needs to explain my presence.

"Don't let—"

"I know the rules," Wren interrupts like a grouchy child.

"Rules?" I ask after we leave the front office area and head back to the big breakroom I met the other guys in when I came here the first time.

"We deal with a lot of sensitive information. She was just warning me to be careful with what you see."

I follow him across the room to the door on the far side.

"This is my office."

A blast of cold air hits me in the face when he swings the door open wide.

"Hey, fucker—Oh a pretty lady."

My eyes snap to the most beautiful African grey parrot I've ever seen, and I laugh when he tilts his little head to the side to get a better look at me.

"Are you here of your own free will?" the bird asks, earning a scoff from Wren. "Do you need assistance? Come here and let Daddy help you."

The bird moves back and forth on a perch that runs the length of the room.

"That's Puff Daddy," Wren explains as he takes a seat in an office chair that looks like it belongs on a spaceship. "I've had him since I was a teenager."

"Puff Daddy?"

My smile grows wider when the bird starts bopping its head up and down.

"I traded him for some work in high school. He already had the name."

"He's cute," I say as I reach up to pet him.

"Don't touch the goods unless you're buying, lady."

I snap my hand back. "He doesn't like to be pet."

"I'm not a dog," he squawks.

"You're an asshole," Wren snaps back.

"He's very fluent."

"Mostly cuss words and inappropriate shit." Wren doesn't even look ashamed to own a foul-mouthed bird.

"Just mad. Just mad. Just mad," Puff Daddy says on repeat.

"For fuck's sake," Wren mutters. "Here we go."

"Why is he mad?" I ask.

"Because my dick's bigger."

I choke on a laugh, covering my mouth with my hand, but Wren just grins and flips the bird off.

"Deacon fucking hates him."

"He lives here?"

"Have a seat." Wren uses the tip of his sneaker to push another rolling chair in my direction. "I take him home when I go, but I spend most of my time up here though."

Puff Daddy calms down when Wren stands and pours some food in a little silver bowl, but there's a wicked grin on his face when he sits back in front of his computer.

"This is a lot of equipment," I observe as he begins typing something.

"Wanna have some fun?"

"I'm not really into online games." He mentioned playing them the other night. "But I guess I could try."

"Not games." He winks again, and I almost open my mouth to remind him that he also told me he's not very good at social interactions with women. "Give me the name of the one guy you dated that you wouldn't spit on if he caught fire."

"Benito Ricci," I respond immediately. "We dated—"

"Your sophomore year of college."

My eyes widen like saucers when I look at the computer screen. "How in the hell?"

Looking back at me is a picture taken at a college football game. I'm looking up at Benny, and of course my ex-boyfriend has his eyes glued to another girl's ass. It's so easy to see how much of a jerk he was now, but back then, I thought I'd marry that idiot.

"Want to know what he's been up to?"

"Not really," I answer truthfully.

"Divorced, twice," he reads from the screen. "Is engaged again. His fiancée and girlfriend don't know about each other."

"Gross," I mutter. "Dodged that bullet, I guess."

"Wow. This guy is a total douche."

"Tell me about it."

"Let's cause some trouble for him."

"Nothing illegal," I hiss. "His father is a high-powered attorney. I don't want you to get sued for messing with him."

He snorts a laugh. "I won't mess with him too bad, but if you change your mind, let me know. I don't get caught."

He types away on his computer, screen after screen flashing too fast for me to be able to tell what he's doing.

"And done." He presses a final key with flair.

"What did you do?" My eyes sweep the three screens in front of us, but I can't decipher the information. It's all written in numbers and the English alphabet, but it still looks like a different language.

"I set alarms on his phone to activate in the middle of the night."

"That's not too bad." He honestly deserves worse.

"And I set up a date with both women at the same time. They'll know about each other by the end of the evening."

"Nice," I praise. "Let's see what else you can do. Look up—"

A phone rings, cutting me off. Instead of picking up a phone, Wren slides a headset over his head and answers.

"Your ears must be ringing," he says instead of hello. "Anna and I were just talking about you."

What the hell? Is Benito calling him?

"Why are you talking to Anna?" The familiar voice fills the room, and it shocks me because I didn't expect for him to be on speaker phone.

Not Benito. Deacon.

"She got bored, so I had her come to the office."

"Take me off speaker," Deacon snaps, and with the press of a single button on his keyboard, I can no longer hear what the jerk is saying on the other end of the line.

Wren frowns as he answers questions, but his responses give me no detail about the topic of conversation. The call only lasts a minute or two before Wren hangs up and pulls the headset off his head.

"Is he always such an asshole?"

"He's the boss," Wren answers diplomatically. "He wants you back at the hotel."

Chapter 19
Deacon

"Anything new?" I rub the back of my hand over my eyes.

I've been gone for a week, but it feels like it's been years since I stepped into Wren's office.

Thankfully the bird is in his cage and sleeping. I just don't have the energy or the patience to deal with it today.

"I've been looking everywhere since you called and told me Dani wasn't in West Africa. I haven't found anything. Other than a little chatter from the Russians about still looking for her, I haven't found shit." Wren cracks his neck as he turns his chair to face me. "I think she's gone underground. Even with no activity on her credit cards, it's still possible. The Russians don't have her."

"Yet," I mumble.

"That still gives us hope, though. All we have to do is keep looking. Give me a little more time, Deacon. I'll find her."

"I'm going to get some sleep," I tell him as I back away toward the door. "I'll check in on you in a few hours."

"Hey," he says before I can make it fully out the door. "I didn't mean to piss you off with bringing Anna here. I know she's off-limits."

"No big deal."

It was yesterday when I called because my mind kept wandering back to her, warring over the regret of walking away when she tried to kiss me. I was livid that he was spending time with her while I was still hundreds of miles away on a plane.

"She's a client," I say, more to remind myself than him.

His eyes search mine, and I know his reference to her being off-limits has nothing to do with that fact. He's implying that she's not an option for him because I have some sort of claim over the woman. It couldn't be further from the truth.

"Right." He nods his head, but for Wren, it's impossible to hide his true thoughts.

I walk away before I lie to the guy.

"Client," I snap at myself as I walk toward the private elevator that will take me to my apartment. I need a shower and a couple hours of sleep, but instead of pressing the button for the tenth floor, I hit the one for the parking garage.

I must be delirious due to lack of sleep because I'm hopping on the elevator in the Four Seasons' lobby without having a clue how I managed to drive across town safely since I can't remember the trip at all.

The hotel suite is bathed in darkness except for a single light bleeding into the hallway from the kitchen. My blood runs cold when I notice the made bed in the middle of the bedroom. I pull out my phone, hell-bent on ripping Wren a new one for letting her leave when I find her curled up on the couch in the media room.

She's wearing twice as much clothing than she was the last time I saw her, but they still leave so much of her perfect skin exposed.

Her tiny sleep shorts have ridden up her thighs revealing at least half of her luscious ass, and the hem and shoulder strap of the tank top she's wearing seems determined to meet in the middle of her body.

What would the skin taste like between her ear and her collarbone?

How much of that thick ass could I cup in a single hand?

What color are her panties?

Is she even wearing any?

I walked in here exhausted, with the intent to look in on her before crashing on the couch, but sleep would be impossible right now. It's the last thing on my mind as I look down at her. I do, however, have a million other things I'd like to be doing.

She stirs, but rather than her shirt hiking higher or the strap of her tank top dropping lower, her eyes flutter. She looks up, her mouth tugging up in a sleepy smile, and I know she's disoriented. It makes me wonder what she was dreaming about, because the Anna I left in the hotel suite a week ago would be terrified to wake up and see a man standing a few feet away watching her.

"What are your dreams about?"

She jolts, her body snapping like she was hit with an electric shock, and when she sits up, regretfully adjusting the strap of her tank back onto her shoulder, the Anna I know is glaring at me.

I knew I should've just smiled back down at her with my mouth shut to see how long her sweet smile lasted.

"What the fuck, Deacon?"

"What the fuck, indeed," I say as my eyes wander down her legs.

I must be more sleep deprived than I thought because normally I would never let her catch me looking at her this way, but damn if she doesn't look like the tastiest snack all rumpled from sleep. She doesn't have a single drop of makeup on her gorgeous face and her hair is a little ratty from the sofa.

When she stands, the glare never disappearing from her face, I look away. My only mistake was looking down first. It's obvious she's not wearing a bra, and one peek at the outline of her nipples in that tank top is enough to make my cock take notice.

I clear my throat, shifting my hips so I'm half inside the small media room and half out.

"Where have you been?"

"Working."

Her jaw clenches, hands opening and closing as if she's trying to decide which fist to hit me with first.

"You didn't call." She inches closer, so close I can smell the sweet scent of her bodywash on her skin.

I'm such a weak man. God, I feel powerless when she's this close.

"You barely texted."

I take a step back, knowing if she gets much closer, I'm not going to be able to keep from reaching for her.

She doesn't take the hint, and before long, she's standing right in front of me, head tilted back so she can shoot fire in my direction.

Her honey-golden eyes are filled with anger and insolence.

"You're a client," I remind her, knowing damn well she's more than that. I ignore the pain that flashes in her pretty eyes because I have to take command over this situation, again. I never should've lost it in the first place. "You're not my damn girlfriend, Anna. I don't answer to you. You're a job. That's it."

Of all the things I could've said, this seems to hit the mark dead center. It's what I needed to say, but I regret the last part immediately. But like pouring rain back into a cloud, it's impossible to take back.

I expect her chin to quiver, maybe a tear to drop down her cheek, but then her lip tilts up in a sneer a single second before both of her palms shove against my chest. Unprepared for this response, I stumble back a few feet.

"A job?" she snaps before walking around me and striding down the hallway toward the bedroom. "I fucking know what I am!"

I follow her, wanting to backpedal.

"Anna."

"No!" she hisses as she swings open the closet door. "I'm a fucking job. Dani doesn't fucking matter to you. This is about getting paid."

That couldn't be further from the truth.

"Well, guess what, asshole? You're fired!"

Uncaring of how expensive the clothes are, she begins to rip them from the hangers in the closet before tossing them all in a pile on the bed. The shoes are next, the boxes flung without concern onto the growing pile.

"What the fuck are you doing?" I snap when she disappears into the bathroom.

"Leaving." Her arms are burdened with beauty products. They end up on top of the other things.

I grab her by her upper arms, not trying to hurt her but increasing pressure when she tries to pull away. I wasn't prepared a few moments ago when she shoved me, but there's no way she'll get away from me right now unless I allow it.

"Let go of me," she seethes through clenched teeth. She jerks so hard, I know if she keeps it up she's going to hurt herself.

In three steps, I have her pinned to the wall. She glares at my chest, refusing to look up at me.

"You'll stay where you're safe, and that's final."

She lifts her chin, finally looking up at me even if it is to glare. Her jaw unhinges, and I know I'm seconds away from getting every ire this fiery Italian can manage.

"Don't open your damn mouth unless it's to—"

I snap my jaw shut, blaming her proximity, the angry inhales and exhales of her breath pressing her breasts against me, and the pressure of her thighs against my own, on what I was about to say.

"Unless what?" she snaps.

Maybe it's the pink in her cheeks. Maybe it's the way her lip quivers as she waits for my answer. Maybe, just maybe it's the fact that

Annalise Grimaldi has driven me crazy with her attitude one too many times.

Or, maybe it's because I can just no longer resist her.

Instead of letting her go, instead of taking a step back and telling her to go about her merry damn way, I inch closer, hovering my lips over hers until her breath becomes my own.

"Deacon," she whispers, but it's not a warning like it should be. It's a plea, her way of begging me to come just an inch closer.

It should've been what made me snap back to reality, but all it does is make me want her more.

I slam my mouth against hers, partly because I can no longer resist the need to know what her lips feel like against mine, but mostly because I'm pissed that I don't have the strength to step away.

She moans, the perfect sound rushing past her parted lips. I slip my tongue inside, my body nearly seizing when she presses her own forward. My fingers tangle in her silky hair as I tilt her head to the perfect angle for me to dive all the way in. Breathing becomes impossible. Thinking took a long hike off a steep cliff.

The only thing that exists is this.

Me.

Her.

The way her lips smile against my own when I inch back to reposition.

The way she tilts her chin, inching closer when she thinks I'm going to end it.

My brain doesn't come back online until her fingers reach under my shirt and trail down my sides.

And then it's like the first bullet of a firefight. It snaps me back into focus. Her hands are on my skin. Her lips are pressed against mine. Every inch I can manage to line up is pressed against her. My cock throbs to be released.

It feels fucking perfect, but we both know just how wrong it is. This can't happen. If she were literally any other woman on this Earth, I'd have her naked with her thighs clamped around my head. I'd bury my cock so fucking deep in her—

"Stop," I whisper, resting my forehead against hers. "We can't."

She takes a long shuddering breath. "I know."

Her hands fall away, and somehow, I manage not to lift them back to my sides. With strength I didn't know I possessed, I untangle my fingers from her silky hair and take a step back.

Her chest is heaving just as hard as my own, and somehow, it's a mild comfort to know that she may possibly be as affected by the kiss as I was.

"Dani wasn't in West Africa. I need you to stay here where it's safe." She nods but refuses to look me in the eyes. "I'm spread too thin. I don't want to have to worry about you, too."

She nods, a mere two quick dips of her head, and I walk away, closing the bedroom door behind me.

Chapter 20
Anna

My eyes blink over and over as if I've just been woken up from a dream. My fingers press to my swollen lips as if I need to touch them for proof that the kiss really happened.

Even with his manly scent still in my nose, infiltrating my brain all the while telling me to chase after him, I can't believe it's real.

He went from get fucked to let's fuck like a lightning flash, and he ended it just as quickly.

I lick at my lips, missing the scratch of his overgrown stubble. I don't think he's shaved in the week he's been gone. It's been forever since I've kissed a man with facial hair, and it wasn't until the rough texture touched my face that I realized how much I actually missed it. God how I've missed it.

I didn't realize how much I missed him, rather than just having someone around. I've ached for his eyes on me. Hell, I would've relinquished my trust fund just to listen to him telling me I'm a spoiled brat.

And now things are ruined.

We can't.

I knew that before he leaned in. I knew it with the very first strike of his tongue against mine. I knew it before my fingers found the heat of his skin. We both did.

Kissing him was wrong. Wanting to keep doing it is a betrayal I'll have to learn to live with. Deacon is a lot of things, but a man who goes back on his word isn't one of them.

It was a one-time thing. It'll never happen again.

I shove the pile of stuff on the bed to the side, moving it only enough for me to crawl under the covers and bury my face. He's not even in the room, and I'm utterly embarrassed, but the increasing heat of my skin still isn't enough for me to shove the blankets back enough so I can breathe comfortably.

This is my own personal hell. I agreed to be here. Truthfully, I want to be here, so long as he's around, but that's a double-edged sword after what just happened.

It was just a stupid kiss, my subconscious reminds me.

But it wasn't.

It wasn't stupid

And it surely wasn't just a kiss.

That kiss was everything. It was the best. It rules supreme over every other kiss I've ever had from Josh in sixth grade straight through to the last guy I dated whose name completely escapes me right now.

Epic.

Fiery.

Passionate.

Too short.

All of it. I groan, grumble about my own stupidity as I bury my face deeper in the pillow. I'm going to have to face that man. I'm going to have to eventually walk out of this room and see him again. Just the thought makes my skin flame even more, both with shame and a level of lust I know I'll never feel again.

It doesn't matter that he kissed me first. I kissed him back. I want to keep kissing him. Forever seems like it wouldn't be long enough.

I punch the pillow hard enough that something rolls off the bed and smacks the floor. Whatever it was sounds broken now, and I just don't have the energy to care.

"Stupid men," I mutter.

It's with regret and sheer will to keep my ass planted in the bed that I manage to fall asleep. I wouldn't even call it sleep. It's that second right on the cusp that you grow weightless when a loud bang wakes me. The sound of something breaking forces me fully upright in the bed, but then silence surrounds me.

I know I didn't dream it. The sounds were too real, as real as the sheer terror that fills every cell in my body. I ease out of the bed, using trembling hands to pull random clothes from the pile still on the bed. I shove my legs in jeans and put on a top before pressing my bare feet into a pair of shoes.

There's nowhere to hide in this room. I discovered that the first night I arrived when Deacon left me here alone for a short period of time. Designer clothes won't protect me, and since we're on the nineteenth floor, climbing out of a window to get to safety isn't an option.

I can hear every breath rushing past my lips, every pound of my heart, every single step I make toward the bedroom door. What I don't hear is a single sound coming from the other side. I scream when the door swings open before I can reach for it, and nearly collapse on the floor in relief when I see Deacon rather than a masked murderer enter.

"Wh-what's going on?"

He's rumpled, sweat dotting his forehead and upper lip. He leans to the side filling the doorway, but that doesn't stop me from seeing past him if only for the briefest of seconds.

A sob escapes my mouth, but my hand isn't fast enough to cover it.

"There's been an incident." How can he be so calm?

"Is he dead?"

I can no longer see the guy on the floor right outside the bedroom door, but the ever-growing pool of blood surrounding his body will be burned into my brain for eternity.

"He's dead."

Deacon fills every inch of my line of sight, and I'm honestly grateful. I didn't want to see the dead man once, much less getting another glance at him.

"Russian?" I manage when it's clear Deacon isn't going to reach out and touch me.

"He's a local street thug," Deacon answers before I feel his arms wrap around me.

He kicks the bedroom door closed before walking me over to the edge of the bed. I sit down; he doesn't.

Before I can ask any more questions, the doorbell to the suite rings.

"Stay here," he insists before walking out of the room.

He doesn't need to worry. There's no way I'm going out there. The door opens again, only it's Flynn walking in, not Deacon. I reach for him immediately, and in kind he doesn't hesitate to cross the room and wrap his arms around me. He doesn't seem bothered by my tears when I sob into his shoulder.

Seeing bloody EMTs and a trashed apartment have nothing on what has happened tonight. Short of deceased, elderly relatives, I've never seen a dead body, certainly not one so recently deceased. Not one that was clearly feet away from getting into this room. Was he coming after me? What if Deacon wasn't here? What if that guy came in here last night or any other night this last week?

This realization makes me cry harder, but Flynn takes it in stride, rubbing my back and assuring me everything is going to be fine. I don't think it will though. How can everything be fine when there was a guy coming to hurt me? How will things ever be normal again with me knowing that?

The doorbell chimes again, causing me to jerk and hold Flynn tighter.

"That's the police."

I snap my head up looking toward the door. I didn't know Deacon had entered the room behind his friend. He made no move to comfort me, and that stings. I've known him for years. He's literally the closest person I have around right now, and he didn't even try to interfere when Flynn took me in his arms.

I shove my face back into Flynn's neck when Deacon's hand reaches for the doorknob. I can't stand the thought of seeing that body again, but it's also nearly impossible to watch Deacon walk out of the room again.

"Are you okay?" Flynn asks. I cling to his British accent as hard as I cling to his arms. Maybe if I close my eyes, I can wish myself away from this moment in time. "Anna?"

"I d-don't think so," I answer honestly. "Will Deacon be in trouble?"

"No, love. He won't be." He pulls back, cradling my face in his huge palms. "We need to pack. Can you help me?"

I nod even though I'm unsure how helpful I'll be right now. He urges me to stand, holding me around the waist when my knees nearly buckle. He's patient, waiting until I assure him I'm okay before he releases me and takes a step back.

He eyes the pile of stuff on the bed before looking back at me. I don't give him an explanation. The kiss I was obsessing over a couple of hours ago seems like a distant memory. How easy it is for one's perspective to change in the blink of an eye, or in this case, the firing of a gun. Deep down I know that first bang I heard was the dead man getting shot.

"Where's your luggage, love?"

I swallow, unsure if I can speak without stuttering.

"I don't have any. Just the bags all the stuff came in."

"Are they in the closet?"

I nod, knowing he's trying to distract me, and I'm grateful for that, but I can't keep my eyes from darting to the closed bedroom door. I move my body to the chair Deacon slept in my first night here. From this vantage point, I won't be able to see out into the hallway if someone opens the door.

Flynn doesn't blush or miss a beat when he begins folding my clothes and placing them with care into the bags. He doesn't bat an eye as he matches each thong with the coordinating bra either. He's clearly a professional, but it's still embarrassing to see a man who will never put his hands on my body in a sexual way touch my undergarments.

I take deep breaths, closing my eyes all the while willing my heart rate to slow down. Just as I'm relaxing, the bedroom door swings open and the trembling doubles again.

Deacon walks in first, and it takes more energy than I can spare not to jump up and rush to him. I want to thank him for saving me. I want to make sure he's okay since I selfishly internalized what happened tonight rather than immediately concerning myself with him being forced to kill someone to keep me safe.

Behind him is a stern-looking man in a white button-down shirt and khaki slacks. The gun and badge clipped to his belt leads me to believe he's a detective, but until I know for sure, I watch Deacon in order to know what to do next.

"Coleman," the newcomer says with a nod in Flynn's direction.

Deacon watches Flynn folding my things for a long while, his jaw clenching and unclenching before he looks away.

"This is Detective Mendoza," Deacon says as he hitches his thumb over his shoulder. "He's got a few questions for you."

Detective Mendoza takes a few steps toward me but stops when it's clear that Deacon isn't going to allow him to get between us. Deacon does turn to face the bed, giving me his back, and I'd pay good money to see the look on his face as he watches his friend and employee folding my belongings before placing them in the retail bags.

"Ms. Grimaldi, I work for the St. Louis Police Department. I'd like you to tell me what happened here tonight."

I glance toward Deacon, and Detective Mendoza tracks the move.

"The truth," he says with a hint of annoyance in his voice.

Deacon's back stiffens, but he doesn't turn back around.

I don't know if it's because it's the middle of the night and they both wish they were still sleeping or if there's bad blood between these two, but neither one is happy right now. Just that thought is ridiculous. There's a dead man in the hall. Of course they're not happy.

"I don't know."

"You don't know?"

"I was sleeping," I begin, somehow feeling like I'm already under interrogation even though I'm sitting on a French silk-covered chair in a posh hotel room. "I heard a bang."

"There's a man lying dead in the hall."

I nod, swallowing again. "I know."

"You know?" Mendoza looks over at Deacon, but Deacon doesn't even turn his head to acknowledge the guy. "Mr. Black assures me you haven't left the room."

"I haven't. He came in here and I saw the guy before he could close the door."

"Do you know the man in the hallway?"

"Don't fucking be ridiculous, Mendoza," Deacon snaps.

"I didn't really look at him. The blood," tears begin to stream down my face, "all I saw was the blood."

"So you've never heard of," he looks down at the small tablet in his hands, "Sebastian Wilks?"

I shake my head.

"Ever heard of the Crips?"

"Everyone has heard of—"

"How much time do you spend in Benton Park West?"

Confusion draws my brows in, but it's Deacon that emits a wild growl. "Wrap it up, Mendoza."

The detective scowls, but he flips his notebook closed without another word. When he pulls a business card from his pocket, Deacon takes it rather than letting him get close enough to hand it to me.

"Call me if you think of anything else," Mendoza mutters before walking back out of the room.

"Fifteen minutes," Deacon tells Flynn before leaving as well. Once again, he doesn't even look back at me before he leaves.

Chapter 21

Deacon

"I can't." She shakes her head to emphasize her refusal.

"We can't stay here," I argue.

"I can't go out there. Is it—is he still out there?"

"Mendoza is waiting for the coroner. He can't move the body."

She begins to tremble all over again. "You had to kill a man because of me."

"He was a bad guy, Anna."

"He's still dead."

I hate that she won't look up. I miss her honey-colored eyes on me. Fuck, this night went to shit incredibly fast. I'll never tell her that the douchebag dead in the hall had to go through me to get to her. Quite literally in fact, because I was standing at the fucking bedroom door contemplating coming back inside to pick up where we left off when the hotel room door fucking opened.

"Dead bad guys don't matter."

"He's dead," she says again. Those two words have been on repeat like even though she knows it's true it still doesn't seem real. "You killed him."

She's a civilian, and people who don't do the work I do are affected differently by seeing shit like dead people with a bullet hole in their heads. Just another fucking piece of scum off the street as far as I'm concerned.

"Wasn't the first, won't be the last," I assure her, but my words aren't calming. If she shakes much more, she's going to wiggle herself right out of the chair onto the damn floor. "Let's get out of here."

"If you weren't here..." her voice trails off, and I know she isn't meaning for there to be accusation in her tone, but I feel the disappointment in myself to the bone. I should've left one of my damn guys here every night last week. I didn't for selfish reasons. She's fucking charmed Flynn and Wren. I know neither guy would lay a hand on her, but when she showed up at the BBS offices two weeks ago, I told myself that very same thing. Yet, I was the one pinning her to the wall just a couple of hours before that dickhead tried to come in here and hurt her.

I couldn't leave my guys alone with her overnight because I'd have to kill one of them if they laid a hand on her. Seeing Flynn with his arms around her crying form earlier nearly upped the body count in this fucking suite.

"I was here," I soothe from two feet away. Touching her would be a mistake. Things could've ended differently tonight had I not been torn between going back to her and getting the fuck out of there. I can't even think what would've happened if I didn't first walk away from her. If I'd taken things as far as my body was begging me to, I would've been several feet from my gun rather than standing in the hallway with it strapped to my hip. I would've been lost in her, lost in her smell, her taste, the sweet slick heat of her—

"I won't leave you alone again."

With that promise, she lifts her head, her eyes searching mine to determine if I'm just placating her or telling her the truth.

"I won't leave you unprotected again," I amend.

"I'm scared."

"I know you are, bab—" I pull my hand back before it reaches her cheek and snap my mouth closed.

Jesus, does tonight have me completely fucked up.

"We need to get out of here."

"I can't walk out there." She inches back in the chair, all the coaxing I've managed the last twenty minutes ruined with my insistence.

It won't look well if I have to sling her over my shoulder and haul her ass out of here. Mendoza is still pissed at me for some shit that went down a couple years ago, but hey, if he didn't believe me when I told him I didn't know that chick was his sister, that's on him. The world's too fucking small if you ask me.

"I'll carry you, love."

My spine stiffens to the point I feel more made of steel and concrete than flesh and bones at Flynn's offer. If I thought I could touch her and not be affected, I would've suggested that from the jump, but contact with her skin makes my body go haywire.

My friend isn't offering to help her to rile me up. I mean he's not above it, but he knows how important it is to get her out of here. The dead guy in the hall isn't connected to the Russians other than being hired for the hit on Anna. The idiot had Petrovich's name and number in his fucking pocket, and Wren was on top of gathering intel long before the cops managed to show up, but pissed gangbangers aren't as willing to take their time with retaliation as other criminal organizations. They're the shoot first ask questions later kind of guys. We've already been in this suite long enough that anyone waiting for that piece of shit is already growing worried about where his guy is at. We should've been out of here half an hour ago.

"You get her bags," I snap without looking back at Flynn. "Come here."

I open my arms, clenching my hands open and closed like I would if I were urging a scared animal to trust me.

She swallows again, but only spends a minute contemplating her move before she stands. I lift her, holding her to my chest like a bride, and when she buries her nose in my neck, I realize just how fucked I really am.

***

She didn't say a word when we got in my truck.

Didn't ask a question when we ended up in a parking garage or when we climbed into a black sedan.

She didn't look confused when we pulled out with five other vehicles identical to the one we climbed in the back of.

I don't know if she's ever participated in a shell game before, but she didn't seem concerned. At least no more than she already was when we left the hotel suite.

The driver drops us off at my ranch three hours after I carried her past Mendoza without a word. I regretted having to let her go when I placed her in the pickup and every second since.

I know she's in shock, and I know how to comfort her, but it's the walking away when she's calm that I'll suffer with until the end of time.

My body is humming with the need to head over to Benton Park West and burn the entire shitty neighborhood to the fucking ground for even thinking they could walk in that room and hurt her.

The police are heading to the address that was written down along with Petrovich's number. If I had to guess, the piece of shit was ordered to get her to that location so she could be tortured until she revealed where Dani is.

I didn't tell Mendoza that my men were already en route to the location before he arrived at the Four Seasons. They found it empty which means they still had someone outside of the hotel waiting for their guy to come out with her. They were tipped off and scattered before my guys could get there. Hence the need for the shell game.

I brought this trouble to her door. They followed me there. I know Anna was worried about the nights I wasn't there with her, but those were the nights she was safest. I put her in trouble this time, and that knowledge sits in my gut like a bomb waiting to explode. The trip back from Cote d' Ivoire gave Petrovich enough time to put measures in place to track me. Wren is working on the hows, and I feel utterly safe on this land. Not only can this place not be tracked by normal means, but I have enough weapons and ammo to overthrow the government of a small country.

Finding Dani is crucial right now. The sooner I can do that, the sooner I can let this woman get back to her regular life without the worry of someone wanting to hurt her. She'll never be safe around me.

I scrub my hand over my face for even considering being around her longer than it takes to track down my ex-wife. It's impossible. My life isn't made to have someone in it. I wouldn't put a woman through that. The loneliness and isolation are what killed my marriage. Anna deserves better than anything I could ever offer her.

I'm wondering when the shift occurred, when I went from hating her to wanting to be around her as I unlock the front door. Anna looks around, taking in the huge wraparound porch and the acres of land surrounding the home before stepping inside.

"Let's get you settled." I head to the stairs, knowing which room I'm going to put her in.

Early morning sun streams into the house as we climb the stairs.

"This room gets the least light in the morning." It's the one that's also the furthest away from my room, not that I anticipate sleeping much while we're here. "I know you're going to want to nap."

"Thank you," she whispers when I drop her bags near the dresser. These are the first words she's spoken since I picked her up and held her to my chest in the suite.

She must know she won't be here long because she doesn't make a move to unpack.

Unsure of what to say to her, I nod and walk out, pulling the door closed behind me. I wait just outside of the door, ready to go back in if I so much as hear a whimper from her perfect lips, but the only sound that makes it to my ears is the creak of the antique metal bedframe.

I feel the burden weighing me down the farther I walk away instead of the relief I expect. I haven't even spent that much time with her since she called me weeks ago, but the draw to her is unmistakable. Anna has always been fiercely independent, and somehow her reaching for me, the need I could see in her eyes when I crouched down in front of her while trying to coax her from the room nearly burned me. I feel the same desire deep inside. I feel the same urge to touch her, to comfort her, to make promises I'm not sure I'd ever be able to keep.

The horses snort, scraping their hooved feet over the dirt of the barn when I enter. It normally calms me, but I can't keep my eyes on the animals long before I'm outside again staring up at her window.

Yep, I'm well and truly fucked.

Chapter 22
Anna

Never in a million years would I look at Deacon and think the man owned a ranch. His tight t-shirts, cargo pants, and combat boots make me think he'd be more apt to live in a tent in the woods than a homestead on so many sprawling acres. I'm sure my guess in size wouldn't do it justice.

The bed I wake up on is old, but the sheets are fresh. The soft fabric enticed a long nap from me, but they didn't keep me from waking with a start with my head tilted to listen for possible threats.

I hate the woman I've become. I've never lived in fear. I've never woken up with a jolt wondering if someone was mere feet away ready to hurt me.

The house is silent except for the wind whistling through the trees outside, but it brings no real comfort. I feel dirty and abused even though I haven't met any real physical harm. My skin crawls from knowing how close that man got to the bedroom back at the hotel.

I dig through the bags in front of the dresser, grateful that Flynn had the peace of mind enough to separate them into categories. Before long, I find my lounge pants and a long-sleeved shirt. A tank would be best due to the heat, but I feel the need for an extra layer of comfort right now.

I don't bother digging through the bag with all of my bathroom essentials, I just slip my hand under the handles and carry it with me into the hall. There's no bathroom in my room, but I noticed one on the way to the room earlier.

Once inside, I lock the door behind me, shaking the entire time at my vulnerability as I strip down and climb in the shower. I tremble the entire time I wash, not willing to take the time to shampoo and condition my hair. I don't want to be trapped naked in the bathroom if something terrible happens. I'm quick and efficient, and I don't think I've taken a shower as quickly since I was in high school and embarrassed that I hadn't filled out yet.

I dress just as fast, uncaring that the fabric of my shirt sticks to my still damp back. After carrying my dirty clothes and bathroom items back to the room Deacon designated as mine, I head downstairs.

Smells strong enough to make my stomach growl hit me before I clear the bottom of the staircase, and I follow the scent to the kitchen. Finding Deacon standing at the stove, stirring something in a large pot, leaves me breathless, and now I understand why Mom was so pleased when Dad was caught in the kitchen cooking on Sunday mornings. We've always had house staff, and they prepared all meals except for Sunday brunch. Dad always cooked for us, and he did so with a huge smile on his face like it was a privilege to prepare a meal for his family.

Deacon isn't smiling when he turns around and notices me hovering in the doorway. He isn't exactly frowning either, but that serious face, the one that tells me he's not in the mood for any bullshit, is chiseled into his features. His gaze tracks all the way down my body, and I cross my arms over my chest in an attempt to stop the shiver caused by his perusal.

"I made chicken and dumplings. That and chili are about the only things I know how to cook, and I didn't figure your stomach could handle my chili right now."

I want to argue that I'm full-blooded damn Italian and no stranger to spicy foods. Hell, I'm first generation American, and my parents brought over their love of food from Pesaro when they immigrated. Hell, there's a good chance if I'm cut, I'd bleed pasta sauce.

But I don't argue.

"I've never had chicken and dumplings," I tell him instead. "Where are we?"

"South east of the city," he answers, but he turns his back to me once again.

"Illinois?"

He grunts, the mmm hmm response enough to make me want to sweep his legs out from under him. Why does he always have to be so damn annoying? A little common courtesy goes a long way.

"Bowls are in that cabinet over there. You do know how to set a table, right?" I know it's another jab at my upbringing, but somehow I manage to keep my mouth clamped closed.

As my frustration grows with him, I realize it helps to alleviate the fear I thought I'd always suffer from, especially with what's happened recently.

Without a word, I reach for the cabinet he indicated, but the bowls are on the top shelf. I can feel his eyes burning into my back as I open the bottom cabinet and use the shelf there to hoist myself onto the counter so I can reach them. He doesn't offer his help, probably knowing I'd hit him in the head with one of the old crystal glasses on the lower shelf if he even tried.

I try to keep my eyes trained on the floor as I climb down, but his imposing body on the other side of the room proves to be too much to resist. His mouth tugs up in a grin when I jump off the counter with a grunt. The cross tattoos on his neck ripple when he turns his attention back to the pot on the stove.

After placing the bowls on the opposite ends of the mid-sized dining room table, I go in search of silverware. He doesn't offer any guidance, and I'd bet money that the man is getting some form of pleasure from watching me open each and every drawer until I locate the eating utensils. I should give his ass a fork just out of spite. It's only because he's been hospitable enough to bring me here to relative safety that I grab us both spoons.

I don't say a word as he carries the pot to the table, filling my bowl with more food than I'll ever be able to eat. In turn, he doesn't speak either. I don't pick up my spoon and dip it into the heavenly smelling food until he sits and lifts his own. He eats with purpose, almost as if he's only eating to survive and not enjoying the food he's prepared.

In my household growing up, food was our love language. It was a time to talk about our day and share all aspects of our lives with our family. Deacon doesn't seem interested in opening his mouth for any other reason than to shovel the food inside.

The quiet is killing me, pushing me close to the edge of insanity.

"Who was that guy?"

Deacon lifts his head but doesn't answer.

"He was there to hurt me?"

He swallows his mouthful of food but doesn't answer.

"I don't associate with dangerous people." I feel the need to tell him this because Detective Mendoza all but accused me of being involved with gangbangers.

He won't answer my questions. He won't respond in any form, and the longer the time ticks by, the more alone I feel. I don't know what to do with these emotions. Hell, I don't even know how to feel right now.

I don't think Deacon would let anyone hurt me. He killed a man tonight before he could breach the bedroom, but it's very apparent he doesn't want to be around me. He doesn't want to be in the position I forced him into. I'm sitting in front of this man unwanted, and that kills something inside of me.

Giving up on trying to get him to engage with me, I lower my eyes to my own bowl and struggle to eat past the lump of sorrow growing in my throat.

I didn't ask for any of this. My life was lonely before Dani disappeared, but I was content. At least I thought I was. My world was normal until Deacon pushed me against the damn wall hours ago and pressed his lips to mine. That one act, that single kiss changed everything. He doesn't feel the same. Irritation is rolling off of him in waves so thick, I feel smothered by them even at the other end of the table.

He instigated that kiss, and yet I'm the one getting glared at and blamed. Tears burn the backs of my eyes, but I fight them off. Not only is he not worth my pain, I refuse to show him that I'm affected by him at all.

I don't lift my head when his chair scrapes back. I sense him moving across the room with his empty dish, but I keep my head down. When he disappears from the room, I wait until I hear the front door open and close before I release the breath I was holding.

I struggle through a few more bites, but when my stomach turns, threatening to expel what I've eaten, I give up and head to the trash. After scraping the rest of my meal into the garbage, I busy myself with cleaning the kitchen. The remaining food goes into a large Tupperware container and into the fridge, and I handwash the dishes since there isn't a dishwasher here.

When I'm done, there's still no sign of Deacon, so I do the only thing I can. I grab a bottle of water from the fridge and head back upstairs. Sleep doesn't come as easy this time around, in part to my nap earlier, but mostly because I can't stop the emotions threatening to take over my body.

No matter how deep I snuggle into the blankets, the shivering doesn't show any sign of vanishing.

Chapter 23

Deacon

"Fucking ridiculous," I grunt as I turn over for the hundredth time since I climbed the stairs and threw myself on the bed.

Sleeping has never been an issue for me. Normally, it takes a few minutes of calm, relaxed breathing and I drift away.

Tonight, a million thoughts and questions infiltrate my head, making it impossible to settle enough to sleep.

I put Anna in the room furthest from mine for a purpose, and even though she's a mere thirty feet from where I lie, it feels like a million miles. Will I be able to get to her in time if the Russians are craftier than I anticipate? Is she struggling to sleep like I am? I haven't heard a peep from her since I climbed the stairs two hours ago, but that doesn't mean that she's sleeping.

I'm such an asshole. She had questions, and I refused to give her the answers she needed.

But what good would it do?

I could explain in detail how her friendship with Dani is what could've gotten her killed tonight. I also know that would make me look like a bitter ex, pointing fingers and assessing blame even though it's the cold, hard truth. Dani is toxic, but there's no way to make her best friend see it. Anna would just wave her hand, like the action relieves Dani from any responsibility, much the same way she did when Dani would stir shit up in high school.

Another long sigh of frustration escapes my lips as I turn over and punch the pillow under my head. I'm fucking exhausted, still having not slept much since I left over a week ago to head to New Mexico to meet up with Cerberus. My muscles literally ache from so much action without the proper recovery time, yet, my eyes just won't close.

I refuse to think about Anna and the kiss we shared, but actively trying to ignore an issue only seems to make things worse. So instead of ignoring the fact that I pressed my mouth to the lips of my ex-wife's best friend, I studiously try to ignore my hard dick when the memory floods my head.

What a damn mistake that was.

I don't really regret the kiss, but I hate Anna a little more than I did because why would someone I hate, someone who has caused me nothing but grief have the softest lips I've ever touched?

Why did the little sigh that escaped her perfect mouth sound like the chiming bells at the gates of Heaven, like it was welcoming me home?

How is it even possible with our size differences that she fit against me like we were made to press into one another, her softness aligning perfectly to the rough planes of my own body?

What did I do in a past life to deserve such torture?

I grind my teeth, the frustration growing to the point that I'm seconds away from climbing out of the bed, redressing and heading to the barn. There's always something that can be done on a ranch. The work is never done even though I have a pretty awesome crew that keeps things in tip-top shape around here.

Then the door to Anna's room opens, the old hinges groaning their disapproval. I train my ears, focusing solely on the soft footsteps she's taking down the hall, but instead of heading to the stairs like I expect, her footfalls cease right outside my bedroom door.

I ignore the soft rasp of her knuckles on the door. I can't deal with more questions right now. It won't take much more pressing from her for me to lay everything right at her feet, and I don't imagine Anna would take that well. It's after midnight, and I just don't have the energy to argue with her when she tries to defend her friend's actions.

Instead of walking away, going back to her own damn room or heading downstairs, Anna twists the doorknob to my room. The ranch house is old, built by my grandfather who passed it down to me in his will several years ago, and that means there are no locks on the inner doors. To my grandfather, a closed door yielded the people inside privacy, and he felt no need to enforce that privacy with a lock. When the door slowly creaks open, I'm regretting not having added deadbolts to my list when I was working through the renovations.

"Deacon," Anna whispers, and I can tell by the tone in her voice that she really doesn't want to wake me.

My back is to the door, but I close my eyes even though she can't see my face. If something was truly wrong, she wouldn't have bothered to knock. She would have shoved the door open or screamed for help from her room.

I continue to pretend to be asleep, praying that she backs out playing on a loop in my head. A ragged, shuddering breath nearly makes me turn over, but I resist. Comforting her right now would be too much for me. It's the last thing I need. We'll find Dani and then we'll be right back out of each other's lives, probably for good this time.

The stupid yearning I've felt for her recently is something I'll have to deal with later, but the longer she stands across the room, the longer I hear her shallow breathing, and the harder it is to keep from adding to my burden. The things I'm going to have to deal with later are growing exponentially, and I know it won't take much before things become impossible.

Anna doesn't back out when I fail to respond. She doesn't head back to her room, putting the distance that I need between us.

She crosses the room, standing at the side of the bed for so long, I nearly gasp because I'm holding my breath. Then she tugs back the covers at my back and climbs in the fucking bed with me.

My chest hurts from the strength in which my heart is pounding. My cock... let's just say he's not upset one bit that the fiery girl with honey-colored eyes is mere inches away.

My eyes snap open, staring into the darkness as she settles, and when she sighs, I can tell she's facing away from me. I hate her in this moment. Hate that her breath isn't warming my neck. Hate that she's maintained some distance and not a single inch of her soft skin is touching me. Hate that my hands aren't roaming up her thigh. Hate that my fingers aren't splayed across the flat expanse of her lower belly.

Fuck, I just hate everything right now.

Then a sob escapes her mouth, and I freeze, her crying and trembling shake the bed, and I can tell she's trying to be quiet. She didn't crawl into this bed as a trick, a way to entice me. She's terrified, or upset, or a little of both.

How could anyone resist that?

I need to ignore the fact that I want to sink inside of her, that I want to watch her lips part on a moan when I shove myself all the way into her. Ignore that my fingers itch to twist her nipples and test her limits. Ignore my body's primal need to make her come.

She's hurting, scared, and unsure of what the hell is going on, and I'm the only man who knows the details, the one close enough to the situation to ease those fears, and I've done nothing but treat her like a hardship. If she were an actual client, I wouldn't be this close to the situation, but I would answer questions. I would explain what's going on.

I've made this situation different, not her.

When she buries her face in the pillow in an attempt to be quiet, I can't take it anymore. I turn on the mattress, immediately wrapping my arms around her and pulling her against my body as much as I can without making it painfully obvious what her being in my bed does to me.

Not a single word is spoken as I lace my arm around her midsection and bury my hand under her side. I press my lips to the back of her head, breathing in the flowery scent of her hair. Thankfully she's still in long sleeves and lounge pants. If she came in here with as little clothes as I saw her wear in the hotel suite while she slept, this night would turn out differently. There are a million things we could do to take her mind off the situation, but I'm trained to avoid unnecessary complications.

And Annalise Grimaldi is easily becoming the biggest complication I've ever faced.

Chapter 24
Anna

I know he's gone before I even open my eyes to the light filtering in from the curtains. I didn't wake when he crawled out of bed, but my body somehow knew. My dreamless sleep turned to images of me running for my life, always looking over my shoulder, watching as the masked men chasing me drew closer.

I could regret coming in here last night. Scratch that. I should regret coming in here last night, but I just can't conjure an ounce of contrition. I slept like the dead in his arms, even though his touching me wasn't what I expected to happen. I wanted to be near someone, even if he was sleeping.

Of course he wasn't sleeping. He's a damn commando. I wouldn't be surprised if he heard me climb out of the bed in the other room.

His arms around me, the heat of his skin, the soft brush of his breath on my neck—

"Nope." I sit upright in bed and stare at the bedroom door.

He didn't close it all the way, but there are no sounds from downstairs filtering into the room.

Leaving his bed in a tangle of sheets is intentional. I don't want him to forget that I was there. No matter how much he tried to keep me from knowing what holding me did to him, the truth was below the belt, his hardness impossible to escape.

As I cross the hall to the bathroom, I run fingers through my tangled hair. I avoid the mirror for as long as I can, but when I face it fully for the first time, I realize that even a good night's sleep isn't enough to keep the purple bruising from under my eyes. My stress levels are through the roof, and the evidence shows. My skin no longer has the same glow, my hair is in desperate need of a blowout, and the paint on my nails is dull. I've never felt so frumpy in my life.

I grab a change of clothes from my room and head back into the bathroom for a shower. This time, in the light of day, I feel safer and manage to wash and condition my hair. A quick search of the cabinets doesn't turn up a blow dryer, so my damp locks just end up in a tangle on the top of my head. I don't bother with makeup, and I frown at imagining what Dani would say if she saw me walking down the stairs in jeans, a loose shirt meant for lounging, makeup-less with my hair a mess.

"She'd probably be more worried about where you slept last night than your appearance," I mumble as I cross the room, heading to the kitchen.

I huff a laugh because I know that's not true. She would cup her hand over her mouth as her eyes skated over my body. She'd expertly somehow insult my appearance while giving me shit about sleeping in the same bed as her ex. She's a pro at encompassing all faults into a single conversation. It's a skill she perfected many years ago.

Deacon isn't in the kitchen, but the note on the counter directing me to the oven for breakfast brings a smile to my face. Having not eaten much last night, my stomach growls when I pull the oven door open and grab the plate of food. I'm not big on eating first thing in the morning, but I scarf down the eggs, sausage links, and toast while standing at the counter.

I wash the dishes and don't waste another second in the house. I refuse to let things get any weirder between Deacon and me and avoiding him all day will only do just that.

For some reason, I expect to find him sipping coffee on the front porch like I've seen men do in western movies, but the chairs are vacant. Lifting my arm to ward off the bright sunlight, I cross the yard and head to the huge barn across the field on the off chance that is where Deacon is. The old truck that was in the driveway when we arrived yesterday is still parked, so that gives me hope that he hasn't left me stranded on the property.

Not only do I find Deacon in the barn, he's somehow poured his thick thighs and perfect ass into a pair of jeans that look like a second skin. I'm struck stupid watching him move, his back muscles rippling under his thin t-shirt, that it takes several long moments before I realize he isn't alone. Only it isn't a person he's mumbling to in a low tone. Gloved hands scratch down the white face of a gorgeous horse. The sight of the huge animal stops me in my tracks.

"Don't tell me you're afraid of horses," Deacon says over his shoulder with a bright smile.

Has he ever looked at me that way before? Has he ever seen me and not felt like running in the other direction?

"She won't bite," Deacon assures me when all I can do is stand and stare.

The horse snorts, lowering its head and nudging Deacon's hand when it stills on her face.

"I grew up in the city," I remind him. "I've never been around big animals."

Or any animals for that matter. My parents love supporting all forms of nature and animals through charity events, but the closest I got to having a pet growing up was a squirrel that would come into the backyard every once in a while.

"No riding lessons for you?"

"No," I answer with a roughness to my voice I don't recognize, my attention torn between the expanse of his back and the beautiful creature he's reverently running his hands over.

I run my teeth over my bottom lip as I inch closer, and Deacon steps to the side, his hand still on the horse's face.

"There you go," he praises when my fingers brush down her jaw. "This is Sweet Pea."

I coo at the animal like she's a baby, and he chuckles.

"Wanna take her for a ride?"

I step away immediately. "That's not—"

"You can ride with me," he offers, and I step back as he opens the fence and begins to put the saddle on her.

My heart is pounding in my chest as I watch him hoist himself on the creature's back. My mouth runs dry when he reaches a hand out for me. I never pictured myself climbing on a horse, but with Deacon's help it doesn't end up as awkward as I thought it would be.

"Hold on to the saddle horn," he instructs, and my hands clasp it without thinking because all I can feel is the heat of his body against my back. "We'll go slow."

Instead of holding only to the reins with both hands like I've seen in movies, he positions the leather in one hand and uses his other arm to wrap around my waist. I'm grateful for the extra safety, but then the manly scent of his skin infiltrates my nose and I'm lost. My body barely registers the jostling as he directs Sweet Pea out of the barn and toward an open field.

"It's a beautiful day to ride."

His words are a whisper in my ear, his chin nearly resting on my shoulder, and I almost let myself take in the green grass and rolling hills, but then his fingers flex on my waist making it impossible to see or feel anything other than where he's touching me.

I don't know how long we ride or the distance we travel because my eyes flutter closed. Wind whips my hair and birds chirp in the distance; the serenity of the moment only interrupted by the occasional snort from Sweet Pea.

"Gorgeous, isn't it?"

"Mmm hmm," I answer without bothering to open my eyes.

"Let's take a break."

I open my mouth to tell him I don't want a break, that I want to be lost in this moment forever, but I understand *he* needs to take a break when he shifts me to help lower me from the saddle. He doesn't mention the erection I felt against me right before I climb off. He doesn't make some crude comment about him getting hard, and it's in that moment that I realize Deacon Black isn't the boy I knew years and years ago. He's a man, one not controlled by his body's reaction to minor friction.

He does keep his back to me when he jumps off, and I turn to face the trickling stream we've stopped at to give him the privacy he needs to get himself back under control.

If things were different, if my best friend wasn't missing and we didn't have such animosity from our past, I would have reached for him. I would've reminded him with my mouth pressed to him just how good our last kiss was. But we are tangled together with a history filled with so many knots, the possibility of having something with each other, the ability to *give* ourselves to each other is an impossibility.

"All of this is your land?" I ask, tossing small stones from the bank into the water.

He coughs behind me, but I still keep my back turned. "Yeah. I inherited it when Gramps died four years ago."

"I'm sorry for your loss," I say instinctively. "Were you close?"

I feel his presence beside me, but the heat in my cheeks from picturing how different this day could be keeps me from looking over at him.

"We weren't when I was younger, but he sort of became my best friend after I got out of the Army." He tosses a larger stone into the water, creating a rippling effect that gives me something to concentrate on until the movement of the stream evens it back out again. "I wasted a lot of time being a hard ass. Had I known he wasn't going to be around longer, I would've done things differently."

Another stone in the water, another reason not to look at him.

"Yeah." I toss my handful of pebbles and rub my hands together to wipe away the fine dirt left behind. "Regret sucks."

I'm no stranger to the emotion. I lived mostly for myself as a kid, but Zeni's death in high school opened my eyes in a way nothing short of losing someone you love could. She was two years younger than me, but that shouldn't have made a difference. Had I not been so selfish, maybe I would've seen the signs, maybe I would've been able to help. I didn't because I was too busy worrying about boys and dances and whether I was going to get to go shopping every weekend.

"You okay?"

I jerk when Deacon touches my shoulder, and he pulls his hand back immediately when all I want to do is wrap my arms around his waist, bury my nose in his shirt, and tell him that I don't care about our past. I want to explain that I don't understand exactly why I feel this pull to him when I spent years actively hating him. I want to beg him, ask him if he feels it too, or to at least tell me I'm crazy and we aren't like two magnets being drawn to each other.

But I don't. I nod and step away.

"I'm fine."

I'm not.

Of course, I'm not.

I'm lusting after Dani's ex. I'm as desperate to get away from him as I am to feel his arms around me like they were last night. I want to feel the stubble on his face rough against my sensitive skin. I want his fingers brushing hair away from my face just moments before he lowers his mouth to mine. I want to curl up in his lap while he tells me that what I'm feeling is okay, that it's unavoidable and worth all the fallout that's sure to come if we don't keep our distance.

He clears his throat again, the awkward silence filling the space between us like a canyon rather than the mere two feet separating us.

"We should head back."

I don't walk toward the horse with the same brand of hesitation that I did earlier. I'm no longer afraid of the animal but afraid of the way I know I'm going to miss him once we arrive back at the barn.

I'm losing my mind, but I don't think walking back is an option. Even suggesting that I do would wave a bright red flag in front of Deacon. I come to the conclusion on the ride back as I try to keep as much distance between our bodies as possible on the small saddle, that it's all in my head.

I don't want Deacon, I want comfort. It's not this man in particular that I crave, but the attention and assurances during the upheaval of my life. It's proximity, not him that has my cravings all out of whack.

When he lowers me from the horse, I arrow toward the house without even looking back at him.

Chapter 25
Deacon

After checking on Anna an hour after she ran out of the barn like her ass was on fire, I discovered her resting in her room. I shoved down the irritation that she was asleep in the spare bedroom rather than in my own bed because the frustration was irrational.

She's keeping her distance like I should be. I never should've offered the horseback ride. Or at minimum, I should've saddled up her own damn horse, but I'm a selfish bastard, and the time she spent in my arms last night wasn't enough. It was better than I imagined when I pictured curling around her in the hotel suite. The images in my head didn't give justice to the warmth of her body or her soft curves.

I escaped to my bedroom much the same way she did after jumping down from Sweet Pea, but something upset her at the stream, and that's on me. I could've asked what was wrong, but I'm an idiot, one that likes to solve my own damn problems and assumed she's the same. Clearly it was a mistake because I fucked up, and I don't have a clue how.

I spent the entire day in the barn, skipping lunch because I'm a coward who knows how hard it would be to keep my damn hands to myself if I went inside.

The rumble of my stomach and the prospect of eating more chicken and dumplings eventually win out over staying out of the house until I get more information from Wren. A couple of days between waves of intel isn't a new thing. Sometimes it takes weeks to build a case before we're able to make a move with certainty, but the minutes just seem to be crawling by.

It's a special kind of torture finding a gorgeous, albeit untouchable woman, standing barefoot in my kitchen. Anna doesn't look over her shoulder when I pause in the doorway and take her in. Tendrils of hair have escaped the pile on top of her head which is all kinds of sexy to me. After Dani, I realized that well-put-together women are nothing but trouble. I don't want a perfect woman. Their focus is never where it should be.

But it isn't just the sight of Anna standing at the stove like she belongs in my space that has me entranced. As if that cruelty isn't enough, she's swaying her hips to music playing low from her phone on the counter. I know exactly how good that thick ass feels. Our sleeping positions somehow changed last night going from me curled around her back to her being sprawled on my chest, leg hitched up. I woke with one hand holding her against me at the knee and the other wrapped around her back and gripping her ass.

I swallow thickly with the memory, and Anna turns around, noticing me with a hitch in her breath before I can run upstairs and take care of the problem arising the same way I did when I left her in bed alone this morning.

"You scared me." Her hand goes to her throat like she's been scandalized, but I can't say a word.

I'm too distracted by the heaving of her chest and the little smile toying at the corners of her mouth. She doesn't seem upset like she was when we finished riding earlier, but I still plan to tread lightly.

"You cooked?"

"Spaghetti carbonara," she whispers as if she thinks I'm going to be upset with her taking over my kitchen.

Maybe I have been too much of an asshole to her, letting our past bleed into the present when I discovered long ago that she isn't the same girl she was back then.

"Smells delicious."

Her grin is electric. "Get cleaned up."

She turns back to the stove, and I only spend maybe another minute looking at her curves and the way the ceiling fan blows the loose strands of her hair against her neck before I haul ass up the stairs for a quick shower.

***

"None?" she asks as she brings the glass of whiskey to her lips.

God, she's fucking distracting. Dinner was amazing, tasting even better than it smelled if that's possible. We ate at the table, chatting like old friends before I insisted on cleaning.

We're sitting on the front porch, where I found her after the kitchen was put back together, as the sun fades over the horizon.

"Deacon?" She uses the tip of her bare foot to nudge my leg from her rocking chair.

"Huh?" I look away, realizing that I just got caught staring at her.

"No college?"

I scrape my hand down my face before looking into my nearly empty whiskey glass. When did I drink most of it? How long have we been drinking? There's a buzz in my head, a flitter of what feels like wings against my skin, but I'm certain it has more to do with her than the amount of alcohol I've consumed this evening.

"No," I manage to finally answer with a shrug. "I mean, I've taken a couple online classes, but formal education was never my thing."

"You made good grades in high school."

I frown, rolling my head on the back of my rocking chair and looking in her direction. "I said it wasn't my thing. I never said I was stupid."

"I didn't say you were." Her frown matches mine, but then her lips turn up into a grin.

"What?"

"So, commando school is more your style?"

"Commando school?" I laugh.

"Yeah." She waves her hand in a sweeping motion to indicate my body.

I want to bite my lip and flirt with her, but I vowed during my second shower of the day, which sadly ended much like the first with me grunting her name and coming into the drain, that I'd be an idiot to pursue anything with her. There are too many women in the world that wouldn't bring the trouble and baggage that Anna would. I wish my body would listen and take heed of that information.

"You're all buff and badass."

It's even harder when she says shit like that.

"I imagine you and your guys whacking each other in the stomach with sticks to see who loses by grunting in pain first."

"Fists," I tell her with a lazy smile. "We used fists in basic training not sticks. God, we were idiots."

Her laugh fills the country air around us. "So, you like pain?"

"Naw. It just felt necessary at the time."

"I understand necessary pain. Even though it hurts, I still show up for my waxing appointments like clockwork."

I cough on my sip of whiskey, but when I look over at her, she's focused on the hills across the pasture. She didn't just lay that information down at my feet in an attempt to entice me. She was just stating a fact, but now I can't keep my eyes from roaming up her body and pausing midway up.

Waxing appointments? Jesus, is she trying to kill my restraint?

She may not be, but fuck if she isn't.

"Life is strange, isn't it?"

"How so?" I ask.

"Never in a million years did I think I'd be sitting on Deacon Black's front porch in the country drinking whiskey while rocking to the sound of crickets." I smile when she does. "I didn't even think commandos liked peace and quiet."

"We can't always be running from a hail of bullets." She chuckles. "What?"

Her eyes sparkle, the light coming from inside the house hitting them perfectly. "I don't see you *running* from bullets. You shot that guy before he could get to my room."

I was between him and the room.

We haven't mentioned Dani or what happened back at the Four Seasons. I thought we had an unspoken agreement to just leave it alone, but it seems to be fading with each sip she takes from her glass. I know she wants to know. I also know that telling her the truth will frighten her even more. I guess it's a good thing I'm here in case she needs me. I struggle for a moment, torn between telling her the full truth or only giving her enough to satisfy her curiosity. If I were in her shoes, I'd want all of it, so that's what I decide to give her. The sooner she faces it and works through it, the better.

"That thug was hired by Petrovich to abduct you." Tears pool in her eyes, and when she lifts her chin, I know she's determined to listen without getting overly emotional. "The intel Wren obtained told us that they were going to take you to a secondary location and get Dani's location from you."

She swallows several times before she speaks. "I don't know where Dani is."

"They didn't know that."

"They were going to hurt me then what? Let me go?"

I shake my head. "They weren't going to let you go. It's very rare someone survives being taken to a different location."

"You were gone for a week." I know she's not trying to accuse me of leaving her unsafe, but her tone is riddled with it.

I set my glass on the porch to the side of my rocking chair so I can give her my undivided attention.

"We raided a compound in West Africa where Petrovich spends most of his time. We didn't hurt anyone in the house, but it landed us on the Russians' radar. You weren't in any danger while I was gone. I put you in danger when I returned." My eyes search hers, and I pray she can see the anguish filling them for doing that to her. "One of Petrovich's men followed me back to the hotel that night. If I had stayed away, it never would've happened."

"Deacon, I—"

"It's dangerous around me. My life is dangerous."

She cuts her eyes away, and I have to grip the arm of the rocking chair to keep from reaching for her.

"Are we safe here?" she asks on a whisper.

"We are," I assure her. "Wren buried this property under so much paperwork, unless the Russians know the elderly lady working at the courthouse, they'll never find this place."

She nods, but I can see the distance she's putting between us. It's exactly what we both need, but it still cuts me like a knife. I've never been so damn indecisive in my entire life.

"I'm going to go to bed," Anna says as she stands, and I don't stop her.

Hopefully, the truth scared her enough that she keeps her distance, because God knows I'm running out of the will to do so myself.

I wait to leave the porch until I'm certain she's safely shut away in her room. I even somehow manage to keep my eyes on my own bedroom door by the time I make it up there. Even with those steps taken, I keep the door cracked, a fucked-up invitation for her to join me again tonight.

It makes no sense. Getting involved with Anna is literally the worst thing I could possibly do, but when that bedroom door creaks open a couple of hours later, I'm grateful. Much the same way it happened the night before, I wait until she's settled before I turn over and wrap my arms around her. This time she clings to my forearm as she cries, and the only thing whispered into the night is my assurance that she's going to be okay.

Chapter 26
Anna

I scrunch my eyes against the sunlight, wanting to yell at Deacon for not having the wherewithal to buy blackout drapes. When I try to roll over, I realize I'm still pinned to him with his arm banded around my back.

I'm no longer on my side, the little spoon in the bed, but sprawled all the way across Deacon's chest with my nose buried in his neck.

My heart begins to pound, more at the possibility of him waking and leaving the room, than the fact that I'm plastered to his side like a second skin when I didn't have any business even coming in here last night in the first place. I can't help the whimper that rumbles deep in my chest when his fingers begin to trail up and down my back, the hope that he was still sleeping flying out the damn window.

Unsure if I'm in the middle of a dream, I lift my head to find him looking down at me. He isn't smiling. There isn't a knowing glint in his eyes or a teasing lift to his lips. The serious face I saw in his office after going over eight years without seeing each other is familiar and makes me feel like a gnat he's getting ready to swat away.

I shift to rise off of him but his other hand caresses my cheek, the one around my back holding me close. My eyes flutter closed before I can stop them, then his lips are on mine, his tongue urging my mouth open.

My fingers clench against his bare chest, nails digging into his skin, and it seems to activate some primal animal in him because the next thing I know, I'm flat on my back and he's hovering above me, mouth still pressed to mine with an insistence ten times greater than what I felt when he kissed me at the hotel. My skin catches on fire, heat spreading like wildfire over every inch of my body.

He doesn't break away when his hips roll against mine, and I swallow the groan that travels up from his gut. I'm in heaven, or at least I think I am, then his hands get involved, one tangled in my hair and the other fishing for the hem of my sleep tank.

Warm rough fingers tease the side of my breast for mere seconds before he pulls his mouth away only long enough to pull the fabric over my head and toss it to the floor. His eyes never open. He never looks down at me, never searches my eyes for answers, but when he lowers his lips to the tip of my breast, I forget to wonder what that really means.

I don't have the ability to worry that we haven't talked, that we haven't discussed what trouble doing this could cause. I'm not concerned about the repercussions right now. The only thing I can focus on is his expert mouth on my breast and biting my lip so I don't hiss too loud, afraid to break the trance we both seem to have woken up in.

The time spent on my breast is limited, a tease of the most erotic kind as distraction draws him lower. The rough stubble on his face abrades the skin of my lower stomach, his tongue dipping into my belly button to tease the jewelry there, his teeth nipping at the skin on my hip.

I'm slick with arousal, ready for any suggestion the man could make, but he isn't asking, isn't giving options. We both know what's going to happen, and this isn't a multiple-choice question. I lift my hips in permission when his fingers twist in the fabric at my sides. The silk sleep shorts and lace underwear disappear with practiced ease. Wide shoulders spread my legs, and only then do his eyes flutter open for the briefest of seconds before he lowers his mouth, sweeping his scorching hot tongue up the length of me.

I bite my fist to keep from screaming, my head angled down so I can watch in awe as he brings me to the brink of release in mere seconds. A commando, covered head to toe in muscles and perfectly tanned skinned with an Olympic Gold talented tongue? Deacon Black is every woman's perfect package rolled up in one man.

He groans, diving in and using most of his lower face to bring me pleasure. The tip of his nose brushes my clit while his tongue works magic on my slit, the scruff on his chin teasing even lower. I want to warn him, let him know I'm only a few short strokes from falling over the edge, but he pulls away, nipping at my inner thigh before tracing the line at my hip with his tongue.

I want to grip the sides of his face or grip his hair with my fingers and insist he continue, but my mouth is dry, words on the tip of my tongue but refusing to form as he works his way back up my body.

His lips brush mine, the taste of my own arousal clinging to his lips as he rolls his hips. I don't know when he shoved his boxer briefs down, but the heat of his erection is right where it's meant to be, and a groan of pleasure rumbles in my ear as he pushes forward. My head snaps back, throat and back arching as he enters me.

I'm lost, unsure of what to do other than take exactly what he's giving, but my fingernails dig into the skin of his taut muscled back, a warning to take things slow because he's on the brink of being too much.

He must understand my warning because he ceases all motion except for biting the skin on my exposed neck. One hand is on my throat, his thumb applying pressure under my chin as he nips at the delicate skin there. The other is tangled in my hair, the bite of pain from the pull managing to increase my desire for him. My legs spread wider, hips opening up as I settle my ankles on his upper thighs, and it allows him to sink even deeper. Another whimper escapes my mouth, but he doesn't move, other than his mouth working against my neck.

When my fingers relax on his skin, he moves. First one slow stroke forward and back, and then another. The third takes my breath away, but he breathes life back into me when he presses his forehead to mine. His eyes are still closed, squeezed tight, jaw ticking as if he's in pain.

"Dea—"

Before I can even say his name, before I can beg him to open his eyes and see me, he draws back, and I'm bereft with him gone. I know what he's going to say, and deep down if I focus on something other than the pleasure he's been giving me, I know it'll be the truth. We shouldn't be doing this. Having sex, no matter how unemotional it is, shouldn't be happening. But he doesn't jump off the bed as if he just realized what he's been doing. He flips me over, lifting my ass into the air and tangling his fingers back in my hair before plowing forward again.

My back arches, and I scream, both in pleasure and from the bite of pain of how much thicker he feels from this angle. Rough fingers dig into the meat of my hip as he pulls my body back to meet his with every stroke.

It's heaven, the thick slide of his cock taking me this way.

It's hell because I know I'm ruined after this. No other man will compare, and that nearly brings tears to my eyes.

I fall forward some when his fingers leave my hair, but then I'm back up on my elbows, shifting my body back to meet his when those fingers find my clit with adept precision.

God, has sex *ever* felt this good? Not that I can recall right now.

"Yes, yes, yes," I pant as arrows of heat shoot down my spine, settling in my lower belly with the threat of an explosion that's sure to leave me unable to walk.

I press my face into the pillows, moaning as he works his fingers and his cock even harder. He must be as close as I am, waiting for me to fall over the edge before he allows his own pleasure to manifest.

I couldn't deny him if I wanted to. He growls, and the unspoken command skyrockets me toward the heavens, my body convulsing, gripping him in rhythmic praise for a job well done.

He holds me up with his hand on my hip, pinching my clit one last time that forces another quake of release from my body. When he pulls his hand back, I can't help but fall forward, but it's only my upper body he allows to move. His grip holds me in place, and I feel the brush of his knuckles on my core as he strokes his cock three times before jets of cum slash across my back, the heat a sharp contrast to the sweat dotting my back.

He doesn't roar like a caged animal when he comes, and if it weren't for the sharp breaths he's trying to take, I would think he was barely affected at all. My eyes are open, staring into the pillow shoved against my face, but I don't move immediately. I couldn't if the house were on fire, but I know I can't stay like this forever. When I finally gain both the strength and the courage to crawl out of the bed, Deacon is sitting on the edge of the mattress with his head buried in his hands.

He doesn't speak a word or look at me when I gather my clothes and leave the room. I don't know how to feel as I cross the hall to the bathroom. Yes, we just had amazing sex. That orgasm was possibly the best I've ever had. He got off, too, but I can't help but wonder as I'm washing him from my skin if I t just made the biggest mistake of my life.

Chapter 27
Deacon

If it wasn't Wren's ringtone blaring from my phone, I would pick the damn thing up and chuck it through the window, but this call could be the one that will help set my entire life back in order.

So why do I falter when I grab it from the nightstand? Why is my heart pounding from more than the amazing orgasm I just had?

"Yeah?" I snap when I answer the phone.

"Rough night?" Wren asks, but he clears his throat when I don't answer. "I've found Dani."

He yawns, and guilt fills me inside because I know I just spent the best night I can remember with a gorgeous woman wrapped around me before waking up and sliding every thick inch I have to offer inside of her, and Wren probably hasn't slept since I got back from West Africa, spending every minute working and searching for my ex.

"Do the Russians have her?"

"Naw, man. She's safe. From the looks of it, she's living her best fucking life."

"Give me an hour," I grunt into the phone before hanging up.

She's not hurt. Living her best life? Typical fucking Dani. She may not be safe after all, because it's likely I'll strangle her for upending my damn life.

I wait for the water in the other bathroom to turn off before I jump in the shower in my room. I just abused Anna's body like I had a right to do so. The least I can do is make sure she has all the hot water she wants.

My shower is quick and efficient, but I take my time drying off and getting dressed. I wanted to find my ex. It's been my primary focus for the last several weeks, but now that it's within my grasp, I'm dragging my damn feet. I'm not delaying because I don't want to face her. I know the woman across the hall has everything to do with it.

Jesus, what was I thinking this morning?

You weren't. You obsessed about her scent for an hour before you drifted off with a hard-on, and when you woke up to her on your chest again, you took the opportunity you squandered yesterday.

My conscience is a snarky motherfucker.

Anna doesn't open the door immediately when I pound on it. I'm not mad at her. I'm mad at myself, but I have no other outlet for it. "Get dressed and grab your shit. Wren found Dani."

I wait for her in the truck like a total asshole, only climbing out when I see her struggling with all of her bags on the front porch. Honestly, knowing that she won't be coming back here hits a little differently than I thought it would. Am I sad to see her go? That can't be it. I didn't even want her here in the first place. I don't bring women to the ranch. It's my sacred place, but it seems to lose a little of its shine when I load all of her things and we drive off the property.

It's fucking typical that I'll no longer have the escape from reality I seek the next time I come out here.

I'm angry, pissed at myself for letting my body win out over my mind as I drive back into the city. Anna doesn't say a word, keeping her focus out her side window for the entire drive. She doesn't bitch at me for what we did or try to fill the cab of the old pickup with mindless chatter. She doesn't sigh or reach for the radio, and with each mile, each strung-out minute, I feel more and more like an asshole.

I'm not some teenager who can't control his cock. It wouldn't have been pleasant, but I could've climbed out of that bed without pressing my mouth to hers. It doesn't matter that it has been months since I've had sex. I've gone longer than that before without any problem. I'm not controlled by my sexual urges and desires. In hindsight, I fucked up, but there's no way to take any of it back now.

She waits for me to open her door but doesn't look at me as she climbs down. Her focus is on her clasped hands during the elevator ride, but by some miracle she comes alive when she enters the breakroom and sees Flynn. Grinning and greeting him with a quick hello makes my jaw clench, and when she follows me to Wren's office, the bird pisses me off.

"Hey there, sexy," the feathered-fucker squawks.

Of all the times I've wanted to kill the damn thing, today takes the cake.

That is until Wren stands and wraps Anna in a hug that lasts a few seconds longer than I'm comfortable with. I can't say a word to either of them. Doing so would raise more questions than just standing here seething until it's over.

"I found your friend," Wren tells her when he knows he should be addressing me with this information.

"Where is she?" I snap, finally having enough of being ignored. First Anna on the drive over and now Wren? Hell, even the damn bird didn't pop off with some bullshit when I entered the room.

"After she wasn't in West Africa, I went back and tracked her travel for the last couple of years." Wren falls into his seat, turning the chair to face the computer screens.

I want him to get to the damn point, but I know this is his process, and the guilt I felt when he called rears its ugly head again. If he wants to spend half an hour walking me through his steps, I'm going to let him.

"It's a lot of damn information because the woman is all over the globe."

"She does travel a lot," Anna agrees.

"She's in the Maldives," Wren finally says after explaining in frustrating details all of the places he didn't find Dani. "She traveled under the name Irina Zappa."

"Her cousin," Anna and I say at the same time.

I can feel her eyes snap in my direction, but I keep my focus on Wren's screen. If I look her way right now, I'm going to tell her that Dani is fine, and it would be in her best interest to just come back home with me. But that's foolish, right? I can't have her in my life. The woman probably still hates me. An orgasm isn't an apology for picking on her and treating her poorly when we were younger, no matter that she gave as good as she got.

"They bear a striking resemblance, honestly." A photo of Dani and her cousin fills the largest screen, and I can see some similarities, but not enough that this shouldn't have been caught by TSA when she was traveling.

"The Maldives doesn't have extradition," I mutter.

Wren clamps a hand at the back of his neck. "Yeah, if I had started with that information and worked backward instead of working chronologically in reverse, I probably would've found her yesterday."

Anna wrings her hands in her lap, and I hate that I can't read if she's happy that he didn't find her yesterday, or if she regrets what happened this morning.

The screen flashes again to video marked from last night.

"You've got to be kidding me," Anna hisses when her friend walks into camera view with a fruity drink in her hand.

She must be on the patio of the hotel because her gauzy dress floats behind her on a breeze as a smiling man walks up to her, his arms circling her waist before he spins her around in a circle.

Anger washes over me, and when I look over and find Anna's eyes on me, I know she's reading the entire situation wrong. I'm not pissed that my ex is wrapped up with another man. That sight might have bothered me six months after our divorce when the wounds were still raw and healing, but eight years later? I couldn't give a damn what she does, other than she endangered her friend. Dani turned my own life upside down with her actions, and she doesn't seem to care.

If Wren found her and she was hiding, hunkered down and afraid she was in danger of getting hurt or killed, it would be different, but here selfish Dani is, true to form, having a grand old time while others in her life suffer with her choices.

"How many of the guys are available to travel?" I ask, sweeping my eyes from the pain I see on Anna's face.

"Other than Gaige who is out of town for the next four days, and Kit who has some kind of convention he asked off for, everyone is here."

I nod, running my hand down the stubble on my chin. I haven't bothered to shave in over a week, and it's really starting to get out of hand.

"I'm going upstairs to change. Have them pack a bag. Tell them we won't be long, so don't plan on bringing a bathing suit. I want Flynn to take Anna to—"

"I'm going with you," she interrupts.

"You're not."

"Deacon." There's a warning in her tone, and I just don't have it in me to argue.

"You don't have a passport on you," I remind her.

"I can fix that in twenty minutes," Wren says with a wicked smile.

Actually, she does have her passport, and it would take about that same amount of time to retrieve it from her apartment that has since been cleaned up and refurnished since it was trashed, but I haven't shared that bit of information with her yet.

"This isn't going to be a vacation," I tell her when she crosses her arms over her chest. It's reminiscent of the way she acted in high school, only now everything is different. I don't want her to go because she gets on my nerves. I'd rather not be enclosed on a small plane with her because there's a fucking bed on the jet. I don't think I can get within twenty feet of a bed with her near and be able to resist the urge to throw her on it and strip her naked.

"She put me in danger," Anna reminds me, and her words hit me in the chest like an anvil. "I have a million questions I need answered. I can travel with you or I can make my own arrangements."

She knows she has me. "Finding Dani hasn't solved the problem with Petrovich."

She quirks an eyebrow up, eyes searching mine.

"Motherfucker," I mutter before I turn and reach for the doorknob. "Wren, go with her and help her get her shit out of Gramp's truck in the parking garage. Pack a small bag, Anna. We'll be in the Maldives in less than twenty-four hours."

I don't have to look over my shoulder to know that she's grinning like she just won a battle as I walk away.

Chapter 28
Anna

Regret.

That's the look filling Deacon's eyes right now.

The sex was amazing, earth-shattering even, but the second it was done, I know he wished it never happened.

How am I supposed to feel about that?

My body still gets tingles when I let myself think of the groan he released when he came. God, that groan.

Tilting my head back on the headrest, I stare at the ceiling of the plane, my fingers clenching the armrests like the tension in my muscles will be relieved if I can just grip a little harder.

He won't speak to me, and believe me, I've tried more than once. I get clipped answers and looks that beg me to stop talking. I'm not a prude. I've done the one-off thing before. I'm able to have great sex and walk away. Well, I've never had sex as good as it was with Deacon, but amazing orgasms aren't the be-all and end-all. I'm thirty years old for heaven's sake. I should be better at being able to chalk it up to what it was, a great night that'll never happen again.

And if that's the case, why can't I stop looking in his direction, hoping to find him looking back at me? Why does the fact that there's a room in the back make my skin heat with anticipation? Why does the sight of his jeans stretched across muscled thighs make me want to lick my lips and suggest dirty things? When did I turn into a sex-crazed animal?

Deacon is bent over his phone less than ten feet away, but we might as well be in different universes with all the attention he's paid me since leaving the BBS office. He doesn't want me here, doesn't want me interfering in going to get Dani, and that makes me wonder what'll happen when we get there.

He's the love of my life. Dani's words echo in my ear, a warning and red flag for the mistake he clearly thinks we made the other night. Eight years is a drop in time where soulmates are concerned, and I'm a fool to think he's over her. He jumped at the opportunity to look for her. He can blame his chivalry to run to her aid all he wants, but deep down I know it's obligation to the girl that got away that had him chartering this jet to the Maldives. He's still linked to her, no matter the time and distance separating them, no matter that Dani goes through men like she's determined to taste every flavor of the rainbow before she dies.

Just that thought has me swallowing against the ball of my own regret swimming up my throat. I don't want her hurt or harmed in any way, but I saw the video Wren presented just like he did. Dani isn't living in fear, hiding from the Russians like we thought. She's drinking fruity cocktails and smiling at handsome cabana boys, charming her way through the good-looking men at her beck and call.

I didn't miss the way Deacon's jaw clenched at her on the computer screen. He's jealous, pissed that she's even entertaining the thought of other men. If we didn't sleep together prior to him seeing her on that screen, I'd say he only did it to get back at her. But we did in fact have sex before this new information came to light, which means he was only sating a need. Men are sexual creatures, right? Keeping in mind the whole *I have an erection, let's solve this problem* mentality, that means I could've been anyone and it would have made no difference.

"Fuck," I grumble, my eyes still tilted to the ceiling.

"Try to get some sleep," Flynn suggests, but that would be an impossibility.

I couldn't sleep while in close proximity to Deacon Black right now without the help of chemical intervention, and I doubt any of the guys have the prescription pills it would require to keep my thoughts from spinning a mile a minute.

As I look around the plane, I have to wonder just how safe we are. If we were only going to the Maldives to get a woman who clearly doesn't want to be found, why did Deacon insist on bringing more than half his guys? There are five other guys surrounding me, including a handsome ginger named Finnegan that has an Irish accent to die for. He winks every damn time I look over at him, but it no longer brings a smile to my face.

All of these commandos with serious attitudes should make me feel safe, but their presence makes me nervous instead. Deacon doesn't seem like the type of guy to overstaff a job, so that means they're here for a reason. It means there's still trouble brewing.

Like a psycho, it scares me and thrills me at the same time. Deacon won't leave a job incomplete, and from the way he's protected me from the second I called him weeks ago, he won't be done with me until he's sure I'm safe. Trouble means more time with him, despite how much it kills me to be ignored.

Unless he's planning to be done with me the second he meets back up with his old flame.

Damn it, why can't I get out of my own head. All these thoughts swirl and contradict each other. I'm starting to hate myself already.

"What's got you stressed, love?"

When I look over at Flynn, I take in his handsome face and the lines that speak of his own stress and battles crinkling the corners of his eyes.

"Life," I mutter.

"Well," Flynn leans in closer, elbows on his knees, head tilting a little to let me know he doesn't want others to hear our conversation.

Instinctively, I lean in closer to him too.

"You're going to be fine," he insists. "Hopefully, all of this will be over soon, and you can go back to your normal life."

His eyes dart up and away, and when I follow his line of sight, I notice Deacon looking over at me for the first time since we took off hours ago.

I ignore the jerk. If he didn't want to look in my direction until his friend started talking to me, that's on him. I'm no longer in the mood to sit silently and stew in my own issues.

"I don't even know what normal is anymore." And damn if that isn't a brutal truth I have to deal with at some point.

Everything has changed. Thinking my friend was dead, getting my apartment trashed, and coming close to being hurt or killed by a street thug has a way of putting things into perspective. Pain and suffering never touched me before. I was living in some protective bubble, never letting the outside world touch me in any way. My life was all fun and games, and I was sheltered to the point that I had no clue such bad things could happen to people. Of course there are always stories on the news, but it was always so easy to turn the station and ignore the stuff that was going on around me. I avoided bad neighborhoods without the consideration of what people were going through that couldn't escape that life. I was all about helping at fundraisers and trying to get other rich people to donate money to save wildlife and art when people practically in my own backyard were suffering.

The realization that I'm as vapid as Dani has hit me harder than I like. Deacon has every right to his opinion of me being a spoiled brat wearing rose-colored glasses. I'm part of the problem, part of the reason people in lower socioeconomic neighborhoods hate rich people so much. I don't spend my time making the world a better place. I only help to create a greater divide.

"Life has a way of throwing us curveballs," Flynn says, making me realize I'm not alone while having my current existential crisis.

"Yeah," I agree instantly.

"But the biggest test is figuring out what you're going to do about them." Flynn leans back, his eyes flicking in Deacon's direction before he clasps his hands over his chest and closes his eyes.

Is Deacon a test?

I huff a humorless laugh as I settle back into my seat. Of course he is. But what exactly is he testing? My loyalty to Dani? My loyalty to myself?

Just thinking of my best friend makes my blood boil. Not counting the fact that I'd never get involved with a dangerous man, I'd never just take off and leave without letting someone in my life know where I was going. If we found her hiding out, afraid for her life, I might feel differently. If that were the case, I could understand her not making contact with me or someone else in her family.

It's hard to feel bad about what happened between Deacon and me when she didn't respect me enough to reach out to let me know that she's not dead, not cut up in tiny pieces and tossed into the Mississippi River because she got involved with the wrong man and then stole from him.

I have a million questions, and it's with that resolve—the knowledge that I'm going to finally stand up to her and let her know what a shitty friend she is—that makes it easier for me to ignore the man a handful of feet away that's glaring out the window and close my eyes.

I'm no longer going to be the friend that gives and gets nothing in return, and I get the feeling that I'll be leaving the Maldives with a little less baggage than I showed up with. As much as that hurts my heart, I feel like it's been a long time coming.

Chapter 29
Deacon

He's just fucking with me.

I've told myself that every time Flynn leaned over and spoke to Anna on the plane, and every time he's whispered something in her ear that made her smile once we landed. It's what keeps me from reaching around his neck and choking the life out of him on foreign soil as he sticks close to her side, leaning in and winking at her every damn chance he gets.

What I hate most is that my oldest friend can read me like a book. I don't even have to say a word and that fucker knows that Anna means something to me. She's more than a client, more than just some woman I knew in a past life. And fuck me if I can pinpoint when that shift occurred. At this point, I don't know if it was a gradual shift, or if it hit me all at one time.

"I'm going to fucking kill him."

"What was that?" The sound of Wren's voice in my ear reminds me that I'm not alone.

"Nothing," I mutter, hating that the Air Pods in my ear picks up every damn sound I make. "Where is she?"

"She headed out the east side about fifteen minutes ago. I lost visual, but the only thing in that direction is the beach."

Dani thinks she's safe here, and as hard as it was to track her, it's possible that she was until we arrived. I'm in the frame of mind to wring her damn neck, too. I might just do that with every one of my guys, so I might as well add her to the list. The hardest part will be deciding who will go first. Flynn is the current front-runner of course, but each time Finnegan cuts his green eyes in Anna's direction or brushes his palm against her lower back he jumps up the list.

Jude and Quinten split off from us a few minutes ago to scope things out and make sure we won't intercept any trouble. I don't anticipate a problem, but it was too damn easy to gain access to this resort. A single reservation for the night is all it took for the security guard lazily working the front gate to allow seven men and one woman to enter the property. I grind my teeth at remembering the salacious look he gave to Anna as we drove through. The glint in his eyes told me that he thinks we're going to have a grand time running a fucking train on her or something, and it makes me wonder just how different my ex-wife is now than she was when we were together. What kind of shit is she into that she's staying on a property that would be okay with a wild orgy? She sure as hell wasn't into any form of kink while we were together. Hell, just convincing her to do more than lay on her back was an exercise in futility.

Goddammit. Why does that bitter memory make me think of the expert way Anna arched her back when I was taking her from behind? Getting a hard-on right now is the last damn thing I need. I refocus on my bitterness, on the anger that's been building up since we discovered just how put out Dani has been since she shot a man in her apartment.

I peer over my shoulder making sure that Anna is close but not in harm's way if some shit goes down. If I weren't struggling with some fucked-up form of obsession over her, I could easily see my guys protecting her, keeping her close, within arm's reach to come to her aid, but all I see are other men encroaching on something that belongs to me.

I shake my head to clear it of that thought. I don't own her, and I never will. She's a person for fuck's sake, not something to claim and own.

Flynn is the closest, his strong arm brushing hers as they keep pace. Finnegan keeps a step and a half back, and I narrow my eyes when he looks down. I can't tell if he's trying to see where he's going or if he's enthralled by the sight of her ass, but I'm murderous with the prospect that it's the latter.

A throat clears, and when I look back, I realize I'm so lost in my head, I walked right past the cabana my ex-wife is in.

My hands clench at my sides because I'm never distracted enough to lose focus, and it's just one more reason I need to get this shit over with. I told Anna the truth when I confessed the danger my actions put her in, and now I can't even do one damn thing right. I can't fucking protect her if she's so distracting, I lose my own damn head.

"Dani," I hiss, standing in front of her lounging body, blocking the sun with my wide frame.

"Hey." The smile she gives me is enough for me to deduce that she's probably been drinking most of the day. Either that or she's high as a fucking kite. Drugs weren't her thing when we were together, or maybe they were and I just didn't know about it. Nothing would surprise me at this point, but her grinning up at me like we're old friends sets my damn blood on fire.

"Having a good time?" I grind out, keeping my eyes on her face and not the male hand rubbing lotion into her lean thighs.

"The best." She lifts a hurricane glass to her mouth, lips wrapping around the straw as her grin grows.

I clench my jaw so hard; I won't be surprised if I crack a damn tooth.

"You're a hard person to find."

Her fingers tease the back of the man rubbing her down, but she's petting him like an animal, not someone she respects on any level, and that's just typical Dani. She's a user, someone who is only about herself, a queen always looking down on people, anticipating what they can do for her instead of caring about their needs.

I thought Anna was the same way, but I knew she was different the second I saw her get upset over the destruction of Zeni's picture in her apartment. Anna and Dani are nothing alike, and I honestly don't know what to do about that.

I step to the side, so my ex can see that her best friend is here as well, and only at the sight of Anna stepping out from around me does Dani's demeanor change. She isn't exactly happy to see her friend, but the irritation only lasts for a second. It's so brief I don't know if Anna caught it or not.

"Is this some sort of family reunion?" Dani asks as she looks at her oldest friend.

"We were worried about you," Anna says through clenched teeth. "Imagine our surprise to find you here."

Dani doesn't acknowledge the sweep of Anna's hand as she indicates the sunny beach and muscled hunk rubbing on her. She simply takes another sip of her cocktail before setting it aside on the table near her lounger.

"Imagine my surprise to see my two favorite people standing here," Dani says, her eyes darting between Anna and me.

Yep, she's definitely drunk. Dani wouldn't spit on me if I were on fire, much less be caught dead calling me one of her favorite people.

"You just disappeared. I was worried about you." Anna looks over her shoulder at me, and her emotions are hard to read. "I thought you were hurt, and I reached out to Deacon for help."

"Help?" Dani scoffs, but it's Anna's reaction to the dismissal that makes my muscles tense. Anna's arms cross over her chest and her hip kicks out a few inches.

With a wave of Dani's hand, the guy with the lotion stands, leaning in close to run his nose up the column of Dani's neck.

"You know where to find me," he whispers loud enough before walking away. His eyes skate over every guy in my crew like he's sizing them up and placing bets on whether Dani will come to him or end up with one of my men.

I ignore him completely, but when Flynn mutters wanker under his breath, it's hard to fight the grin.

"I'm fine," Dani says, her eyes darting suspiciously between her friend and me. "Is that all you came for?"

"Wow," Finnegan mutters from behind me, and it's then I realize I've had enough. I can't stand here a second longer without bitching my ex out, and I'm not that guy. I gave up on trying to reason with Dani years ago, and it's no longer my place to make her see the error in her ways. She was never good at doing anything other than pleasing herself as it was.

Without another word, I turn and walk away. Flynn trails closer behind as the other guys give the women some space without going too far.

"That one's a piece of work," my old friend says as we cross back inside the hotel.

The cool air should bring some relief from the blazing sun, but I feel like I'm on fire from the inside out. This problem could've been solved from a simple damn phone call. There was no real reason to load everyone on a damn plane and fly over here to confront Dani. It's not like she'd change a damn thing. She isn't remorseful for hauling ass out of St. Louis, and I don't know why I thought things would be different.

I used a favor with the Cerberus MC to make sure she'd be safe. I kept her best friend close to my side for weeks to make sure that the fallout from her bad decisions didn't hurt someone she supposedly cared for, and it was all for nothing. Dani doesn't worry about anyone but Dani, and I knew that from the jump. So why was I in such a hurry to help out?

"Fucking Anna," I mutter to myself.

She's the reason.

That damn phone call and the fear in her voice.

The way she reacted at her apartment.

The crying I heard from outside of the hotel room that first night.

The legitimate fear in her eyes when she saw that guy dead at my feet.

The sobs wracking her perfect body when she climbed in bed with me.

The way the sun sparkled in her honey-colored eyes when she woke up in my arms and I discovered I couldn't resist her any longer.

The soft, silken glide into her body.

All of it was the reason I kept going.

And none of that had to do with Dani.

Not one single thing.

I'm not here for Dani.

I'm here because it was more time I got to spend with Anna.

I've spent weeks and tens of thousands of dollars for just a little more time with a woman I haven't given a single thought to in the better part of a decade.

So tell me how she's managed to invade every single damn waking thought I've had since I heard that first whimper when she called?

Chapter 30
Anna

"Nice choice in bodyguards." Dani tilts her head before giving Finnegan a little wave. He doesn't even acknowledge her, and it takes great restraint not to smile. "They seem a little more severe than the ones you've had before."

"They're not my bodyguards. They work for Deacon."

"Ah." She takes another sip of her stupid drink before looking back over at me. "I heard he had a business. Security or something."

I clamp my jaw closed against the urge to explain what the man does. Security or something doesn't even come close to explaining what these guys do. I haven't seen much, but what I have witnessed makes her description seem disrespectful, like they're guarding a shopping center during Black Friday or something.

"What the hell happened, Dani? I was sure you were dead somewhere."

"Why are you here with Deacon?"

Classic Dani, avoiding my concern in order to appease her own curiosity.

"I told you. I was worried."

"My dad hired him?"

Because there's no way I'd reach out to her sworn enemy? I'm sure that's her reasoning.

"You and I both know your dad doesn't have the money to look for you."

She glares at me as if it's in bad taste to mention her family's money troubles.

"But financial insecurity doesn't seem to be bothering you much." I wave a hand toward the private beach and the personal waiter waiting to the side to serve her every need.

"I have my own money," she seethes.

I can't help but laugh at this. "Says the woman who has only dated guys who are capable of lavishing her with gifts and attention."

"I've always dated men with money." She states the fact like I'm being irrational.

She hasn't though. The man she told me she was planning to spend her life with didn't have money. He didn't grow up dirt poor, but Deacon was raised by two working parents that couldn't just hand everything to their son.

"And how many of them have you stolen from?"

She doesn't react at all. Her eyes are glued past me at the waves rolling lazily against the sand.

"How many of them have you left for dead?"

Her right eye twitches, and if I didn't know her well enough, I'd think she was affected, but Dani and I have been close since we were kids. Her masks, the ones she wears to keep others at arm's length don't hide her from me as much as she wishes they would.

"He's not dead," I hiss. "Nikolay Petrovich didn't die in your apartment, Dani. Hell, he checked himself out of the hospital over a week ago."

Dani and I have been through so much together. Happiness, and fear, several times when we thought we'd end up dead from drinking too much and the one time we got lost in a part of town we had no business being in. She handled thugs on the street once when we were in college much the same way she lived her life, with indifference and an air of superiority that would make dignitaries stand up and take notice.

That bravado disappears the instant she hears my news.

"Wh-what?"

"Not dead," I repeat. "The bullet you shot into him missed every single vital organ. He's alive and well. He's looking for you. He trashed my apartment, sent some gangbanger to kill me."

A wave of confusing emotions contorts her pretty, tanned face. First, she seems relieved, and I have to wonder if the fear of killing someone managed to infiltrate her *who gives a fuck* demeanor, but then I see her skin turn ashen.

"Alive?" she says as if she can't believe what I'm telling her.

She doesn't even look at the drink that topples over when she stands.

"Where are you going?"

She looks all around as if she expects Petrovich to pop out from behind a palm tree and surprise her. I'm barely able to keep up with her as she hauls ass toward the resort. She frowns at me when my hand slides between the doors to stop the elevator from moving before I can climb on with her.

"What's going on?" I ask when she just stands there watching the numbers flash as we ride up.

"He'll kill me," she whispers. "He's a dangerous man."

"I know," I say and reach for her hands. She lets me clasp them but it's easy to tell her focus isn't inside this elevator. "That's why we came to get you."

She doesn't look grateful. If anything, she looks terrified and bordering on agitated that we had the nerve to dip into the fun she was having. As if us showing up caused all of her problems, not the fact that she got tangled up with a dangerous man, stole his diamonds, and then tried to kill him when she got caught.

Dani uses the keypad on one of the two doors on the floor and shoves inside. I tell myself that she's scared. I know just how dangerous a man like Nikolay is. He sent a man to hurt me after all, but my friend hasn't once acknowledged the damage done to my life because of her. I don't know why I expected anything different from her. God, why has it taken me so long to see through her bullshit?

"What are you doing?"

Dani paces back and forth, and I know her mind is going a million miles an hour. "Maybe you should pack. Deacon hired a private jet. We can go back home and get to the bottom of this."

"Why are you here with Deacon?" I glare at her. Has she not heard a damn thing I've said? "Why him? Is there something going on between the two of you?"

"What? Are you kidding me right now? We need to get you out of here. He can make sure you're safe."

"You aren't denying it." Dani stops in her tracks, giving me a look I've seen a hundred times when she thinks I'm trying to encroach on someone she's claimed, and if this situation were different, I'd be able to remind her that we have opposite tastes in men.

I can't do that right now, can I?

I've slept with her ex-husband, felt him inside of me, and I know what he sounds like when he comes. I shake my head. Now, isn't the time to come clean. Now isn't the time to think about the night we spent together and how the brush of his fingers on my cheek left me confused because it felt like more than just a one-night stand.

"There's nothing going on between Deacon and me."

It's possibly the truth. After all, he hasn't made any overtures. If he wanted more from me than a way to get off, he wouldn't have retreated into himself right after he came on my damn back.

"You're certain Nikolay isn't dead?"

For once I'm thankful for how easily distracted she is when a conversation isn't about her.

"Yes. Deacon was able to keep him in the States, but I don't think they can keep him there forever." I instantly feel guilty for disclosing information I overheard Wren talk about during a conversation while I was there. "He took his team to West Africa to find you. He thought you might be in Cote d' Ivoire."

"He can't find me, Anna. I'm as good as dead if he does."

I step closer to her. "He won't. Deacon will keep you safe."

She steps away, continuing to pace the room. She's legitimately terrified, and that only ramps up my own terror. Dani doesn't get flustered and seeing her this way makes my skin crawl.

I gape at her back when she turns toward the hotel room door.

"Where are you going?"

"To blow off some steam."

Before I can tell her that a massage isn't the answer right now, she disappears.

Some things never change, and Dani, no matter the trouble she's in, will always only think of herself.

Chapter 31
Deacon

Nothing has ever had the ability to piss me off the way my ex-wife can. I didn't realize how much of a hair trigger I had where she was concerned until I saw her lounging on the damn beach like she doesn't have a care in the world, like she hasn't put her best friend's life in jeopardy more than once since she pulled her most recent shit.

I was so mad at seeing her sitting there, fruity cocktail in hand, unconcerned about what she's done, I didn't even realize I forgot to bring up the fucking Russians and stolen diamonds until I walked away and had a few minutes to calm down. "They aren't on the beach," I hiss into my Air Pods as I walk to the cabana I left Dani and Anna at minutes ago.

"Dani is registered to room 1401," Wren informs me.

I hang up, not needing any more of my frustrations being witnessed by my guys. Flynn followed me around for a few minutes after I walked away, but he eventually got tired of trying to calm me down and split off somewhere else.

I find Finnegan outside of room 1401 when I step off the elevator, and he disappears when I nod at him. He won't go far, but at least he doesn't give me shit when I lift my hand to knock.

Dani doesn't answer the door. Instead, it's a frustrated Anna who pulls the door open.

"I didn't talk to her about the diamonds," I explain because the last damn thing I need is Anna thinking I'm here to speak to my ex-wife about anything other than the issue at hand.

"She isn't here." Anna doesn't seem happy that her friend is gone, or maybe she isn't impressed with me standing here even with my truthful explanation.

"Where did she go?"

Anna shrugs. "Who knows? She said she was going to blow off some steam when I told her that Nikolay was still alive."

"Can I come in?" She hasn't budged from blocking the door, but I can tell she's upset.

How Dani treated her and everyone around her hasn't changed, but I can see that there's something different in her eyes, as if, just maybe, Anna can finally see through her friend's bullshit. I know it took me years and hundreds of miles of distance to see the real her. It wasn't a pretty realization for me, and I know it won't be for her best friend either.

Anna steps to the side, allowing me entry, but she doesn't reach for me when I pass. God, how did this woman get under my skin so easily? When did frustration being in the same room with her transition into needing to touch her just because she's near?

"How did she take it?" I could walk across the room and get comfortable on the sofa, but she doesn't move, so staying close to her is my only option.

"She seemed relieved at first, like she was happy that she hadn't killed someone, but then she was terrified. She said he'll kill her if he finds her."

Her chin quivers, and I can tell she's scared for what this may mean for her friend but also because Dani has endangered her as well.

"Hey." I lift her chin with my hand, forcing her to look up at my face. "I won't let anything happen to you."

Man, I wish I could keep the promise, but I've already failed her more than once. People wanting to hurt her have gotten close more than once, and it guts me to think the next time I may not be there to protect her.

"She doesn't even care about the trouble she's caused for me." True sadness fills her tone, but I know now isn't the time to explain that Dani is just being Dani, and she shouldn't expect more from her friend.

"I care," I say instead. "I care what happens to you."

Her eyes search mine, and I don't know what she sees, but whatever it is it has her letting the door snap closed and her feet carrying her closer to me.

I wrap my arms around her, tugging her against my chest. My nose immediately plants into the top of her head so I can breathe her in.

How do I tell her I missed her warmth? How do I explain that she feels a million miles away when we've been right on top of each other the last couple of days?

I can't. I don't. I simply hold her tighter and relish the feel of her body against mine. I need this woman like I need air, and that spells a million kinds of trouble for me, but I can enjoy this one moment, this one blip in time where we have no other problems, where there is nothing that can cause us problems.

"Anna," I whisper when she takes a step back and looks me in the eyes.

She swallows, her eyes focusing on my lips for a second too long to mean anything other than what I want most.

I don't hesitate, lowering my mouth to hers and pulling her back against my chest where she belongs.

She clings to me like she doesn't want to let me go, and a fire I can't ignore burns inside of me.

"Off," I grunt, pulling my mouth from hers and lifting the hem of her dress until it's over her head and tossed to the side. "Fucking perfect."

My hands immediately pull down the cups of her lacy bra until her tits are spilling over the top. She moans low in her throat when my tongue strikes at the pebbled tip of her right breast.

"Come here." With sure hands, I grip her ass and lift until her legs are wrapped around me and I don't have to practically bend in half to get to her.

She squeals like she's afraid I'm going to drop her when I spin to sit us on the couch, but the laughing stops abruptly when my fingers dig into her ass and my mouth explores her chest.

I'm in heaven with her fingers digging into my scalp, egging me on. Her hips roll and I hate that I'm wearing jeans, even if I can feel the heat between her legs like a scorching fire. I want to be against her naked skin, inside her tightness.

"Wait," I hiss, my mouth popping off her breast and hands lifting her a few inches over my lap.

I just want to look at her, maybe slip my fingers into the slickness that's darkening the fabric between her thighs, but she has other ideas. When she reaches for the button and zipper on my jeans, I let it happen. I even lift my hips so she can maneuver the denim down my thighs, but I draw the line at letting her slip out of my lap so I can get them all the way down. I've never hated the time it takes to take off combat boots more in my life, but we'll manage. She doesn't shove my boxer briefs down. She's perfectly content to slip her little hand inside the fabric and wrap it around my shaft.

"Mmm," she moans, dropping her mouth back down to mine.

I didn't tease her much when we were back at the ranch, and I've regretted that every second since. You'd think I'd be in a better position to take my time right now, but then again, I've been inside of her before. My body knows what it's been missing rather than just having a fantasy of what she feels like gripping my cock when she comes.

Taking a deep breath, I let her free hand roam down my chest while the other works some kind of voodoo on my cock that has me nearly to the brink of exploding.

"Anna," I hiss. "Wait."

She smiles against my lips, ignoring the warning, and since turnabout's fair play, I press my fingers to her clit while the other arm wraps around her back. Her hand stills on mine, but just the pressure of her grip makes me grit my teeth.

"I'll come," I warn before nipping at her breast and sucking the nipple back into my mouth. She moans when my cheeks hollow, her head rolling on her shoulders like she's in heaven.

"So come," she manages, but her grip has lost its strength.

"You first."

Crooking my fingers, I find her wet heat and press inside of her, my thumb making maddening circles on her clit.

God, she's everything. She's not shy, tilting her head down to watch my hand exploring her. She's willing to let me dirty her up right here on the sofa in Dani's room, and fuck if I don't want to just lift her until we're standing and impale myself right into the little slice of heaven I've been craving since the last time I was allowed to visit.

I have a million things to say to her. A thousand different ways I've started the conversation in my head. More than a hundred scenarios of my counterarguments when she tries to back away and tell me that what's happening between us isn't real.

It has to be. I feel it in my gut in a way I've never felt once before in my life. She's perfect for me, and if it wasn't because of our complicated past, I would've told her so. But, I'm tired of fighting it. Tired of worrying about how it looks to outsiders. Tired of some archaic code that says because I was married to her best friend a lifetime ago, that what we could have is wrong.

"Anna," I pant against her mouth. "Please, baby. Give it to me."

I use my free hand to pull the black lace of her panties to the side so I can have better access, and that seems to do the trick. Her body bows over mine, pussy clenching on my probing fingers as she comes apart.

"That's it," I praise. "So fucking perfect."

She clings to me, both hands over my shoulders, fingernails digging into my skin, the tiny bites of pain making this more real than I ever thought it could be. I give her a minute to come down, loving the sex-drunk look in her eyes when they finally flutter open.

"I need you," I whisper. "I want—"

Before I can tell her all the dirty things I plan to do to her starting today and never stopping, the hotel room door swings open, and it's just my luck that my ex-wife is standing there staring at me, seconds away from ruining my life once again.

Chapter 32
Anna

I don't even realize the door has opened until I see Deacon's face fall. The needy look in his eyes drops in an instant. His eyes narrow mere seconds before I hear a feminine huff behind me. He doesn't seem too quick to pull his fucking fingers from inside of me, and I read that, along with the fact that if I look over my shoulder that I'll find Dani standing behind me as a way for him to get back at his ex for leaving him. I've become the pawn in this scenario when moments ago, I thought the look in his eyes was pure lust and need.

It kills a little part inside of me if I'm being honest.

"Oh, God!" I yelp, trying to scramble off his lap.

He doesn't try to hold me against him. Doesn't open his mouth to explain or tell her to leave because she's interrupting a private moment. While I'm frantic and looking for my dress, he stands from the sofa lazily as if he wants Dani to get a real good look at him, slowly pulling up his jeans.

"Nothing going on, huh?"

I feel his eyes burning into my back, but I can't face him right now. It's already taking everything I have to keep from crying, and I don't know if the misery stems from her catching us or him not opening his mouth to defend what we were doing.

Why would he defend it? He's exactly where he put himself. I believed his explanation about needing to talk to her about the diamonds, and that makes me a fool.

"It's not what it looks like." I pull my dress over my head, realizing too late that it's on backward.

"So, you weren't fixing to fuck my ex-husband?"

I can't even look at my friend. The best I can do is look in her direction, keeping my eyes trained over her shoulder on the door I so desperately want to make a run for. The situation doesn't even need explaining, so I clamp my lips closed. We won't be able to ignore it for long, but Dani eyes Deacon warily as he makes a production of zipping his jeans and adjusting his cock. Of course he'd still be hard. I'm sure this went exactly to his plan, and that's the kind of shit that turns him on. It doesn't matter that I'm probably going to lose my friend. Yeah, she's petty and vapid, but we're like sisters.

I know I shouldn't have been on his lap, mere seconds away from freeing his cock and sliding down onto it. I shouldn't have done a lot of things these last couple of weeks, but nothing makes me regret what I've done more than watching Deacon walk across the room before disappearing into the bathroom.

Is he waiting for me to leave so he and Dani can have it out before hate fucking each other? I wouldn't be surprised. No matter how much I've tried, I can't keep her voice out of my head, the one that bragged about his prowess in bed when we were teens. It nearly made me gag in disgust then, but now I know exactly what she was talking about, even more so because I'm certain he has skills now that he didn't years ago.

The heat from Dani's eyes draws my attention back to her, and she's standing with her hip cocked, eyebrows raised as she waits for me to speak, and I hate that I meet her gaze because now I can't seem to look away.

She doesn't say anything, and neither do I.

It's not what it looks like.

Isn't that what every person who gets caught red-handed says? I said those words moments ago. I've turned into a fucking cliché and I can't stand myself.

"Dani," I begin, but the words just stop.

As much as I want to tell her how I feel about him and explain that it honestly did just happen, I can't. I have real feelings for the asshole even though he will never feel the same for me. Actions always speak louder than words and the way he just sat there with me on top of him without telling her to leave until we were decent is screaming from the top of the mountain right now.

I should've listened to my gut when it told me to run far and fast after he shut down the first time we ended up in bed together, but then he looked at me, held me when I was upset, and I told my inner voice to shut up. When his lips met mine, I knew I wouldn't be able to stop.

My friend holds her hand up, and instead of getting irritated, I snap my mouth closed.

"I'm not discussing this with him here," she says after a long moment and quick look toward the bathroom.

The toilet flushes and water runs in the sink, but he still doesn't exit the bathroom. I can't help but wonder if he has his ear to the door and a grin on his face as he waits patiently for Dani to rip into me. Is this retaliation for invading his life, for taking up his time? Is it some form of manipulation to get Dani back and finally get me out of their lives for good?

If I hadn't spent so much time with him recently, that's exactly what I'd think was going on, but I can't discount his sincerity when he spoke to me earlier.

I won't let anything happen to you.

Those words, although they feel like a million years away, were spoken less than a half an hour ago. He meant them. I could see the truthfulness in his eyes. Emotion clogs my throat because I'm so damn torn. It's the unknown that I can't stand. If I thought I owned even a part of him, some fraction of certainty that if I stand up for what he and I have that he'll be by my side, I'd do it in a heartbeat, but I don't. All I have are doubts. I don't know where he stands. I don't know if he wants something from me. All I know is he got up and walked away, just like he has more than once, and that screams at me to keep the one friend I have left even though she's done a terrible job so far.

"Listen, I'm sor—"

Before I can spit my half-hearted apology, because honestly the only regret I'm feeling right now is not opening my mouth to figure out what's going on between Deacon and me, the hotel room door crashes open.

I duck my head, crossing my arms over my face when splinters of wood from the door frame fly into the room. Dani spins around to face the threat, and my heart nearly pounds out of my chest when I see two men standing just inside of the room with guns drawn.

One of the men I recognize as Nikolay Petrovich and the other I presume is one of his henchmen.

"Daniella," Petrovich hisses and the air around us crackles.

Before Dani can even gasp, the bathroom door bursts open, and Deacon emerges with his own gun drawn.

He must have mad skills because if I were armed, I think I would've already unloaded the entire clip in fear. I can't reason at all right now, and I commend both sides for not covering the room and all of us in it in a wall of bullets.

Slowly and with precision, Deacon crosses the room, and I ignore the fact that he's standing closer to me than his ex. I'm simply closer than she is.

"Petrovich," Deacon spits, and my eyes volley back to the Russian to see his response.

Nikolay eyes Deacon from head to toe, clearly not impressed with what he's seeing.

"Black," he spits in an accent so heavy it's almost as if he's literally spitting the name at our feet. "You disrespected my home."

He must be talking about the raid on the compound in West Africa that I know little about, but no one expands on the statement.

I'm waiting, pulse hammering in the hollow of my throat while waiting for something to happen. It's like we're stuck in some sort of limbo, each side waiting for the other to act first. Seconds seem like days as Nikolay turns his attention from Deacon back to Dani.

There's a softness in his eyes I didn't expect from a man tracking a woman for theft and nearly killing him. The second Russian keeps his eyes trained on Deacon.

"Where are they?" Petrovich finally asks, and even though I hate the sight of Dani trembling, I can't honestly defend her right now.

She took something that didn't belong to her, and the fallout has been trouble of epic proportions.

"I-I don't have them."

Both Deacon's and Nikolay's jaws tense with irritation, and I'm thinking it's a very bad idea to piss off a couple of guys with guns, but Dani doesn't look like she's going to budge. Is death better than having money? I know what my answer would be, but my friend doesn't seem too quick to come to the same conclusion.

"Dani," Deacon hisses. "Give the man his fucking diamonds."

"I don't hav—"

Dani's jaw snaps shut when Deacon's commandos fill the doorway. The Russians don't seem bothered. Nikolay doesn't pull his penetrating gaze from Dani, and his comrade doesn't lower the gun pointed at Deacon.

Chapter 33

Deacon

I should feel calmer with the arrival of my men, but I don't. Anna is directly in the line of fire, and that makes my blood fucking boil. I promised that woman I'd keep her safe, yet here we fucking are once again.

The look both Flynn and Ignacio are giving me tells me they're ready to act with the slightest indication, but I know there's a good chance that if bullets start flying, there are going to be casualties. The Russians look like they've made their peace with God and don't really give a shit about the outcome. They've been slighted and they want retribution for that.

A second look at Nikolay tells me something I didn't initially see moments ago. He isn't looking at Dani like she's at the top of his shit list. There isn't murder in the man's eyes. He's watching her the same way he was in that picture Wren showed me. This man is head over fucking heels in love with that woman, and he honestly looks more hurt that it's come to this than anything else. He doesn't want this to end badly. If anything, he looks like he wishes it never happened to begin with. I can work with that.

"Dani, give him the damn diamonds," I insist as I position my feet to jump in between the second Russian and Anna.

"I don't—"

"Right fucking now," I snap. "Lie again and I'll become a bigger problem than these two guys."

I wiggle the tip of my gun for emphasis because they have three guys each with them in their sights.

Dani never pulls her eyes from Nikolay.

"Kitten," Nikolay coos at Dani. "Where are they?"

His voice is heated, a burning ember evident of the way he feels for her. He's not done with her by a long shot. He's fucking on fire with need for her, but it doesn't seem to be the need to punish her for wrongdoings like one would expect. I somehow feel sorry for the bastard. Loving Dani will be his downfall.

Dani isn't scared either, which says a lot because the woman has a gun pointed at her chest. I could never convince her to go shoot with me when I was on leave, no matter how adamant I was that she should know how to protect herself, and here she is not even trembling as her life is threatened.

"What's the move, boss," the second Russian asks with irritation in his voice. Now this motherfucker is ready to spill some damn blood. He's the unknown, the loose cannon that will cause problems.

Flynn inches forward while the man is distracted, but he stops in his tracks when I tilt my head.

"What do you say, Petrovich? You get the diamonds and end this shit today?"

It's a ridiculous hope. We invaded this man's privacy, stormed into his house and held his house staff hostage while we looked for my ex. I know that can't go unpunished. Hell, I don't know why bullets aren't flying already, but I also know I have to try. Dani has made her bed, and on the plane ride over, I made peace with that. It's Anna that I can't stand to see hurt because of her friend's bad choices in men.

"Niki," Dani whispers, and I'll be damned if she doesn't have the angry Russian by the balls.

The longing in his gaze is almost enough to make me want to turn my head and give them some fucking privacy.

"The diamonds, Kitten," he urges, but the threat in his tone speaks more of a cat-and-mouse game they're both familiar with rather than anything else.

"I need them," she argues. "You know I do."

"And I needed you, *lyubovnik*. I think we're both going to be disappointed."

I cock an eye at Ignacio, but he's focused on Petrovich's back and doesn't look my way. I'd bet money that it was a term of endearment.

I take a step forward, and the second Russian curses in his native tongue, aiming his gun from my chest to my forehead. "Boss?" Flynn grunts, but I simply shake my head.

My guys are nearly perfect aims, but this issue is bigger than the people in this room. Killing these two guys won't end the problem. Other than the thug sent for Anna and the blood Dani spilled in regard to Nikolay, no loss of life has happened yet. There's no telling the fallout if we drop these two fuckers here today. I imagine it would be catastrophic, and I'm not looking to put Anna in anymore danger than she's already faced.

"The diamonds, Dani."

My ex-wife snaps her eyes in my direction, and I gain Petrovich's scrutiny as well.

"Kitten," he urges, his eyes still locked on me.

"Get the man his belongings so they can be on their way."

Anna trembles even harder when the second Russian seems to grow anxious as Dani crosses the room to the safe hidden behind a painting on the far wall.

She seems put out, agitated at having to relinquish her stolen spoils while her best friend is probably near a stroke due to fear. I can't believe I ever thought I loved that woman. Life partner, my ass. If we had stayed together, Dani would've already sucked the life out of me. The only thing I regret about the entire relationship is taking so long to finally open my eyes.

I brush the back of my free hand against Anna's arm and she startles with a gasp.

"Shh," I urge. "It's almost over."

The fear in her eyes tells me she doesn't believe me at all, and that fucking kills me. She isn't meant for this type of life. She needs calm and serene. Hell, she deserves that and more.

"I assume this is the end of it?" I glance at Petrovich who can't seem to take his eyes off Dani. "You won't send someone else to hurt Anna?"

"I have no trouble with her or you," Petrovich says, but he doesn't make any promises about Dani.

I don't know exactly how I feel about that, but I'm close to calling it a win. Then Flynn curses under his breath.

"Again, *lyubovnik*?" Petrovich lowers his gun, crossing one hand over his heart. "Won't you ever learn?"

"*Day slovo, boss, i ya broshu suku*," the second Russian hisses, his aim leaving my head and shifting to Dani on the other side of the room.

"Give the word, boss, and I'll drop the bitch," Ignacio whispers with a Russian accent. The man is a savant when it comes to language.

I take the opportunity to lower my own weapon and move Anna to the side. I may not be able to prevent something from happening to Dani, but I'll be damned if Anna is hurt ever again because of her.

"*Net*, Ivan. *Opusti oruzhiye.*"

To my surprise Ivan lowers his weapon even though it looks like he's biting the inside of his cheek hard enough to taste blood. He's ready to kill Dani for her disrespect, but Nikolay won't have it.

"Please?" Dani begs, and when I turn my eyes to her, she's standing there with a handgun, pointed in her former lover's direction. Just what we need, an emotional woman who thinks she's at the end of her rope.

Anna clings to me, quiet sobs escaping her lips, warm, salty tears running down her cheeks. I want to wrap my arms around her, comfort her and promise her everything will be okay, but I can't. I have to get a handle on this situation before I can drop my guard.

"Pull the trigger," Petrovich says with his arms splayed at his sides. He looks utterly broken. "Or get the diamonds, Kitten."

The gun in Dani's hand trembles uncontrollably, but in a matter of seconds she drops it to the floor with a gasp before turning and pulling a black bag from the open safe behind her.

Tears are streaming down her face as she walks the bag across the room, and I can see right through her. She isn't upset for the trouble or the harm that has fallen at Anna's feet. She's upset that she's having to relinquish her payday. She's going to eventually be forced to go home broke, facing a reality she never thought she'd encounter. I don't feel sorry for her one bit.

Petrovich takes the bag, clasping Dani's hand in his. He pulls her close, leaning down to brush his lips across her damp cheek. She leans into his touch just briefly, but I don't miss it. If I had to guess, I'd say she feels more for him than she ever did for me.

"*Moya krovat' ne takaya zhe bez tebya, kotenok,*" he whispers before he releases her and turns to leave.

"This is over, Petrovich," I say to his back as my guys part so they can walk out.

Petrovich spares Dani one more glance before he looks in my direction. A single dip of his head is all I get, but I guess I'll have to take it.

With a gasping sob, Dani rushes from the living room of the suite and slams the door to the bathroom as she enters.

"What did he—"

"My bed isn't the same without you, Kitten," Ignacio answers before I can finish my question.

"That was fucking intense," Flynn says as he steps further into the room. He doesn't put his gun away. None of them will until we're sure that the threat is eliminated.

"Wren?" I ask

Flynn nods. "He saw them coming through the lobby. The guy has got a wicked sense for trouble."

I knew Wren wouldn't let his guard down while we were still here. We had a long conversation about the possibility of Petrovich following me to the Maldives like he did to the Four Seasons. It's why I brought as many guys as were available.

"Seems too easy," Ignacio says before stepping out into the hallway.

"His problem isn't with us," Finnegan mutters, his eyes darting to the closed bathroom door. "Her on the other hand…"

Anna gasps, finally giving her sobs permission to escape.

I reach for her, determined to pull her against my chest. She can't protect Dani from herself, and I'm willing to bet that Petrovich wouldn't hurt Dani. He's madly in love with the woman. If shooting him and stealing his bag of diamonds wasn't enough to put a slug in her head when he first walked in here, I don't imagine that it'll ever happen.

She doesn't give me a chance to hold her. Anna shrinks away from my embrace before I can get my arm all the way around her. My guys disappear like shadows, and I'm grateful they don't give me shit about my girl pulling away.

She denied being with me when Dani busted in on us earlier, and at first, I understood, but the longer I stood, staring at myself in the mirror, the more pissed it made me. She didn't stand up for me, for *us*. She went with her gut, which was to deny everything, no matter that we got caught seconds before I shoved my dick inside of her. She doesn't want anything to do with me, and I'm a fucking fool for even entertaining the idea that she did.

I clear my throat, taking a step back. Without looking in her direction, I walk across the room.

"We're leaving first thing in the morning. You and Dani can be on the plane for a ride back to the States or not. Either way, I don't care."

The busted door swings right back open when I walk out and slam it. Of course, I can't even have the satisfaction of hearing it snap closed behind me as the final punctuation on whatever this shit was that I started with Annalise Grimaldi.

Chapter 34
Anna

I couldn't bear to watch Deacon walk out again. It's a situation of my own making, but he's proved over and over that walking away is what he does. I'm an idiot for not letting him comfort me. I'm well aware of that, but I didn't expect him to give up so easily.

I haven't had time to evaluate what is really going on. One minute no one else in the world exists but Deacon and me, the next, Dani is busting in on us. Seconds later, we're being ambushed by two angry Russians. My head is spinning, and I don't know where to place my focus.

I could've been killed... again.

I don't want any part of this life. I don't feel a need for an adrenaline rush. I'd prefer my heart racing the way it did when I rode in front of Deacon on Sweet Pea, or the way excitement fills my blood on Christmas morning. The threat of death? Yeah, no, don't sign me up for that ever again.

Deacon remained calm, and it didn't go unnoticed that he kept closer to me than he did Dani, but in my head sometimes I can be reasonable. My brain is telling me that I was closest to him, the easiest to defend. My heart wants to believe that he was choosing me over my best friend.

My chin trembles in fear, the spike of epinephrine refusing to subside even when the danger has dissipated.

But has it really?

I thought it was gone days ago when Deacon brought me to the ranch. I didn't feel an ounce of it when he had his arms around me, but now I'm understanding that his embrace was only false security.

Wanting to get stuck in my head isn't an option any longer because Dani pulls the bathroom door open and pokes her head out to make sure everyone has left. She doesn't even seem pleased to see me standing in the middle of the room.

There's an ache deep inside at the realization that maybe no one wants me. Everyone seems to give up on me so easily. I straighten my spine. Feeling pain for rejection of my own making is ridiculous. I made a choice, and even though I didn't even want to consider the consequences at the time, I knew they would be coming. I just thought I'd have a little more time to prepare. I thought I could deal with them individually rather than being slapped in the face with them all at once.

"Are you just going to stand there? Or are you going to tell me what the hell is going on?"

I frown at my friend, but typical Dani is quick to put the focus on what she walked in on rather than the danger she's put everyone else in.

"It just happened," I lie.

There's nothing positive that will come from confessing the slow build to the intimacy I shared with Deacon. Not when it's clearly over. I blame my loneliness, albeit it, mostly self-imposed, for being untruthful, but I don't have Deacon, and Dani is the closest friend I've ever had. Toxic friendship or not, she's the only person I have left. She knows my secrets, my fears, and losing her would be a pain I'm not willing to face so soon after losing a man I was thinking I could love for the rest of my life.

"Really?" She's not acting like a woman who just had a gun pointed at her head. She seems inconvenienced at most.

"I promise," I lie again. "Maybe it was relief with finding you safe or something."

My cheeks heat because I've never been good at lying, but thankfully Dani doesn't exactly pay much attention to those around her.

"I can't be friends with someone dating my ex." And there's the ultimatum I knew was coming.

"We're not dating."

I don't bring up the boyfriend she took right out from under me in eighth grade because let's face it, dating a guy before high school and hooking up with a friend's ex-husband are on two different playing fields. Deacon and I knew crossing that line was wrong, no matter how right it felt at the time. Plus, he didn't defend what we were doing. Didn't make a single overture to explain. Simply, I was revenge, a way to stick it to Dani one last time for her leaving him, and that cuts in a different fashion than just being used for a quick release between two willing partners.

My hands tremble as I cross the room, but Dani takes a step back. She's not upset about what just happened, but she's not willing to offer comfort to me either. She's still mad, and that's understandable.

"Deacon said the plane is leaving in the morning."

"And?" Dani snaps as she crosses the living room to the bedroom of the suite.

Just like I have for years, I follow her.

"It means we have a free ride home if we want one."

It goes without saying that she just lost her payday by handing over the diamonds, and she's left without a financial lifeline, but maybe she'll continue to be stubborn. She could possibly turn down the generous offer and stay on the beach until her funds run dry. Knowing Dani, she won't be without money for long. She has a knack for seducing men until they're practically begging her to take their money in exchange for a little attention. I'd always thought it was funny before because if men want to be stupid and not see through her act, then that was on them, but my eyes are open a little more these days.

I can't think of Deacon right now or how I'd never do something like that to him because it makes me acknowledge the feelings still swirling around inside me that are forbidden. It would make me want to walk out of this room, walk away from my best friend and chase after a man that has proved time and time again that he has no interest in me other than sating a sexual need. Just like I wouldn't use a man for riches, I won't be used for sex.

"A private jet or commercial?"

It takes all my strength not to roll my eyes and huff at her question. "Private."

She perks up at this, a slow smile spreading across her face.

"Just how much money is that business of his making?"

My skin crawls with the salacious look in her eyes. When she and Deacon got together, he didn't have much, and what? Now that he's successful in life he's an option once again?

I clench my hands at my sides, but she has her back to me as she pulls expensive clothes from the closet, placing several pieces on the bed before her nose scrunches up.

"Can you call housekeeping to pack all of this up? I just don't have the energy for it after what happened today."

She turns, walking past me without looking back.

"And have them do something about the broken door," is what she tosses over her shoulder before walking out of the suite.

"With friends like you…" I mutter before picking up the damn room phone and doing her bidding.

I have some serious reevaluating to do when I get back to the States, but I'll keep my mouth clamped closed, jaw aching with the force until then. I don't want to make any more trouble for Deacon, and pissing Dani off more than she already is only means trouble for everyone involved.

***

I'm not surprised that Deacon won't look in my direction on the flight home. It honestly fits his MO perfectly. If I caught him glancing in my direction even once, it would probably send me into arrhythmia.

I'm also not surprised to watch Dani flirt with him like eight years and a divorce doesn't separate them. She came back to the room last night drunk, skin flushed and smelling of men's cologne, and I let my mind go wild with the possibilities that she spent the hours she was gone in Deacon's arms, but the way he seems disgusted with even the sight of her today has alleviated those questions. But then again, I spent a night in his arms and got the same response, so who freaking knows.

Any attempt to sleep is thwarted by her incessant need to make every second about her. If she isn't cooing at Deacon's guys, no doubt trying to get a rise out of her ex, she's insisting on engaging me in conversation loud enough for every person on the plane to hear. I'm surprised the pilots haven't closed the door to the cockpit to get a little peace and quiet.

"Have you picked your dress for the Grand Gala?"

"No." The Grand Gala is months away, and fortunately the very last one of the year that I'm obligated to attend. Even with the loads of fun I had with Wren, they no longer have the appeal they did weeks ago.

"Really?" She snaps her head back, aghast that I haven't taken time out from the recent attempts on my life to go shopping for a damned gown. "Whatever you pick it better not be emerald. Mine is, and I don't want people to think we're dressing like twins."

I turn in my seat, lips in a thin line and lean in closer to her. "My apartment was trashed by your Russian friends. Some street thug broke into my hotel room with the intent to abduct me and beat your location out of me. I had a gun pointed at my face just yesterday. No, Dani, I haven't had the chance to go shopping for a gown."

"Trashed?" Her face falls, and it's the first time she's shown an ounce of care for what others have been going through while she was drinking cocktails on the beach and entertaining buff cabana boys.

"Torn to shreds," I explain. "They destroyed everything. Ripped my couch to shreds. There wasn't a thing left to salvage."

Her hand covers her face, and for a split second I think she's going to have some empathy.

"That couch was hideous. So maybe it's for the best."

I do my best to hide my disappointment, but it's impossible.

Dani merely chuckles absentmindedly when I huff and turn toward the front of the plane. Maybe complete isolation from everyone is best.

Chapter 35

Deacon
One Month Later

"This is fucking subpar work," I snap, tossing the dossier back at Gaige.

He glares at me, but he's a smart man because he keeps his mouth closed.

"Get me more."

I stomp out of his office, only feeling mildly guilty for getting on his ass. Gaige claims to be the best acquisitions guy around, but his half-assed list of materials we need isn't going to cut it. I don't care about the recent climate and social issues the world is facing right now, we don't deal with low-level material.

"What the hell was that about?" Flynn matches my stride as I walk down the hall toward my own office.

The lights are low, and I growl when my friend tries to open the damn blinds. I don't want sunshine or happiness floating through here. It might actually force me to climb out of the shitty mood I've been in since... fuck, I don't even want to think about the Maldives and how easy it was for Anna to shift right back into her place behind Dani. I say behind because they've never been equals. My ex-wife would never allow that.

"He was trying to shove pine down my throat rather than the cedar I asked for," I mutter.

"Fencing? You're getting on his ass about fencing?"

"It's fucking important." I shouldn't have to explain this to him.

"There are shortages. Shit is going down in the world. There are many people waiting for things they want that they're unable to get right now."

"I don't want to fucking wait. I want to work on that damn fence this weekend."

"You sound like a spoiled, entitled brat right now. Get a fucking grip, man."

I can't confess that I've been waiting for everything else in my life right now, and the damn wood sent me over the edge. That would reveal too much about me, but the look in Flynn's eyes as he shakes his head in disappointment at me tells me I don't even need to open my mouth right now for him to know exactly what's been going on.

I never have to wait for things. My success means most everything I could ask for is right at my fingertips, sometimes before I could even express my need for them, but not Anna. No, she's across town, living her life. I can't even consider myself waiting for her because she's never coming back, and the things I should've said back in the Maldives successfully keep me up every damn night.

"I'll personally kick your ass if I see you talking to another one of the guys like that."

I cock an eyebrow at him. "Have you forgotten whose name is on the fucking door of this place?"

I don't often have to pull rank, but there's no way Flynn is going to force me out of my month-long bad mood. If anything, he's only making it worse.

"That shit again?" He rolls his eyes, flopping into the chair across from my desk as if he were invited to stay. "Maybe if you let some light in here and do something other than work eighteen hours a day, things would get better."

"That's why I need the damn wood. I'll get plenty of sunshine while building that new paddock."

"You need to go watch a movie or eat something that doesn't get delivered in a Styrofoam container. When was the last time you had a steak? Maybe you're low on iron."

"Are you fucking kidding me with this shit right now? Low on iron? You sound like Pam."

"Listen," he leans forward, and I know this conversation just took a damn turn. It won't be the first time someone in the office has tried to convince me to stop being a dick. "We care about you."

I cross my arms over my chest, leaning back in my office chair so I can glare at him better. "And now you're Dr. Phil? Lay it out for me."

His head tilts, and I don't miss the clenching of his jaw. "Lay it out? You really want that?"

"Whatever gets you the fuck out of my office and back to work."

He rolls his lips as he takes a deep breath, and I'm already regretting tossing the challenge at his feet. It'll be just my luck that he starts and doesn't stop for hours.

"Getting your heart broken sucks."

"I didn't get my heart broken."

Obliterated more like it, and I know I'm just as much to blame for the outcome, but hindsight is always twenty-twenty.

"My ass," he scoffs. "Dani was no good for you."

"Dani? She has nothing to do with..." A slow smile spreads across his face, and I'll kick my own ass later for stepping right into the damn trap he set.

"Anna is an amazing woman."

"I fucking know that."

"Then why are you being a brooding asshole here when all you have to do is drive across town and make her yours?"

"Make her mine? Have you ever been in a fucking relationship before? That's not how it works. A man can't just show up, throw a woman over his shoulder, and claim her. That caveman shit doesn't work. That's how you end up in a jail cell with kidnapping charges."

His chuckle makes my eyes narrow.

"But you want to?"

"Fuck no."

God, if I had even the slightest indication that some bullshit like that would work, I would've done it when she climbed off the private jet and refused to look back at me.

"Liar."

"Are you done? I have shit to do."

"I'm not done, and no you don't. It's Sunday, and until Wren gets the information on Jefferson, we're all in a holding pattern. Since you've so kindly worked every one of us to the bone the last month, we're completely caught up."

I release a very slow breath through my nose and close my eyes.

"You need to either lay all of your cards at her doorstep and take your chance or you need to get over it."

We've been volleying back and forth which is typical of what Flynn and I do. The man knows he can approach me with anything. All the guys do, but the sincerity in his voice this time is eye-opening. I'm pushing them too hard, treating them like they don't deserve and that's on me.

"Fine," I grunt.

"Fine? As in you'll stop being a complete dick? Because Pam asked me to show her how to make a noose the other day. If you don't make some changes, she may end up trying to kill you."

I huff a laugh for two reasons. Pam would never hurt a fly, and with my attitude lately, I also don't doubt that my friend is telling the truth. The woman hates dissension in the office, and it hasn't been an easy ride for anyone lately.

"I'll do better." Saying the words is acknowledging that I've fucked up. "Tell Gaige that we can wait on the cedar."

"Tell him yourself, asshole." Flynn stands, stretching his arms over his head. "I'm not your fucking servant."

He waits for me at the door, unwilling to let me stop being a dick on my own timeline, and I stand, obliging him. There's no time like the present, right?

Gaige is no longer in his office, so Flynn forces me to the breakroom where everyone congregates, compelling me to interact with my men, something I've avoided unless absolutely necessary recently. A hush falls over the previously boisterous room when I enter, and it speaks loudly of the jerk I've been lately.

"What the fuck," Wren spits, his head lowered over a recently opened delivery box.

He gains all of our attention, but Finnegan is the first to move.

"Is it a fucking bomb?" the Irishman asks as he approaches. His already freckled cheeks pink even further as he looks inside before he bends over with a laugh.

"What?" Brooks asks, smiling before he even knows what's going on.

Wren flips the flap on the box to look at the address.

"I just picked this up from the front desk at my apartment."

"The suspense is fucking killing me," Flynn says as he also approaches. "Holy shit! I knew you were into some weird shit, but this is eye-opening."

"This isn't mine," Wren hisses as Flynn reaches for the box and upending it.

"Wow," I mutter, but the grin is slowing spreading across my face, and I don't even try to stop it. "Might as well be a bomb. If you can handle that, call me impressed."

Wren glares at me before reaching for the item Brooks picks up from the pile.

"*Dios mio,*" Ignacio hisses with a chuckle. "That thing is huge!"

"Twelve inches," Flynn says holding the giant dildo to the side to read the label, "and ribbed for her pleasure."

"The things you learn about people even after all the years of working together," Gaige tsk-tsks.

"I didn't order this shit!" Wren snaps as he gives up on getting the huge cock from Flynn and runs his hands over his head.

"Like hell," Brooks chuckles as he holds up the box. "It says right here that it was delivered to W. Nelson. Apartment number 913."

"I'm in apartment 1213, dick." Wren snatches the box from Brooks and examines the label. "They gave me the wrong box."

"Are you sure?" Ignacio moves the other items around on the table, spreading them out so everyone can see. "I'm sure you can find uses for this ball gag."

"Use it on the fucking bird," I offer.

"Or this feather tickler," Ignacio continues.

"I've used that lube before but the cherry flavored is better," Brooks adds.

"If you need lube—" Gaige begins, but Brooks throws a butt plug at him, pegging him in the chest.

"Don't judge me. This is about Wren."

We all turn our attention back to the flustered guy, but he's already across the room, deserting the sex toys on the table.

We're all invested, so of course we follow him to his office, cramming into the space that's not meant to house more than a half-dozen curious guys.

"What are you looking for?" Ignacio asks.

"Doesn't matter to me at this point," Gaige says with a laugh, "I'm already invested."

We all nod in agreement as Wren's fingers work their magic on his keyboard.

"Is this real life?" he mutters when a smiling woman's face fills the largest screen of the three he has in front of him.

"Major has great tits!" Puff Daddy squawks.

"Major?" Brooks asks before I can, but it's clear we aren't the only two confused looking at the purple-haired girl on the screen.

"A character from *Ghost in the Shell*," Jude explains which draws every eye in the room.

"You into anime porn, too?" Wren asks, with weird hopeful surprise.

"I'm into Scarlett Johansson, not anime," Jude amends.

"Can we get back to what's really important?" Finnegan prods. "Who is that chick?"

"Whitney Nelson," Wren says as he turns back to the screen. "The W. Nelson in apartment 913. They gave me her box of stuff."

"You have to return it," I tell him.

We all laugh at his discomfort when he turns back around to glare at me.

This little incident couldn't have come at a better time. I've spent way too much time acting like an asshole, and thankfully when I find Gaige later to apologize, he just slaps me on the back and tells me to get fucked. Ah, now life is back to order.

Chapter 36
Anna

"We should do this more often," I tell Dani as I bring my fourth, or is it fifth, martini to my lips for a long sip.

Dani doesn't respond. She's bopping her head to a tune that isn't even close to the slow jazz playing through the hidden speakers of the lounge.

This is the first time we've gone out together since we got back from the Maldives over a month ago. I've barely seen her in passing and was shocked when she knocked on my door earlier, asking me to go out.

"How have things been with you?" Slowly, she rolls her head in my direction.

We're both tipsy, filling our time with tossing back drinks rather than actually catching up on girl talk, something she used as the reason for wanting to hang out tonight.

"I'm still fucking broke," she mutters, holding her hand in the air to flag a waitress after she drains her drink.

"I can ask Dad about a job at the firm," I offer. "You graduated with a business degree same as me."

"Work?" she scoffs, and it makes my hackles rise.

I've taken an entry level position at my dad's office, and I have to say I'm enjoying myself even though I'm not much more than an errand girl right now. He may have spotted me the job, but he doesn't believe in nepotism. I'm going to have to work my ass off before I can advance.

"I'm not going to work." She rolls her eyes, giving a lazy glance to the guy across the room that's been trying to get her attention. The man doesn't stand a chance. The Brooks Brothers suit he's wearing may turn eyes for other women, but anything short of Brioni wouldn't impress her.

"I love my job there," I interject.

"Well, you're more suited for manual labor."

I could argue that it doesn't even come close to manual labor, but she's never listened to me before.

Conversation once again comes to a standstill, and she doesn't speak again until we've both downed two more drinks.

"I can't believe I gave up Deacon, and I'm still poor."

The words come out as a self-reflection rather than a conversation starter, but she has my complete drunken attention. There are two concerns at play here, so I address the one that could cut me the worst first.

"You still love him?"

She huffs again, and it's one of the disrespectful reactions I've come to expect from her lately.

"Love?" Another eye roll. "Deacon was the best lay I've ever had until Nikolay came along. Now that Russian god knows how to make a woman purr."

"Deacon was the love of your life," I remind her.

"I never said that." Her words are low and indignant, the slur of her tone almost enough to make me believe her.

"Yes, you did. Numerous times. At the aquarium, at prom, and about a thousand other times." I'm blaming the extensive alcohol intake for being unable to just leave well enough alone.

"In high school?"

She actually laughs at me, or maybe she's laughing at the idea, but I keep my mouth shut. If there's anything I've learned about Dani, it's that she loves to hear her own voice, and that need only increases when she's been drinking.

"No one finds their true love in high school, Anna."

I could argue with her. My parents fell in love in school and have been married for decades, happily to boot.

"I felt more for Nikolay than I ever did Deacon. Hell, I still do and that man tried to kill me."

The waitress delivers fresh drinks, and I reach for mine faster than any self-respecting woman should, but even with the copious amount I've consumed already, it isn't even close to being enough to deal with what she's telling me.

Wouldn't not loving Deacon or not counting him as her soulmate, the one that got away, make a difference for me? If I could find happiness in his arms when she doesn't miss his embrace be okay? Wouldn't a real friend see how much I've been hurting for weeks with his absence?

Don't even get me started on returning to my apartment to find it completely cleaned and refurnished. On top of that act of kindness, he even had the painting Zeni gave to me restored as best he could considering the damage that was done to it. He even returned the check I sent to cover the hotel expenses and shopping I incurred while I was there. That last one hit differently than the kindness. It was a slap in the face, the final *I don't want you in my life*. The one reason I haven't reached out to him since we've been back.

"But seriously, had I known Deacon was going to end up rich, I never would've left him."

As if she didn't just explode a bomb in front of me, Dani winks at the guy across the bar.

I take a long slow breath, wanting to just get up and walk away. In doing so, I know I won't be just walking away from tonight. When I leave, I know that will be the end of this lifetime friendship, if you can even call it that.

"You left him because he wasn't rich?" My tone is as calm as the gin will allow.

"Anna, seriously? Didn't you see how I was living?"

"You mean the cute house he used his enlistment money to put a down payment on?"

"Cute? The square footage of that house was smaller than my suite at my parents' house."

"I thought you were happy there?"

She shakes her head, a look of confusion on her face. I know I would've been happy there. She had three bedrooms, and an amazing backyard. I distinctly remember a conversation we had about how much fun their kids would have playing in the fenced-in backyard.

"I wasn't happy. We were even poorer than I am now, and that's saying something because if that guy over there doesn't pick up my tab, I'm going to need you to pay for these drinks."

So, reading between the lines, she wanted me to come out tonight to foot the bill. Wow, things just keep getting better.

"You know," she leans in closer, her actions slightly sloppy, "I told him I needed more money for groceries, and he had the nerve to suggest I clip coupons from the Sunday paper."

"No!" I hiss dramatically, covering my mouth.

"See? Now you understand just how bad things were." I'd blame her being drunk on her inability to detect my sarcasm, but alas, she still thinks I'm completely on her side and would even if she hadn't been drinking.

"So you divorced him?"

"Daddy wouldn't let me come home if I was still with him." She takes another long drink, once again draining her glass and flagging down the waitress. I tilt mine back just to keep up. "Plus, Charles had a better offer."

"Better offer? You didn't start dating Charles until after you and Deacon split."

My blood runs cold when she rolls her eyes at me again.

"You cheated on Deacon?" I nearly scream in disgust.

Her head snaps in my direction faster than I thought possible. Usually her reactions are lazy, a little fuck you to whoever may have upset her, because she'd rather be caught dead than having a visceral reaction.

Instead of opening her mouth to speak, she curls her lip in a menacing sneer.

"Did he cheat on you first?"

The sneer turns into a frown.

"Really? I had that man wrapped around my finger. If he sucked in bed, I would've denied him access to my body, and he'd still follow me around like a lost dog looking for scraps of affection."

"Th-that's disgusting, Dani."

"Still the truth."

"How did I never see the real you before?"

"I've always been real."

She can't even be bothered to look me in the eye right now, and it's not because she's ashamed of her confessions. No, Dani just doesn't give a shit about anything or anyone. She claimed to love Deacon, wanted to spend the rest of her life with him and have his children, when from the sounds of it, she never really cared at all. It's almost as if he was a way to piss her parents off until her father maintained his side of the threat and cut her off. Maybe out of spite, she kept Deacon on a string for the six years they were married.

"I can't believe I chose you over him."

"Chose?" she snaps, her eyes finally showing some heat. "Has he contacted you over the last month? Deacon doesn't want you. Whatever you two had, even though you're continuing to lie about it, wasn't real. If anything, he tried hooking up with you as a second-place replacement because he lost me."

Slap, punch, kick.

That's exactly what it feels like she just did to me.

"Wow." I turn up my drink, draining the last of it before flagging down the waitress. I hand over the payment for my drinks, making sure she knows I'm not paying for Dani's. It's a petty move, but this woman has sucked enough from my life already. If I'm going to walk away with a clean slate, it starts here and now.

"You can't be serious," she hisses when I stand and offer the credit card slip back to the waitress.

"That guy over there will probably help you out. Let him know before you climb into his bed tonight that you don't love anything or anyone but yourself."

She has the audacity to chuckle at me.

"Anna, wait!" I don't get more than a few feet from her before she's calling after me, but when I turn her way, it isn't the death of our friendship that has her beckoning me. "Are you really not going to pay for my drinks?"

"Fuck you, Dani."

Like I've told a hilarious joke, her laughter follows me out of the bar.

I'm gutted for the second time in the last month. I knew the "breakup" with my oldest friend was coming. Honestly, I'm shocked it took me this long to stand up to her when the regret of being linked to her started the day my condo got trashed. Dani will be just fine, however. She's like a cat with nine lives, and she always lands on her feet.

What kills me most when I walk away is the hate and disgust I had for Deacon because he had her attention for so long. Now I feel sorry for the guy because he was somehow the long con, living his life through her manipulation. I never should've pulled away from him when he reached for me. If things were different, if I could turn back time, I would've asked for privacy without even climbing off his lap when Dani barged into that hotel suite.

Now I've gotten rid of the most toxic thing in my life, only I wasn't brave enough to do it before it poisoned what Deacon and I could've had.

And that's a regret I'll have to live with forever.

Chapter 37
Deacon
Another Month Later

"I've been wondering where you go every evening."

"Shut up," I hiss.

"I'd like to say I would never have predicted this, but honestly I'm not surprised at all."

Flynn's British accent is even more annoying than normal for some reason today. If cuffing my hands over my ears wasn't immature, I'd do it just to be able to sit here in silence for five damn minutes.

"Are we expecting a problem?"

"You said you'd keep your damn mouth shut if I let you tag along," I mutter. "Do I need to shove you out of the fucking car?"

"I thought we were going to a movie. My silence would be required for that. This?" He points toward the building I've become all too familiar with over the last couple of weeks. "This doesn't require silence. How often are you doing this?"

I don't answer him, but that in and of itself is his answer. His chuckle tells me so.

"Every day?"

"Not every day," I argue. "Some days I'm caught up with work."

"And?" he asks with a snort because he knows me all too well.

"On those days, I have one of the other guys do it."

"You've never asked me. I think I'm offended by that."

"The other guys don't give me shit."

"To your face," he clarifies.

I wouldn't doubt that the guys are gossiping about me behind my back, but I don't even look over at my friend for confirmation. Taking my eyes from the front of the building means I may miss the ten seconds I've grown to live for.

"And why do you sit outside of Anna's building every evening?"

I narrow my eyes but don't take them from the man holding the front door open as the chauffeured sedan slows to a stop in front.

"I don't think this is healthy."

"Shh."

Another laugh I refuse to acknowledge.

"Ahh," he nearly whispers when the back door of the sedan opens and a tanned leg emerges. "She looks amazing."

I'd have to agree with him, but that doesn't stop the growl that rumbles from my throat. I still haven't forgiven him for walking into the hotel suite and seeing him running his hands through her long, dark hair. I didn't feel for her then as strongly as I do now, but it still pissed me off like nothing before. Now? Well, let's just say he better snap his jaw closed or it'll end up needing to be wired shut.

I contemplate that, knowing it would be beneficial to me if the fucker couldn't talk for six weeks as I watch Anna smile at her doorman. Even Genaro, the man old enough to be her grandfather holding the door, can't resist letting his eye drop to her shapely ass as she walks by.

"A jury will hang you if you kill an elderly person," Flynn says, reading my mind.

"Might be worth it," I grumble, angling my head as if it would make it possible to keep my eyes on her for a single second longer.

It doesn't and before long, she disappears into the building.

"Are you fucking kidding me?"

I may not have shocked Flynn by what I'm doing right now, but he does sound surprised when he watches Ignacio drive by with a wave as he passes my parked SUV.

"You have them follow her from work?"

I shrug. "I want to make sure she's safe."

"Wren has kept tabs on the Russians for the last two months, and there hasn't been a peep of trouble. Are you lying to me, or worse yet, are you lying to yourself?"

"Did you forget about the gangbanger?" I'll never be able to, especially with the nightmares that wake me up when I do get tired enough to sleep. That guy got too close for comfort, and it still haunts me.

"Did you forget the raid that St. Louis PD did? Those fuckers are running scared from the heat on their little organization. They don't have the time or the energy to worry about revenge."

"Stupid people do stupid things."

He snorts another laugh. "You don't say?"

His eyes dart from me to the quiet front of Anna's building.

"Do we sit here all night, or are you done stalking her until tomorrow?"

I'd argue that I'm not stalking her, but even I can see the creepiness in my behavior.

He doesn't say a word for the next hour and a half as I sit and wait to see if Anna is going to go out this evening. It's Friday night, and although she hasn't gone far from her building in the last month, I know she's a social person. For all the grief she gave me while she was holed up at the Four Seasons, she's not been socializing as actively as I had originally predicted.

"You know it would be easier to have Wren keep track of her."

His words startle me. With my focus on her building and the swirling thoughts in my head, I'd forgotten I wasn't alone in the vehicle.

"That would be too creepy."

"Says the man watching a front door. What if she leaves from the parking garage or the rear entrance?"

I swallow, but don't answer his question.

"Jesus, really? Who do you have back there?"

I flex my jaw, not wanting to answer but knowing he'll hound me until I do. "Ignacio is in the garage. Gaige is on the back entrance."

"And you don't think this is a waste of BBS resources?"

I crack my neck, hands tightening on the steering wheel. I placed them there fifteen minutes ago when the voice in my head almost won out over my need to sit and wait, but I haven't gotten the resolve to put the SUV in drive just yet.

"They're my resources to waste."

He grunts but doesn't say another word for the next five minutes.

"Why do you sit out here when the girl you love is inside?"

"I don't—" I clench my teeth. Denying it wouldn't matter. We both know how I feel, and despite what Flynn said earlier, I'm not lying to myself about any of it. No sense in trying to deny it to him.

Flynn turns slightly in his seat, angling his body so he's facing me better. I already know what's coming, and maybe that's why I allowed him to tag along this evening. Maybe I've tortured myself long enough. He's either going to encourage me to go up and plead my case or he's going to tell me to nut up and get over it.

"This isn't healthy."

His tone is lower, comforting almost, and I let my eyes close because this could still go either way.

"Your attitude has been better this last month." I've just gotten better at hiding it and actively not taking my frustrations out on my men. "We all see how much it's costing you."

"I'm fine," I tell him instinctively. I haven't let my personal issues interfere with the job, and even though he's my closest friend, I haven't come to him for advice. I haven't reached out to anyone. My parents have noticed the distance, and even though my guys have been trying to get me to do stuff outside of work like they did in the past, I just can't bring myself to do it. Focusing during work is one thing. Having a few drinks with the boys would probably end up with me getting emotional over losing her. I swallow again, frustrated, but not really with Flynn.

"You haven't shaved in weeks. You look like a yeti."

I got the impression from my interactions with Anna that she liked facial hair, so I've kept it. Also, it's almost impossible to garner enough strength to care what I look like these days. Fuck, if I were on the outside looking in, if I were watching Flynn go through this, I'd probably have his mental health evaluated.

My friend sighs when I don't respond, but being the nosy dick that he is, it doesn't deter him.

"I watched her on the plane ride back from the Maldives." Another flex of my hands on the steering wheel. Another clench of my jealous jaw. "She watched you."

"She was too busy playing into Dani's hands for that," I argue.

"She loves you, too."

Damn it. If she only did, that would change everything.

"You're letting her slip away. The longer you sit here instead of going to her and laying it all at her feet, the greater risk that she's going to find someone else who's man enough to speak his mind." I resist the urge to pull my gun from my hip to shut him up. "She's a fucking ten, man. Probably a fifteen for any man who has fuc—"

I snap my head in his direction. "Finish that sentence and I'll tell your mother you died in a training accident."

There isn't a smile on his face. He isn't trying to goad me, and that hits a little harder than if he was.

"You know she's going to move on. One day while you're sitting outside of this building, she's going to start entertaining the idea of finding someone else. You have an opportunity. Don't waste it."

I mull over his words for a while. If anything, it gives me a little more time to watch the doors to make sure she doesn't leave.

"So tomorrow, I'm supposed to just walk up to her and lay it all out?"

"No. She has plans tomorrow night."

"So Sunday? Monday?"

"Why put off 'til tomorrow what you can do today."

"Thomas Jefferson? Who knew you were such a patriot?" I mutter.

Chapter 38

Anna

"Are you getting enough sleep?"

I give my mom a practiced smile, but like any good mother, she can see right through me.

"If work is too much, I can ask your dad to cut you some slack."

If work were my only problem, I'd be just fine. It's the insomnia I can't seem to manage without a few drinks each night that I'm struggling with. Since I've cleared out all the alcohol from my condo as a precautionary measure to not become an alcoholic, I'm left restless each and every night.

"I stayed up too late watching TV last night," I lie. Well, it's only a partial lie. I did lounge on the couch for countless hours with the television on, but I couldn't focus on the home renovation show that was on mute.

She frowns at me briefly before plastering another smile on her pretty face, knowing I'm not being completely honest, but this isn't the time or the place for confrontation.

"Ah, there are the Westons. Try to have a good time, dear." Mom pats my arm before gliding away to mingle.

Since it's a social event and expected, I have a glass of champagne in my hand. When I lifted it from the server's tray, I told myself it was only for show. Drinking hasn't had the same appeal it had in years past, but I'm giving myself a pass tonight, praying I can leave at the height of my buzz and actually manage some sleep tonight.

I know why I'm restless, why I toss and turn even when actively trying to keep my head clear of where my brain constantly insists it should go. It's exhausting, but even yoga and meditation can't keep him from creeping inside of me. I bought a ton of craft stuff from a late-night infomercial, intent on doing something to take my mind off him, but it became clear very quickly that buying craft things and doing craft things are two totally different animals.

"I could say I'm surprised, but I'm not."

I grind my teeth at the familiar voice, deciding to stand my ground rather than walking away.

"You never could resist the urge to mirror everything I do." There's laughter in Dani's voice, but the insult speaks louder.

I cut my eyes to her when she stands by my side, Cosmo in hand. Her daring midthigh-length dress sparkles under the soft lighting, but it isn't emerald green like she insisted it would be on the plane ride back from the Maldives two months ago. Nope, of course it isn't. Her dress is white, just like the floor-length one I'm wearing.

"Mirror?" I scoff, lifting my drink to my lips, all the while contemplating if being a petty bitch right now would be best. I know what my mother would say, *be the bigger person*, but the way Dani is holding her mouth in that way that tells me she still thinks she's better than me makes the decision for me.

See, classic Dani will stand here and chitchat with me, making rude comments camouflaged by her smile and tinkling tone, but after taking a step back and evaluating many of the conversations we've had in the past, I've come to realize, she's always been a bitch. Before, I thought she saved her cattiness for everyone else, and since I was part of her innermost circle, she didn't treat me that way. Let's just say I've seen the light.

"How can I mirror you tonight? I never would've thought you'd wear the same dress twice."

Her head snaps back, and it makes my petty little heart sing, even though I'd never call someone out the way I just did her. Honestly, who cares if she's wearing a recycled dress. I've wanted to wear the same thing more than once because I have some killer dresses that deserve to shine multiple times, but the fear of being gossiped about kept me from doing so. Thankfully, this is the last event I have to worry about for the year, and I've already trimmed down next year's calendar.

"I'd never." She glares at me over the top of her drink before her eyes roam the room to see if anyone else is thinking the same thing.

"You wore that very same Dolce and Gabbana to the Spring Fling last year."

She swallows her vitriol as two tuxedoed men walk past, and I know it's just killing her not to immediately spit some bullshit my way. I've never been in a fight in my life, and I would never intentionally embarrass my parents, but Dani has the ability to make both of those things change tonight. Fire is raging through my blood. Add in the fact that I've slept like crap for the last two months, and I'm seconds away from an episode of *Snapped*.

"They're similar, but not the same," she argues.

I just drain my glass. Arguing will get me nowhere, and I've wasted years of my life on this woman. Thankfully, a distraction approaches.

"Good evening," I say, doing my best to hide my smirk as Dani practically twitches beside me.

Charles Warren leans in to kiss both of my cheeks before stepping aside so his beautiful wife, Brooke, can greet me with a quick hug. Both ignore Dani, and I hope she's dying inside from the mistakes she's made. I imagine it's another slap in the face for the man you left your first husband for to saunter up with his gorgeous wife. The huge diamond on her finger sparkles in the chandelier light, and I do a little happy dance to see that it's an upgrade from the stone he presented Dani with years ago.

"I hear you're working with your father," Charles says, his arm wrapping tightly around his wife's back.

I'm so grateful he was able to break free of Dani. It would be a shame for another man to get tangled up in her selfish web.

"Working for my father," I clarify with a bright, genuine smile. "It's entry level."

"Builds character," Charles responds. "Brooke has decided to stay home once the baby gets here."

Dani gasps, but the couple standing in front of me don't spare her a glance. Dani tried pulling the *I'm pregnant, don't leave me* card when Charles caught her cheating, and even back then I was shocked how easy it was to purchase positive pregnancy tests online. But Charles is a smart man, and after insisting on a visit to his personal doctor, the lie was uncovered and he walked away.

"Congrats!" I hug Brooke a second time, truly happy for them. She isn't showing yet, but that doesn't keep her hands from roaming to her lower belly protectively.

We chat for a few moments longer before they say their goodbyes.

I don't move a muscle, knowing what's coming next. Regardless of our conversation last month at the martini bar, Dani can't resist the urge to gossip, and she's so self-centered she can't operate in a life where I'm not stuck right by her side. I honestly don't think she believes that we're no longer friends even though I haven't spoken to or seen her since I walked out of the bar until tonight. I'm not missing from her life. I'm sure she thinks I'm still in her corner because she hasn't needed me at all this month.

"She's going to look like a cow in a couple of months."

Right on cue.

"Her face is already bloated."

It's not, but even if it was, Brooke would still look amazing.

"She's absolutely gorgeous. She and Charles are going to have beautiful kids." I lift my champagne glass to my lips, finding it drained. Instead of flagging down a waitress, I set the flute down on the table beside me and clasp my hands. So much for my goal to drink more this evening. I can't lose my wits around the vile woman standing beside me.

"What is wrong with you?"

I smile, giving a quick wave to another couple as they walk past, and I can practically feel Dani growing even more agitated beside me. It's the little things in life, the cheap thrills that I live for these days.

"Seriously?" she spits when I continue to ignore her. "Is this still about Deacon?"

My heart gallops with his name. Although I've been unsuccessful with keeping him from my mind, I'm not in the same circles as he is. I haven't heard his name spoken once since the night I walked away from Dani, and it hits me square in the chest.

Dani must register my reaction, as a little laugh slips past her overpainted lips.

"Is he here?"

My spine stiffens, shoulders rolling back as I do my best to build my defenses. I'm a strong woman, but there are still a few things that can bring me to my knees. Unfortunately, Dani just honed in on the easiest one. I hate being so vulnerable around her.

Dropping her as a friend has been the best thing I could've ever done, and after tonight, I won't have to see her ever again. Her father was arrested last week by the feds, and I know she's only here as a last-ditch effort to snag a rich man who can take care of her. She must not have many options, however, since she's been stuck by my side for the last hour.

"I'm talking about Deacon," she clarifies when I don't verbally respond. "He isn't, is he?"

My eyes scan the crowd, and I refuse to feel guilty when I locate a server and get his attention. I'll give myself one more hour of being here before I fake a headache to my parents and leave. The server approaches, extending his tray, and I thank him as I grab a flute. Dani rudely drops her empty glass on it, nearly toppling the full ones, but the server steadies the tray as she lifts two flutes.

Double fisting her drinks right now is more telling of her downfall than the recycled dress, and I don't even hide the smirk when I reposition my body so I can see her better. I wouldn't put it past this woman to pour a drink down my dress. Pettiness has always been her go-to when she feels bested.

"So, you decided to stop being my friend for a man who doesn't want you? Classic, Anna." Her eyes sparkle with venom as she lifts one of the flutes to her lips. "You must be so lonely."

"I'm not—"

Her gasp stops me short, and I take a step back defensively, waiting for her to splash the front of my dress with her drink, but I see her eyes focused over my shoulder.

My heart pounds. The only person who I'd expect to cause that sort of reaction from her is Nikolay Petrovich, and I'm terrified for my life even before I spin to see who has shocked her.

Only when I turn, I don't find and angry Russian. If it weren't for the sparkling blue eyes pinned to mine, I wouldn't even recognize the bearded man dressed in a solid black tuxedo.

Chapter 39
Deacon

Bright honey-colored eyes follow me as I make my way across the room. I don't even hesitate after seeing that Dani is standing beside the girl I'm after. If anything, my ex witnessing this makes it even more perfect.

My hands are trembling, fear of rejection swimming in my gut, but I have years of practice at not letting my feelings show. I drop every one of those walls when I reach her. I had a speech planned, a long diatribe of reasons she should let me love her, but words fail me when she's within reach.

Instinctively, my hand caresses her cheek, and even though it's clear she's shocked, she leans into the touch like she's been drowning without it.

Instead of words, I use my lips to speak my truth. Her chin is quivering with emotions, but this beautiful woman kisses me back. The slow glide of our tongues says a million things. They confess the things I'll make sure she's certain of before we close our eyes tonight.

"Anna," I whisper against her mouth, and she responds by twisting her fingers in the front of my shirt.

Dani gasps beside the two of us, but I don't spare a single second on my past. I'm looking forward, looking to the future, and if I somehow get lucky enough, that's going to include the woman in my arms.

"How are you here?" Anna asks when I inch my face back just enough to look into her beautiful eyes.

"Wren synced our calendars," I confess.

This party is what Flynn was talking about last night when he was trying to convince me to make my move. The image of her bringing a different man tonight ate away at me all fucking night, and I'll examine why it took jealousy for me to take this step at a later point.

"I've missed you."

"Baby," I whisper, pressing my mouth to hers one more time. "I've been miserable. I wanted to do what was right. I didn't want to interfere with your life, but I've been regretting every single second since I walked away from you. I regret the time we've lost, the things we could've been doing. I miss having you in my arms. I miss your sass, and the way your eyes sparkle after too much whiskey. Everything. I miss fucking everything."

Her eyes search mine, darting back and forth as if she can't believe I'm real. Hell, I'm terrified this is another dream because there's no way she's clinging to me right now. There's no way all it was going to take was to come to her and tell her how I felt. Could I have ended this misery months ago? Will she ever be able to forgive me for not being man enough to admit how much I need her?

"Are you fucking kidding me right now?"

Anna keeps her eyes on me, ignoring the angry woman at her side. Dani no longer exists to her, and that fact is clear in her eyes.

"You haven't been sleeping well," I observe, running a thumb softly under her eye. She's glowing, don't get me wrong, but even makeup can't cover the slight bruising.

"You either," she whispers looking at my own face.

"Is that going to change?" It's an indirect question, and I hope she understands the significance of it.

"I want it to."

I kiss her again because how could I not? I hate that we're in public. I hate that there are too many layers of clothing between our bodies right now. I hate that I didn't go to her last night at Flynn's insistence, but being here is a statement of its own. I hate these kinds of things. I hate the restriction the tie is causing around my neck. I hate shiny shoes and fake-ass people with more money than sense. But I'm here, proving a point. If this is part of her life, then it's going to be part of mine as well, if she allows it.

"I love you," I confess.

Dani gasps again, but Anna doesn't seem as surprised as a gorgeous smile curves her wicked mouth.

"That so?"

"I've never loved someone as much as I love you."

Her throat works on a swallow as her eyes turn glossy. One single tear pools on her lower lash, but I kiss it away.

"I can't promise you an eternity because my job is dangerous, but I promise to love you every night my head hits my pillow and every single day I'm granted the opportunity to wake up."

"Deacon," she says, her voice cracking, filled with emotion.

"Everything before you was smoke and mist, inconsequential distractions from what I really needed. I see you, Annalise Grimaldi, and I'll never let anything make me lose sight of that again."

"I never should've denied what was happening betwe—"

I press my fingers to her lips. "No going back. We're only moving forward."

She puckers her lips, kissing my fingertips before turning her head to press those same petal soft lips to the inside cuff of my wrist.

"I love you, too."

I swear angels are singing, serenading us with joy.

"Yeah?" She nods her head. I pull her against me, leaning down so I can bury my neck into the soft fragrant curls of her hair.

***

"We can go slower," I pant the second I open her condo door, but she's ravenous, tugging my mouth down to hers while tugging my shirt out of the stupid black pants I'm wearing tonight. I'll never love getting dressed up in a penguin suit, but maybe one day, I won't completely hate it.

"I don't understand the question."

I laugh, my hands going straight to her ass. The pull of her against my now bare chest isn't exactly comfortable. The sequins or beads or whatever it is on the front of her dress abrades my skin, but maybe I deserve the bite of pain for staying away so long. I know I want to whip my own ass right now. Sixty-six days have passed since the diamonds were handed over to Petrovich, and I've counted each and every damn one because it meant lying down in my empty bed without her.

"You're like a crazed animal right now," I hiss when she tears at the buttons of my slacks to get to the hidden zipper.

"Calm down."

I placed my hands over hers, clasping them until she looks up at me. Her face falls, and I wonder if she thinks I'm going to put a stop to this. For the record, there isn't any way to stop this train. I'm simply trying to prevent it from breaking down long before it reaches the station. I haven't had her in months, and even though I've only had her once, the memories of that glorious morning are imprinted in my head. I want to create a million more, starting tonight.

"You're fucking gorgeous," I tell her, one hand positioning her arms behind her back, and the other looking for the zipper of her dress.

She looks fucking bridal in all white with her tanned skin glowing. The sight of her from across the room earlier made all sorts of thoughts swim through my head, a couple of questions I plan to ask, but I think right now may be a little too soon for that, no matter if she told me she loved me.

"On the side," she urges when I run my hand down her back for the third time. "Let me help you."

I grip her just a little harder. I can't have her hands on me right now. I'm barely clinging to my control as it is. Hell, if it wasn't for the sake of her modesty and the threat of getting arrested, I would've laid her out on the damn floor at the gala and devoured her.

Anna breathes a sigh of relief when I lower the side-zipper on her dress, but I'm the one at a loss for words as the fabric pools around her feet. She was a fucking sight in the dress, but the devil-red lace remaining makes my mouth run dry.

"Fuck me."

I take a step back, sweeping my eyes up her body, letting my gaze linger at the triangle of fabric between her thighs before lifting my eyes enough to notice her peaked nipples straining the lace covering her breasts.

"You are fucking glorious."

"Take it off," she urges, her hands reaching back to unclasp her bra.

"No fucking way." I reach for her hands, but she's faster.

I watch, torn between absolute awe and disappointment, as the strapless garment falls to the floor. The wicked gleam in her eyes tell me she knows she has the upper hand right now. She's so much in control, I don't realize she's moved until the cool air of her apartment hits the tip of my cock.

"Commando?" I look down at her, the height difference between us drastic while she's standing so close to me. "That's hot."

"I... umm... couldn't." I swallow, trying to remember what I was going to say. "The pants were too tight on my thighs."

Hopefully, that explains enough. Her grin tells me it doesn't even matter right now.

"You tasted me at your ranch."

"Dying to again."

"It's my turn."

This woman has been sent from heaven. Of that I'm certain. I can't take my eyes off of her as she lowers to the floor in nothing but a scrap of lace covering her heavenly treasure. She keeps her head tilted, eyes locked on mine as her tongue snakes out, swiping away the desire that has beaded at the tip.

Of its own volition, my body jolts, the sensation of that one lick taking over my entire body.

"Fuck, that's good," I praise when she sucks the head.

God, I'm going to fucking embarrass myself in minutes, but she told me she loves me, so that's got to help when I have to apologize, right?

How did I keep my eyes closed the entire time we were together that first time? I knew even then that being with her was different, and I tried to keep inside of that dreamlike state, but man did I miss seeing her. Never again. I'll never close my eyes because I can't miss a second of this. Her cheeks hollow as she sucks me down as far as she can manage, but she's too eager for her own good.

When she pulls her mouth from my cock, I want to hug her to my chest, hold on to her and never let her go, but she isn't having it.

"Kick off your shoes. Get that shirt all the way off. Hurry."

My hands immediately start to do her bidding. "Are we going to do this right here in the foyer?"

She looks around us from our feet to the sofa on the other side of the room, and then down the hall. I hate this apartment, condo, and to fully rid ourselves of the toxicity that lives next door, she's going to have to move. I'm wondering how many orgasms it will take before I can convince her to move to the ranch with me?

"I want to make love in my bed," she says, decision made.

I watch as she walks away, the movement of her curves too much to resist. I don't snap out of the trance until she winks at me over her shoulder before disappearing into her bedroom. It takes a millisecond before I'm turning the corner into the room, but she's a speed demon because I find her lace panties discarded on the floor and she's splayed out like a dessert buffet on her bed.

"Fucking heaven on earth," I mutter as I make my way across the room, stroking the length of my dick.

A cursory swipe of my tongue up her slit is all I can manage right now, and after a brief apology and a promise to make it up to her on round two, I position myself between her legs.

"I love you," I vow as I shift forward and sink inside.

"Too," she says with a groan, and I take a little pride that she's disoriented right now. God, I hope this never changes.

We cling to each other, my hips moving and hers answering in kind until our bodies are so slick with sweat that it's hard to hold on. With her legs wrapped like straps around my hips, I cover her body with mine, slowly rocking into her with our mouths fused together.

"Deacon," she whispers. It's both a plea and a warning, but my girl knows I'm going to get her there.

She whimpers with the first clench of her core, but that keening cry turns into a moan that will feature in my fantasies for years to come when I increase not only the length of my stroke inside of her but the power behind it.

"Oh shit!" Her fingers slip on my back, nails unable to find purchase in my skin as I bury my nose in her throat and follow her over the edge.

Chapter 40
Anna

I don't wake this morning with the same dread as I have for weeks, but that still doesn't keep me from frowning when I roll over and face the empty side of the bed. If it weren't for the warmth still clinging to the sheets and the glorious smells coming from my kitchen, I might possibly lose my shit.

After cleaning up last night, an act that had Deacon leaning over my back as I scrubbed makeup from my face while promising all sorts of wicked things, we fell into the bed, an exhausted pile and promptly passed out.

My phone buzzes on the bedside table twice before I pull my nose from the sheets Deacon slept on all night. I'm obsessed, totally gone over that man, and I don't feel an ounce of shame about it. We have a ton of things to talk about. I have apologies and assurances to make, but the world waits for no one I realize when I look down at the text message on my phone. The outside world is going to come in and invade our bubble whether we want it to or not.

I groan after walking into the bathroom. My hair is an absolute mess, and I didn't do a very good job cleaning my face last night because clumps of mascara still cling to my lashes. I spend a few minutes rewashing my face and taking care of my morning business before joining Deacon in the kitchen.

Much like at the ranch, I stand to the side, watching him as he cooks at the stove. His tuxedo pants hang loosely on his hips and the muscles of his broad back flex and twist as he shifts a spatula around a frying pan.

"I thought you only knew how to cook chicken and dumplings and chili."

He doesn't even jump at the sound of my voice. Of course he knew I was approaching, commando that he is. At least he gave me the opportunity to ogle his toned, male perfection. It's the little things that will keep the thrill of being with him alive.

Love!

We both said it last night, but I would've been able to read it in his gorgeous eyes even if he didn't make that confession beforehand. Maybe that's why he refused to look at me the first time we slept together. Maybe he was afraid of what I would've been able to deduce. He wasn't ready then, and I can say I may not have been either, but losing two months that we could've spent together sucks no matter how you cut it.

"I don't know if you'd call this cooking." Deacon grins over his shoulder as he lifts the skillet from the stove, angling it so I can look inside.

I wince, my head pulling back before I can stop it.

"Wow," he says with a chuckle. "I thought couples were supposed to build each other up, not cut one another down."

"And I didn't think you'd try to kill me less than twelve hours after confessing your love for me." I run my hand down the length of his back, letting it rest just an inch or so above his perfect ass because I know neither one of us will be eating actual food if I let it drop lower. "Eggs aren't supposed to look like that."

"By all means, master. Show me how it's done."

He moves the skillet of inedible food to the side so I can take over, but the entire time I'm making breakfast, he doesn't drift far. Unless he's grabbing something from the fridge or pulling dishes down from the cabinets, he's plastered to my back in the most erotic way possible. He doesn't even try to hide the erection that's straining in his slacks or stop his hands from roaming down my body. I nearly ruin the second attempt at breakfast when he begins licking my neck and teasing the tips of my breasts at the same time.

"It's never been like this for me before," I confess nearly breathless from his touch.

"Mmm." His mouth is once again on my neck, and thankfully the eggs are done and I can remove the pan from the fire. "I sure hope not."

"This isn't eating breakfast." I roll my neck even further to the side to give him better access.

"It's going to lead to my breakfast." His fingers release my aching breasts, traveling down until his thick fingers are slipping past the loose band of my lounge pants.

"Deacon, we should eat." I haven't popped our little love bubble, but it's coming.

"It would be easier to listen to your words if your pussy wasn't spasming around my fingers."

"I can't help it." I moan again, swiveling my ass in an attempt to tease him just as much as he's teasing me.

"So needy." His words are a growl in my ears, but then his harsh pants fade into the distance as my body obeys the commands his fingers are demanding. "Give it to me."

If it weren't for his arm banded around my waist, the orgasm would make me crumple to the ground.

"Fuck, how did I keep my hands off of you for so damn long?"

I hiss, oversensitized, when he pinches my swollen clit before pulling his hand free.

I clear my throat to cover a laugh when I try to stand up straight and my knees don't want to work.

"You okay there?" The laughter in his tone makes me reach back to smack at his chest, but the sight of him sucking his fingers clean when I turn around leaves me breathless once again.

This man is a walking orgasm. How did I get so lucky to call him mine?

"My turn," I whisper, pressing my mouth to his, but he stops me before I can drop to my knees. I've yet to get him off with my mouth, and I can't wait to see how delirious he gets when his pleasure is the only thing he has to worry about. "What?"

"Let's eat."

My brow furrows. "You want to eat right now?"

"I'm hungry." There's a teasing twinkle in his eyes as he takes a step back.

"So that's how you're going to play it?"

He presses his lips to mine once again, but steps back even further when I try to deepen the kiss.

"You're cute when you pout." His fingers run down my cheek, and the warmth makes me feel like I've finally made it home.

When did I get so corny? I'd say about the time he walked up and kissed me without a word last night.

He purposefully sits on the opposite side of the table from me after we plate our meal, but his eyes never leave my face. I can't even begin to explain how important his eyes on me are. I want his focus. I want to be able to see in his eyes what I mean to him, and from the way he's watching me right now speaks of the truths his mouth whispered last night.

"Okay," he mutters, letting his fork drop to his empty plate. "I want to spend the next week in bed with you. Eat up."

I look down at my plate, realizing I've spent the last ten minutes watching him rather than eating.

"Can't," I tell him before stuffing a forkful of eggs into my mouth.

"Like hell you can't. It's happening. I'll tie you up if I have to."

I bite the corner of my lip, loving the threat.

"It would be a shame to not touch you while you're inside of me, but I guess you don't like it when my fingernails dig into your skin."

His eyes heat, promises swirling in the blue. "Hurry and I won't have to do it. I love that you express your pleasure with a little bit of pain."

I begin to eat faster, gaining a quick laugh from him.

"I've spent the last month sitting outside of your apartment."

My fork clatters to my plate. "What?"

He nods his head, eyes darting to the side as embarrassment pinks his cheeks. "Yeah. Every day since you started working for your dad. I waited across the street just so I could see you for ten seconds every day."

I have to cough to clear the emotions clogging my throat. "I've been so lonely."

"I know, baby." He stands from the table, coming around to my side and I don't waste a second wrapping my arms around his shoulders as he lifts me from my seat like I don't weigh more than a feather.

Man, I love how strong this guy is, but more importantly, I love that he isn't afraid to show his own emotions now that he's accepted his feelings about me.

"I don't ever want you to feel that way again." His tongue traces the column of my neck as he walks us back to the bedroom. "And you won't be lonely when you move to the ranch with me."

I smile, because once again he isn't giving me an option. Even while he's making promises of forever, he's telling me what to do. I honestly love it.

He tosses me on the bed, and a laugh nearly bubbles out, but it stops before it can gain traction because a second later, he's covering my body with his.

"My mom insists we come over today."

He groans. "Can we not talk about your mom while my cock is seconds from fucking you?"

"She texted," I continue as if I didn't just ruin the mood. "She and Dad want to meet the man I snuck off with last night."

With a mildly frustrated sigh, Deacon backs up, leaning back on his haunches as he stares down at me.

"I've met your parents before, Anna."

I know he has, but I'm not going to open my mouth and remind him that it was on his wedding day when he was marrying another woman. Everyone has a history. Ours is just a little more tangled than most.

"They want to meet my man," I clarify instead.

His grin is radiant as he leans over, pressing his mouth to mine.

"They're going to have to wait until this afternoon."

I squeal like a schoolgirl when he strips me down.

We don't make it out of my condo until the sun is sinking low in the sky.

Chapter 41
Deacon

"Can you not walk like that? You might as well be waving a huge red flag right now."

Anna grins over her shoulder as I slowly trail behind her up the front walk of her parents' home.

When she spins to face me, she catches me staring at her delectable ass.

"One, stop staring at my ass." I grin, not looking even a little remorseful. "Two, if we hadn't spent the day in bed, maybe I wouldn't be a little sore."

I grin down at her before cupping her cheeks in my huge hands as I drop a sweet kiss on her mouth.

"Which reminds me, we need to grab condoms on the way back tonight."

I swallow. "You're not on birth control?"

She shakes her head, and I can tell by the apprehensive look in her eyes that she's wondering if I'm on the verge of freaking out.

"No condoms."

"Really?" Surprise fills every feature of her face.

"No condoms."

"No condoms means babies."

"No condoms." My smile grows wider each time I repeat the words.

"No condoms," she agrees.

This is a monumental conversation. It's a need for celebration, and hell, getting started right away as far as I'm concerned, but just as I lower my mouth to hers to seal it with a kiss, the front door swings open wide. I'm not lucky enough to get caught kissing Anna by someone on the house staff. No, both her mother and her father are standing in the doorway watching us. Her mom is smiling with her hand over her heart, and I know she's going to be easy to win over. Her father, always a serious man, is watching us with a stony look on his face.

Anna clears her throat, pulling a foot or so away from me, and I want to remind her that she's thirty years old, but then I remember that

I'm thirty years old as well and mauling a grown woman in front of her parents may come off a little disrespectful.

This will literally be the very first time I've met someone's mother. I married Dani at eighteen, but neither of her parents came to the wedding they didn't support. The first time I saw her mother was in court the day of our divorce. The only time I came face-to-face with Dani's father before we were wed was the time he shot me down in his office.

I don't have the best track record where women are concerned, but I'd do anything for the woman at my side. I want her parents to like me, if only so she doesn't have to choose. It didn't go so well for me the last time when Dani left me to have her trust fund reinstated.

"Mr. and Mrs. Grimaldi."

I walk forward and hold out my hand to her father first. Surprisingly, he takes it immediately, albeit gripping it a little more than necessary. I grip in turn and think I see a hint of respect in his face when the corner of his lip twitches.

"Ma'am." Mrs. Grimaldi swats my hand away and surprises me with a hug.

"I thought we agreed to hold out a little longer," her husband mutters with a laugh, and when I look over, his face is bright with an easy smile.

"You guys are jerks," Anna says with a laugh. "Can we get inside before you start giving him a hard time?"

When Anna's mom releases me, she doesn't go far, keeping one arm wrapped around my waist as she turns to lead us into the house.

From the outside, the home is stately, but to my surprise it's very welcoming on the inside. It's lived in with shoes lined up near the door and a visible coat rack most rich people would refuse to have in their homes.

"We expected you sooner," Mr. Grimaldi says as he leads us to the sitting room, a cozy den with a wide-screen television and a coffee table littered with financial magazines and a deserted half-empty water bottle.

"We already ate, but we can whip together a snack."

Anna doesn't protest for a second and in the blink of an eye, that traitor walks off, leaving me alone with her dad. He points to a spot on the sofa before turning around to sit on a worn recliner. I move in that direction.

"Mr. Grimaldi—"

"Alessio," he corrects.

"Alessio," I amend. "You have a beautiful home."

"We can skip the small talk, Deacon. What are your intensions with my daughter?"

A chuff of laughter escapes my throat, and I pray like hell he doesn't see it as a form of disrespect, but his aggressive words contradict the humor in his tone and the bright light shining in his eyes.

"I love her, sir." He sits back, arms clasped over his rotund stomach, and I know it's hard for him to keep a serious look on his face because his lip keeps twitching like he wants to grin. "Do you interrogate every man she brings home?"

A serious look makes the humor fade away. "Annalise has never brought a man home for us to meet."

I nod, swallowing as I make a mental note to pay extra attention to all of her erogenous zones with my tongue later because I've never felt more special as I do right now in my entire life.

"Never?" I finally manage, and he responds with a quick shake of his head.

"So, if you could just let me have this moment without giving me shit, that would be nice."

I cough to cover a laugh and draw on all my years of training to school my face as best as I can.

"Yes, sir."

"Your intentions?"

"I intend to love her for the rest of my life. I intend to marry her the first chance I get. I intend to make her a mother."

"Hmm." He lifts his clasped hands to his mouth, but his smile is too wide to cover. "Is that so?"

"It is, sir."

"Anything else?"

"I want her to be happy, and I plan to spend every single day making sure that she is."

"Well," he leans forward in a rush, slapping his knees with his hands. "If my little girl is happy, then I'll be happy."

"I appreciate that, sir."

Tears glisten in his eyes, and it's easy to see he never thought the day would come when someone made declarations for his daughter. I'm just so fucking lucky some other guy didn't get here first.

"I think we should rush the wedding. The sooner the better."

I want to argue, tell him that the timeline is up to Anna, but I'm a selfish bastard, and I want to be able to legally call her mine. Plus, no condoms...

"How did it go?" Anna asks with a wide smile as she walks in carrying a tray of drinks. Mrs. Grimaldi walks close behind with finger foods.

"We were just discussing the wedding," her father discloses, drawing a squeal from her mother.

"Wedding?" Anna looks in my direction, but she doesn't seem offended that I haven't asked yet. "Is that so?"

"How does the seventeenth sound?" This man wasn't joking.

"That's only three weeks away," her mother says, somehow putting down the tray and looking down at her phone in the matter of seconds. "But I think it could work."

"Why do I feel railroaded right now?" Anna's eyes are wide as she looks at me. "We can't plan a wedding in three weeks. I don't even have a ring."

"Actually..."

A collective gasp rings out around the room as I stand and shove my hand in my pocket. Dropping to one knee in front of everyone last night was one of the options, the other being the long speech I'd planned. I didn't get to do either one since I was left breathless at the sight of her.

"Really?" Tears fill Anna's eyes, and her mother is crying before I can drop to one knee.

I smile up at my girl. "I promised to love you for the rest of my life, right?"

"Yes," she gasps, her eyes on mine and not the small box in my hand. This is already going ten times better than the last time I did this.

"Will you love me for the rest of yours?"

"Of course." Anna chuckles when her mom exhales a loud sob.

"Marry me?"

Her answer is a kiss to my lips, and the salty tears running down her cheeks taste like a million promises I can't wait to hold her to.

When we finally pull away and I manage to get the ring on Anna's finger, there isn't a dry eye in the house.

"God, I can't wait to start my life with you," I whisper into her neck as her legs go around my waist.

"Deacon," she whispers as she holds onto me even harder.

"Anna," I warn when she moves just a little too much.

God, this is all so damn new, I'm going to have my invitation to the family rescinded if she doesn't settle down. She chuckles, but eventually releases me. Alessio shakes my hand, pulling me in to slap my back heartily.

"So?" her mother prods as she wipes tears of joy from her eyes. "The seventeenth?"

Chapter 42
Deacon

"Is it too much?"

"It's perfect." Anna looks down at the ring on her finger for the hundredth time since leaving her parents' house a couple of minutes ago.

"You're perfect."

"I'm far from perfect, but so long as you keep thinking that, at least until I'm Annalise Black, I think it'll work out."

Fuck, I love the way that sounds.

"I hope you don't feel like I put you on the spot."

"You didn't."

Her eyes are still on her ring, her finger wiggling as the diamond catches the light coming from the dash.

"You'd tell me if it was?"

"I wouldn't have said yes if I didn't want to spend the rest of my life with you."

"You have three weeks to change your mind." I look over at her as we brake at a red light. "After that, I'll never let you go."

There are no doubts for me where she's concerned. I never knew what I was going to get from Dani, and I thought asking her to marry me before leaving for basic training was the right thing to do. I knew if I went away before officially making her mine, I wouldn't have someone to come back home to, and if that isn't fucked up, I don't know what is. Anna is the complete opposite. She isn't with me for anything other than love, and even though we've made numerous declarations in the last day, I don't have a shred of doubt that she's being a hundred percent honest.

"You're not getting rid of me, Deacon Black. I'm yours."

Her hand runs up my thigh, and I can't wait to place the matching wedding band to her ring on that very same finger. I'd suggest getting married tomorrow if I didn't suspect that she has her dream wedding to plan. Three weeks doesn't seem like enough, but maybe she doesn't want the extravagance a longer one would take to plan.

"We have to head to the office. There are a couple of things I need to wrap up before we go on vacation."

"Vacation? I thought we were heading to the ranch."

"We are." I give her a salacious grin. "But we aren't leaving for the next week at least. I nearly embarrassed myself at your parents earlier."

"And you think a week is enough time to get better control over your body?"

I love that she knows exactly what I'm hinting at, but maybe it's because I've been hard nearly every second since I slipped that jewelry on her hand.

"Not nearly enough time," I confess. "But maybe just enough to take the edge off."

"Hmm." It doesn't sound like a consideration, and the way she's watching my face right now has me seconds away from pulling the truck over and proving just how hard it is to wait.

The parking garage is dark and deserted when I pull the truck in, and Anna's head must be in the same place because she's straddling my lap the second it's in park.

"I have an apartment on the tenth floor," I murmur against her mouth. "I can always deal with the office shit tomorrow."

"We're spending the day in bed tomorrow," she reminds me.

"If that's the case, I need you to get off my lap."

"Don't want to."

The way she kisses me makes every cell in my body spark to life, and since the tint is so dark on my truck, I'm honestly considering tugging her jeans down and slipping inside of her right here.

Banging on the window startles her, but I saw Flynn's shadow in the side mirror before his knuckles could meet the glass near my head.

"Go away," I hiss loud enough for him to hear.

"Wren is watching you on the camera. Says he's going to upload the video to the BBS website."

Anna's cheeks burn with embarrassment, and she buries her face in my neck.

I roll down the window, glaring at my friend for interrupting, but at the same time grateful. I know Wren wouldn't really upload things to the Internet, but the man lives behind a computer screen. Anything he watches through his computer screens has a lack of reality behind it.

"Oh, hey there, love." Flynn winks in our direction.

"Hey," Anna mumbles from the crook of my neck.

Flynn disappears, giving us the chance to drop back down to earth.

"Your hand is still on my breast," she reminds me.

I twist her nipple for the humor in her voice.

"We need to get inside."

"To the tenth floor?" she asks with a devious roll of her hips.

"The ninth," I clarify as she rolls back into the passenger seat.

"And how long will we need to sit here before you're presentable?" Her eyes on the erection straining behind the denim of my jeans isn't helping the situation.

"I'll be fine," I assure her as I readjust and climb out.

She gives me her hand, the one with my ring sparkling on it, when I help her out of the truck.

I'm on edge, needing relief the entire ride in the elevator, and I hiss in disappointment when the car stops on the ninth floor. It's late in the evening, so Pam's desk is empty, but the breakroom is filled with my guys.

"I hear congratulations are in order," Brooks says as soon as we walk in, his eyes going straight to Anna's left hand.

"How in the hell?" she gasps when the guys swarm around us.

"Wren," I mutter.

"Don't blame me. Her mother is the one who posted it on social media half an hour ago."

We left the house twenty minutes ago, so that tells me the sly woman did it while we were still at her home.

The guys slap me on the back and give Anna hugs. I have to growl at Flynn when he holds on a little too long, but I find him whispering in Anna's ear, and from the look on her face and the brief nod of her head, I can tell the man isn't trying to give me a hard time. I wonder what words of wisdom he's imparting on her.

He presses a swift kiss to her cheek before clearing his throat and backing away.

"He's been a dick for the last two months," Ignacio says as he approaches. "I'm hoping that changes soon."

"Soon," Gaige says as he claps me on the back. "Do you see the stupid grin on his face? It's already happened."

I can't even argue with him because he's absolutely right. I haven't been able to stop smiling since I walked out of the gala last night hand in hand with the woman I'm going to spend the rest of my life with. Corny as fuck, but hey, if the fucking combat boots fit.

Anna chats with the guys while I head to the office and get some paperwork done. I don't want anything to pull me away from her. Flynn is my second in command, and I know he'll handle business as usual while I'm gone, but there are several things that require my attention before I can go dark for the next week.

When I make it back to the breakroom, the crowd has thinned some, but Anna is sitting on one of the sofas with a large cup of coffee in her hands. Looks like she's smart enough to know she won't be getting much sleep tonight. Flynn chuckles when he notices me looking at the cup.

"Need a cup of coffee, also, boss?"

I flip him the bird before going to my girl.

"Almost done?" Once her hand is in mine, I can't seem to let it go, so I pull her along beside me as I cross the room to Wren's office.

"Put your dick away!" Anna laughs at the bird, but I've learned to start ignoring him.

"What's going on?" I ask when Wren starts a second before his computer screens all go black.

"It's not what it looks like!" Puff Daddy assures us.

"Who were you watching?" All I caught was a glimpse, but it was clear he was watching some form of CCTV when we entered.

"No one." Wren is a worse liar than Anna is, and that's saying something because she couldn't be dishonest if someone threatened her with bodily harm. I've known that as long as I've known her.

"Who's the girl with purple hair?" Anna asks, and if I've ever seen a look of betrayal, it's coming from Wren's blue eyes right now.

"Nice, Anna. Thanks."

After a few clicks, the screens come back to life, but at least Wren seems a little embarrassed to be caught watching Whitney Nelson. My eyes dart around the office, and lo and fucking behold, the box of sex toys he got over a month ago is still sitting in the fucking corner.

"Wren." He swallows with the warning in my voice.

"Uh oh!" the bird squawks. "Busted!"

"You still haven't given that girl her stuff?"

"She's pretty," Anna says as she leans in a little closer to the monitor. Whitney is at the gym, running on a treadmill with a look of pure hatred on her face.

"Wren," I repeat.

"I can't!"

"What's going on?" Anna looks around, confused.

"You have to," I tell him.

"I can't just walk up to a girl and hand her a box of dicks!"

Anna laughs, which sets the damn bird off. Puff Daddy throws his head back and cackles like a fool.

"You can't stalk her like a damn creep either!"

I point to the screen and notice one of the monitors is pointed directly at a door with the numbers 913 on it.

"Is that her fucking apartment?"

"It's not *in* her apartment," he argues as if it makes a fucking difference.

"You need to get this shit straightened out."

"He's in love!" Wren glares at his gossiping bird, but the feathered creature doesn't look a bit put out.

"I mean it, Wren. Give that girl her stuff and stop being a creep."

"So it's okay when you do it? But no one else is allowed?"

Anna chuckles, placing her warm hand on my chest. It calms me, but even as crazy as this situation is, I can't even be mad about it. If Wren even feels an ounce for Whitney that I feel for Anna, then I know trying to force his hand will be hopeless.

"Stop living in your computer, and get out into the real world," I insist. "It's making you weird."

Anna offers to help him get his girl, but he just grumbles as he shuts down the video feeds to the gym. He looks truly distraught when the camera in front of her apartment door winks off.

"Let's let him grieve," I tell her as I pull her out the door. "We have a lot of time to make up for."

Anna couldn't keep her hands off me on the way to the ranch, and we finished what we started in the parking garage right in the middle of my driveway before we could climb out of the truck.

Life is going to be amazing with this woman, and I plan to prove to her every day that she means more to me than any other person could.

THE END

Social Media Links

FB Author Page
FB Author Group
Twitter
Instagram
BookBub
Newsletter

OTHER BOOKS FROM MARIE JAMES

Standalones
Crowd Pleaser
Macon
We Said Forever
More Than a Memory

Cole Brothers SERIES
Love Me Like That
Teach Me Like That

Hale Series
Coming to Hale
Begging for Hale
Hot as Hale
To Hale and Back
Hale Series Box Set

Cerberus MC

Kincaid: Cerberus MC Book 1
Kid: Cerberus MC Book 2
Shadow: Cerberus MC Book 3
Dominic: Cerberus MC Book 4
Snatch: Cerberus MC Book 5
Lawson: Cerberus MC Book 6
Hound: Cerberus MC Book 7
Griffin: Cerberus MC Book 8
Samson: Cerberus MC Book 9
Tug: Cerberus MC Book 10
Scooter: Cerberus MC Book 11
Cannon: Cerberus MC Book 12
Rocker: Cerberus MC Book 13
Cerberus MC Box Set 1
Cerberus MC Box Set 2
Cerberus MC Box Set 3

Ravens Ruin MC

Desperate Beginnings: Prequel (Book 1)
(Not a romance, but gives all of the back history on the club)
Book 2: Sins of the Father
Book 3: Luck of the Devil
Book 4: Dancing with the Devil

MM Romance
Grinder
Taunting Tony

Westover Prep Series
(bully/enemies to lovers romance)
One-Eighty
Catch Twenty-Two

Printed in Great Britain
by Amazon